The Rake Who Rescued Me

SAMANTHA HOLT

Chapter One

Hampshire, England 1815

Reed slung his shirt over his bare shoulders and headed downstairs. The plush red carpet cushioned his feet and he squinted at the glittering chandelier in the main hall while it reflected far too much daylight for his liking. He paused to peer at the grandfather clock and grumbled when he noted the time.

Two o' clock. Mid-afternoon.

He never usually cared if he slept away the day but for a change, he had things to do.

"Good morning, Your Grace," Mosley greeted.

"Christ, Mosley," Reed grumbled.

He twisted to view the butler as the stern-faced man stepped out of the shadows. The damned man had to have the ability to pass through walls, such was his ability to slip into rooms unnoticed. For as long as he could remember, the butler had been lingering in corners and watching over every aspect of the running of Keswick Abbey.

"Must you skulk so?" Reed demanded and pushed an arm through one shirt sleeve.

"I never skulk, Your Grace." The thin man's white eyebrows rose. "Your valet was not available this morning?"

Mosley did a slow perusal of Reed's person, no doubt taking in the bare feet, the open shirt, the mussed hair. The truth was, Reed's head was thumping, and his stomach grumbled. All he wanted was coffee and sustenance. Then he would worry about his appearance.

He waved a hand. "I'll dress properly later."

"Indeed."

Reed narrowed his gaze at the butler, whose lips remained pressed into an implacable line. "It was a late night, Mosley. I could do without your silent judgement."

"A butler never judges."

"This one does."

"Will you be wanting breakfast, Your Grace, or lunch? Or perhaps supper?"

Reed laughed and shook his head, hearing every drip of disdain in his butler's voice. Despite it all, Mosley had been with the house for nigh on twenty years and would never go anywhere else. Nor would Reed wish him too. Sometimes it was interesting to have some starched old stick of a man give him a little moral guidance. He rarely paid attention, but it could be amusing.

"This is not the latest I have ever risen, and you know it." He eyed the door to the breakfast room. "A light breakfast, I think. I shall take it in the drawing room. Eggs, sausage, bacon. Some toast I think. Lots of coffee. Tomatoes. Ask Mrs. Harris if she has any black pudding. Oh, and some of those pastries she makes so beautifully."

"Of course, Your Grace. A nice, *light* breakfast. I shall see to it at once."

"Is my brother around?"

"Lord Courtenay has been up for several hours, Your Grace. He is likely in the study."

Of course Noah was hard at work already. His younger brother had embraced the running of the estate years ago and could still not let the reins go. It rather suited Reed, frankly.

"I shall hunt him down after sustenance I think."

"Very good, Your Grace."

Reed waited for the butler to move away silently before shoving his arm into the other sleeve. He did not bother doing up his shirt. He would get changed shortly, though not into his finery. He had a task to fulfil and breeches and tailcoats would not do the job.

He pushed open the door to the drawing room.

A woman screamed.

He cursed.

The woman in question scrabbled to standing and nearly toppled over the back of the Louis XIV chair on which she'd been sitting. Reed instinctively leaped forward to aid her, but she screamed again so he retreated whilst his head panged in protest.

Damnation, he should not have drunk so much at the Ellis' last night. He knew full well he had a busy evening of it tonight, yet he had been unable to resist drowning away his boredom at the dinner party in an attempt to make the evening pass quicker.

It worked relatively well but it seemed the alcohol could not have been of brilliant quality because it had left him with a damnably dry tongue and fuzzy head.

And this woman was not helping one bit.

"Who the devil are you?" he demanded, fumbling to do up his shirt. And why had Mosley not warned him he had a visitor?

She turned her gaze to the molded ceilings while he tried to make himself presentable. Not an easy task when merely wearing a thin shirt and breeches. He shoved the shirt into the waistband and grimaced when he realized the placket was fully open. Hastily doing it up, he then thrust a hand through his hair and turned his attention to the woman.

Woman was perhaps a little generous. Though technically old enough, she was a fragile young thing. Thin, bony, with no breasts to speak of. Her summer gown hung from her like a pair of curtains and the print was not much more flattering. Her face spoke of youth and innocence but not in the appealing *I should quite like to test that innocence* way. More like that of a child.

If the spots of color on her cheeks and the way her body trembled lightly was anything to go by, her innocence was likely far too embedded for his liking. He doubted she had ever seen or done an interesting thing in her life and conversations with this stranger would amount to nothing other than her agreeing with every damn thing he said.

Not that it mattered. Because as soon as he had established why she was in his house, unescorted and apparently unknown to his staff, he would send her on her way.

"Well?" he demanded when he had finished righting his minimal clothing.

The fair-haired girl caught his gaze and the blush on her cheeks spread down to her chest. With a lack of bosom to intrigue, he found following the color easy enough to resist.

"F-forgive me, Your Grace."

Her body gave a tiny judder that wracked her frame. He held back a sigh and motioned to the seat on which she'd been sitting. "Do sit."

The strange woman did so but not before glancing at the chair, as though checking it was indeed a chair and he was not playing some heinous trick like a child might play on his governess. Not that he ever did such things, he thought with a slow grin. His governess had never quite been able to prove that he was behind about every bit of mischief she'd suffered.

She eased herself down and Reed eyed the sofa opposite. He should remove himself from the room really. If he remained much longer, they would be discovered and for all he knew, she was some fortune hunter, looking to snare him and force him into a marriage.

However, when he glanced into pale eyes, he saw nothing but horror and utter innocence. This was no scheming woman.

There was one woman in his household who was, though.

Understanding dawned.

"Did my mother invite you here?"

The woman nodded slowly.

"Ah."

"She-she asked me to come early. I have been waiting some time. No one attended to me."

He should not curse the woman who had labored hard to bring him into this world, but he would today. He did a circle of the room and skimmed a finger over the gilded fireplace. "No one has seen you here?"

She shook her head. "No, Your Grace."

His mother likely wanted her to remain unseen—at least until they could be caught together in some compromising situation.

"Where is my mother?"

"She said she had to leave." The girl-woman twined her hands together.

He resisted the urge to roll his eyes. Ever since he'd returned from France, the dowager duchess had been determined to see him married off. For the most part, her antics had revolved around forcing him to dance with every woman in England, but she had manipulated a few meetings that made him grateful he did not embarrass easily.

The last one had been when one of his mother's guests had accidentally fallen in the lake. And needed carrying. By him. Because according to his mother, it would be utterly scandalous for anyone else to touch the young lady. It was a minor miracle his mother had not insisted he strip off her wet clothes and warm her up.

He had to confess, that woman had been slightly more appealing than this one. Dark and comely. He peered at his unexpected guest again. She was not unattractive but certainly not his type. Apparently, his mother was trying out a nice mix of women on him, hoping one might stick.

"What is your name?"

"Lady Edith, Your Grace." She offered an awkward curtsey which seemed ridiculous in the circumstances.

He narrowed his gaze at her. "You're Lord Selfridge's daughter?"

"Yes, Your Grace." A nervous smile quivered on her lips.

"Forgive me, I did not recognize you."

"It has been many years, Your Grace."

Yes, since France. He had only been back a year and had hardly spent much time with the local families. Something else for which his mother scolded him. It was preposterous really, being four and thirty and having one's mother treat one as though one had never grown out of little breeches.

Not to mention being the seventh richest man in the country. How many other wealthy men had their mothers bringing in strange women and forcing them to social events that they had little interest in? Surely so long as he ensured the estate ran well and made money, all the socializing could be ignored? After all, if he was a tenant, he'd far rather his master spent less time partying and more time working.

Not that he objected to fun. Not at all. In fact, he missed it. But there was only so much fun to be had with the bores that lived in Hampshire. God, what he would not give to be back in France, tangled up in the excitement and thrill of war.

He drew in a breath and considered how to politely rid himself of his mother's surprise. "I am afraid, Lady Edith, that my mother had been trying to play some trick on us." He smiled. "I fear old age is taking its toll on her."

There. His mother might not be here for that comment, but it was a small amount of petty revenge. The truth was, his mother was as spry and intelligent as ever. And far too good at meddling with his life, it seemed.

"Forgive me, Your Grace. I would not have come, had I known..."

"But one cannot very well turn down an invitation from the duchess. I do not blame you one bit."

Reed paced over to the window and peered out. The gardeners were attacking the front gardens with gusto, making the most of the sunny spring day.

He looked over his shoulder at the frail young thing. "Did you walk here?"

Lady Edith nodded.

"I shall have to ask you to slip out quietly, I am afraid. I would not wish to mar your good name, my lady."

Color blossomed on her cheeks again but from the slight smile on her face, she was either relieved or had found his manner charming. He suspected the latter. He could hardly help himself most of the time. Since he had been a growing boy, he had this innate ability to look and speak to people and instantly charm them. For the most part, it was a handy skill, particularly when he'd been knee-deep in espionage for His Majesty's Secret Service. However, it was not so useful when he was trying to throw a woman out of his house.

"I-I could stay, Your Grace. Perhaps we could take tea."

He arrowed his gaze in on her. Apparently, this frail young thing was not as sweet and innocent as he had assumed. More fool him.

"You could, Lady Edith, but I am horribly late. Doesn't do for a duke to be late, you know. I shall bid you good afternoon and ask that you use the rear entrance. I should hate for any-one to see you and make any incorrect assumptions."

He swiveled to leave but a blur of muslin flung itself at him. Lady Edith flattened her mouth to his and gripped his neck with surprising strength. He forced her off him and she tumbled back.

"You kissed me! You shall have to marry me now!" she de-clared triumphantly.

Reed perfected his coldest look. It was one that few peo-ple ever saw. "I can assure you, I have kissed many a lady and, as you can see, I am still not wed. I am afraid you shall be dis-appointed to know that *you* shall not be changing that."

Her wiry body seemed to deflate. "But your mother said..."

"My mother is close to being put in a lunatic asylum at this rate." He straightened his not very straight shirt and mo-tioned to the door. "Good day, Lady Edith."

"But..."

"Good day," Reed said firmly.

Lady Edith lifted her chin and gave a little sniff. Snatching up her bonnet, she strode past him and made a fine attempt at slamming the door. Thankfully the large white and gold door merely squeaked shut and Reed released the air from his lungs.

Rubbing a hand across his face, he silently cursed his mother. He was of a mind to remain forever a bachelor and his brother could inherit when he died instead. That would serve her right.

Slumping onto the sofa, he scrubbed a hand across his face and searched for signs of his lingering headache. He couldn't say he'd enjoyed his meeting with Lady Edith but apparently surprise had cured him of that, at least.

Reed tilted his head back and eyed the cornicing on the ceiling. It was something he'd done since he was a child—traced the patterns over and over. Except when he had been a boy, he had usually hung backward off the furniture and was scolded for getting his feet all over the furnishings.

Staring at the ceiling had allowed him time to plot. How would he sneak into the kitchens? How many more tricks could he play on the maids? Would Mosley ever notice he had switched the sugar for the salt?

Now he was using the time to plan his evening. The missive he'd received from London only two days ago had come as quite the pleasant surprise. Until he had realized what a bore the task was to be. Gads, what he would not give to be in France or the underbelly of London society. But once Napoleon was defeated and exiled, they had no use for him. He had to go back to his Ducal duties.

Reed forced himself up from the chair and made his way to the morning room, where hopefully his meal would be ready. Then he would look to getting on his disguise and slipping out unnoticed. A smile crept across his face. Investigating a gypsy fair was hardly the same as mingling with the upper echelons of French society or becoming a French peasant in a dilapidated inn but at least it was *something* for him to do. With any luck, if he did an excellent job, the Secret Service might find more work for him. One could only hope, after all.

Chapter Two

S nores echoed from the wagon. Orelia shook her head to
herself.

"Mama?" she tried. But there was no response.

Sighing, she made her way up the steps and eased open the door. Her mother laid slumped across their shared pallet. She gave another sigh. "Oh, Mama."

Further noises that sounded more like they might escape from a beast rather than a fairly small, if plump, woman emanated from her mother's open mouth. There would be no waking her. Which meant Orelia would be telling the fortunes tonight—again.

Orelia climbed down the steps and made her way to their tent. Visitors were already beginning to fill the land on which the travelers had parked their wagons. Some came out of curiosity, others to make fun of the Romani. Others would enjoy the food and hospitality and spend a little money on crafts. Orelia and her mother usually made their money from fortune telling and selling lucky heather. Unfortunately, since Mama had decided she was in love with Simen, she had taken to drinking more heavily.

Orelia set up the sign and tied back the curtain before ensuring everything was in place. The dark tent housed only two chairs and a rickety table. It was up to her to create some magical effect. What a shame she had no ability to tell fortunes at all. Her mother had all the skill but no interest in ensuring they had food in their bellies and a wagon that did not leak. No, she was far too interested in Simen, Orelia thought bitterly. Heaven forbid her daughter might need something.

"Tell your fortune?" she asked a passing man, but he ignored her.

Of course, this was how it had always been, had it not? Her English father had overlooked her then left to fight in the war. Her mother had ignored her unless she could somehow use her to get some drink. As half-Romani, she was either disregarded or spat on by others. She could not even say her community cared that much about her. After all, they were too busy trying to make a living too, and many did not trust her thanks to her mixed blood.

She tried again. "Good lady, tell your fortune? Will you find love? Wealth? Happiness? I can tell all."

The lady in question ignored her too.

"Well you won't find any with a face like that, I can tell you that for free," she grumbled.

"What of my face?"

Her heart thudded against her rib cage and she whirled to come face to face with a pirate. No, not a pirate. A man. But he had an eyepatch. She glanced down. No wooden leg as far as she could see. And, actually, in the torchlight, he was too handsome to be a pirate, even if his curly moustache did him no favors. Perhaps she could tell him that his future prospects would improve without the facial hair?

"You have a very fine face, sir. And an excellent future ahead of you, I suspect. But I can only say for certain if you allow me to tell you your fortune."

"How can I resist?" He flashed a smile at her. She suspected he was trying to be charming. Unusual for a *gadje*. Few outsiders were interested in Romani women.

"Have you coin?"

"Of course."

She skimmed her gaze over his clothing. Despite the eyepatch, he was dressed well enough. He would have coin and likely more than she would ever have.

"Please enter."

Orelia motioned into the tent and adjusted her headscarf. Her mother had always dressed deliberately with large earrings and bright scarfs, so she attempted to do the same. Unfortunately, most visitors expected some wise old woman to tell their fortune and even a few scarfs would not make up for her lack of wrinkles.

The man sat on the tiny chair. He seemed to occupy her tent to capacity. His shoulders were broad and filled the deep brown wool coat. His legs were long too and when she sat, her bare feet brushed his shins. His teeth flashed again.

She turned up the lamp and held out her hands. This was always the difficult part. She was a fairly talented liar—it came with the territory—but she sensed this man would not be easily fooled.

He offered her his hands, but she shook her head. "You've never had your fortune told before, have you?"

He chuckled. "No. I suppose I tend to make my own."

"You must cross my palms with coin."

"Well, that is one way of saying I must pay you." He pulled out a coin and held it for a moment. "But if I do not like my fortune?"

"I can only tell you what I sense. That is what you pay me for. Whether you take away a positive experience, that I cannot guarantee."

He placed the coin in her palm and she closed her fingers around it before slipping it into the purse on her belt. Then she laid out her hands again and motioned for his. They were warm and soft, far softer than her own. The hairs on her arms prickled, and she had to glance away from him for a moment to gather herself.

Orelia looked back at him and at the confident, slightly lopsided smile on his face. He didn't look away. She closed her eyes, unable to stare into that one eye for any longer.

Using the moment to gather what she had seen of him, she took deep breaths and rolled her head from one side to the other. "What is your name?"

"Shouldn't you—?"

"Your name."

"N-Noah."

There was uncertainty there. Strange for a man who walked and talked as though he owned the world. His accent was refined too. From his soft hands and nice clothing, she imagined he worked with words. A lawyer perhaps. A writer. Or perhaps a doctor.

No, he was too young for that and far too handsome. Doctors, in her limited experience, were old and ugly, and terrifying.

"I sense that you are reaching a busy time in your life."

He said nothing, so she opened her eyes to gauge his reaction.

"You use paper a lot in your daily business."

"I suppose."

"And ink."

Though there were no ink stains on his fingers. Oh dear, had she been wrong? Why could her mother not have done this? Why did everything always have to be left up to her?

"I write letters at times, yes."

"You work with numbers too."

He lifted a shoulder. "Certainly."

"An accountant," she announced.

He grinned. "You are very good."

Orelia relaxed a little. What a gamble that had been. "You have had trouble with women, though."

"That is true."

"You would like to find your true love."

"Always."

Was it her imagination or had his grip on her hands tightened ever-so-slightly?

"You need patience, but she is waiting for you. It shall take time, however."

"How might I find her?"

"Wait. She shall come to you."

"And what of my work? Shall I find success there?"

She paused for effect and closed her eyes for the briefest moment. Then she smiled. "You shall indeed. I see a great need for your line of business. You shall find yourself busy and wealthy too."

"Goodness, wealth and love. It looks as though I am in for a lucky year."

"You are indeed, sir."

She tugged her hands away from his and he leaned against the table. "If I am in need of more advice, should I return?"

Orelia clamped down on the tiny whirl of excitement dancing in her stomach. She was merely excited about the prospect of more money. That was all. It had nothing to do with his deep, enchanting voice or that dashing smile.

"I am always happy to offer advice."

She would have to spend the rest of the night considering what else she could tell him, however. Most of those who wanted their fortunes told were usually happy to hear they would find love and grow richer. But not this man. She tilted her head to view him. He really was not at all the usual sort of man to frequent her tent, so what did he think he would gain by returning?

Chapter Three

Well Reed could thoroughly blame himself for making no progress with his investigation yesterday.

He slipped on his cap and adjusted his eyepatch before slipping out of the back of the house. The gypsy fair was two miles down the road, hence the quartermaster asking for his help. He'd rather prefer to think of himself as indispensable to the Secret Service—especially considering all the successes he'd had in France, exposing Napoleon's plans and tracking down French spies deep in the gut of England—but the government's attempt at stopping Napoleon being murdered was half-hearted at best. At least if they put him on the job, they could say they tried, but he suspected they would not much care if he was killed while under their care, even if it did cause contempt between their two countries.

He strolled down the village lane and admired the golden light flickering across the countryside as the sun lowered. Slashes of pink mingled with it, meaning they were in for a wet day tomorrow. He would not much like to be living in a gypsy camp when the skies opened. None of those wagons looked particularly cozy or watertight.

Setting a brisk pace, he came to the outskirts of the field on which the gypsies had made camp. Reed shook his head at himself. He was losing his touch. He should have come away with enough information to move forward in his investigation. Instead, he'd spent too long listening to that girl's terrible fortune-telling. He had little idea if such a skill existed but if it did, she certainly did not have it.

Several locals milled around the camp. Since the gypsies had come to Hampshire they'd been greeted with a mix of fascination and fear. Some demanded they move on instantly while others wanted to watch them, a little like a circus act or stage play. Reed was aware that some of the finer ladies in the area visited because of some morbid fascination with the Romani way of life. A drop of excitement in their dull lives perhaps. He couldn't blame them. Not long in England and he was already seeking out adventures.

And certainly not those of the marriage variety.

He picked his way across the camp and found himself heading directly toward the girl's tent. He'd hardly been aware he was doing it. A smirk lingered on his lips. What would his mother say if she knew he was spending time with a gypsy girl rather than some fine, well-bred, and dull lady? After their argument yesterday about her antics, she had upped and left for London. With any luck, she would stay there for some time. As much as he loved her, he could do without her interference, especially during an investigation.

The tent flap remained closed and he picked it aside only to find it empty. He tried not to be disappointed. After all, it merely meant he could find someone else to question. What would a young gypsy girl know of plots to kill emperors anyway? The scent of flowers and heather lingered in the tent.

The smell had remained on him last night too. He had gone to bed, breathing it in, and recalling how attractive the girl had been. Her skin was dark, though not as dark as many of the gypsies. He had to wonder if she was all Romani or if one of her parents was English. And her hair... It was glossy and brown, with wild curls in it. He'd longed to thrust his fingers into it and feel its texture.

Reed forced himself past the tent and into the maze of wagons. The wooden vehicles were of varying colors and worn from travel. But the interesting style of them distracted from the chipped wood and dilapidated wheels a little. To most of his fellow countrymen—who were a darn sight less travelled than he—they would look exotic with their curved roofs and wooden decorations.

He eyed the vehicles, glancing between them. He wasn't entirely sure what he was searching for. Someone to talk to, perhaps. Mingling with gypsy society was not nearly as easy as slipping into French society. The gypsies did not trust outsiders. He could not blame them really. They had been treated poorly indeed in the past and would likely continue to come up against discrimination in future.

French nobility, however, was much the same as the English. They admired courage, arrogance, and wealth. He had all three and was quite apt at showing it off. None of those would appeal to these folk, however.

It had not even seemed to appeal to the girl.

Damn it. He needed to focus.

A scream pierced the air.

His heart immediately took to hammering, his senses on alert. Reed twisted in the direction of the sound and raced through the maze. He barreled to a stop when a man burst from one of the wagons. The fortune-teller from yesterday was already on the ground, hands shielding her face. An older woman stood at the top of the stairs to the wagon, screaming at the girl, but Reed could hardly make out what was being shouted.

The brute of a man, who appeared unsteady on his feet, bore down on the girl. Reed could wait no longer.

He sprinted forward and placed himself between the girl and what was surely a drunkard. The haze of alcohol was so pungent that he had to wonder if the chap had not bathed in the stuff. The man's eyes focused in on him.

"Get out the way, *gadje.*"

"If you have a problem with the lady, you can take it up with me."

He snorted. "Lady?"

"Do we have a problem?" Reed asked, his voice cool. The man was wide, though not as tall as Reed. Still, Reed had every confidence he could lay him out with one punch, particularly given his drunken state.

"Get out the way!" the drunkard demanded, a pungent breath escaping him. "This has nothing to do with you."

"If you are trying to harm the lady, it certainly does."

"Noah," came a feminine plea from behind him.

He almost forgot he'd told her that was his name until she tugged his arm. The brute attempted to push him aside to get to her so Reed came at him with a swift punch. It was not intended to do damage, just stop him in his tracks. And it did. The man staggered a little and stumbled back onto the steps. The woman screeched and hastened down to his side.

"Look what you've done, Orelia," she wailed at the girl.

Reed turned his attention to the girl—Orelia, he assumed. An ugly bruise was already rising on her cheek. He curled a fist and faced the man. Thrusting a finger out at him, he snarled, "Touch her again and you will pay for it."

The drunk, nursing a sore jaw while the woman fussed around him, narrowed his gaze. "She is a little whore. Needs a good beating. You cannot stop me."

"Bast—"

Orelia yanked on Reed's arm and tugged him away. He wouldn't fight her, not after what she had just been through. When they were far away from the scene and tucked between the wagons, he turned her to face him. What little glow from the various vehicles there was revealed the full extent of her injury. He lifted her face and she let him.

"That's a mighty fine bruise."

She curled her arms around herself and shrugged. "It will fade."

"Does this happen a lot?"

A sad smile curved her lips. "Not often."

"But it does happen."

"Simen is a terrible drunk."

"Is he your husband?"

"Certainly not!"

"Your father."

She shook her head. "He is my mother's lover. My father died years ago."

Reed studied this beautiful woman. And she really was beautiful. Her hair hung loose around her shoulders and she wore that ridiculous colored scarf around her head and those huge earrings but there was no distracting from the striking look of her features. Wide, full lips, and dark, almond-shaped eyes framed by arched eyebrows that gave her this ridiculously exotic look. Her lashes were long too and every time she fluttered them, she appeared to be beckoning to him.

"He's a brute."

Orelia nodded and chuckled. "That he is. I thank you for your help."

He took his cue to step back though he could not help wanting to touch her face some more. Her skin was so damn soft. "You could do with a cold steak to press against that." He nodded to the bruise on her cheek.

She laughed. "And where should we find one of those?"

Likely at his house, but he could hardly tell her that.

"The river then, the cool water will help."

"It will be fine. I should get back to work."

"You still owe me another fortune telling."

Inwardly, he kicked himself. His mission had not changed. He still needed to find out who these gypsies were that had been on the ship bringing supplies to Napoleon. If he could track them down, he'd have his culprits.

But Orelia flashed a bright smile. "So I do. Come on then." Then she grabbed his hand.

It was such an innocent move. A delicate palm in his. He'd had women thrust their breasts at him, even grab his hand and press them against their curvaceous bodies. He'd experienced enough sordid pleasure to taint everything. Yet he could not deny the touch of her hand, curled trustingly in his, sent a torrent of heat through him.

It had been the same when she'd been telling his fortune. That ribbon of desire had woven carefully through him, entwining around his insides and making him forget himself. Of course, he had gone along and agreed with everything she had said. If she knew who he really was, the game would be up. He doubted she would recognize him without the ridiculous fake moustache and eyepatch, but some people would.

She led him into the tent and lit a lamp. They were enclosed in their own tiny world and he could not think how easy it would be to...to what? Kiss her? Perhaps.

He suspected she would like it. But he did not need the distraction. He had to remember that.

Palms open, mischievousness glinted in her eyes. He gave an exaggerated sigh and sat. Offering the coin, he pressed it into her palm and closed his hand over hers. "I hope this wealth I have been promised appears soon. I shall find myself desperately poor at this rate."

"Well, if you do not let me tell your fortune, how can I say?"

He released her hand and immediately missed her touch. Thankfully she took his hands again, staring deep into his one eye. He suddenly longed to be rid of the damned disguise. At

Samantha Holt

least if he wasn't wearing an eyepatch, he'd be able to stare back properly.

And admire her fully.

She went through the same act as the previous day, closing her eyes and taking deep breaths while smoothing her fingers over his hands. Her own hands were work-worn but pretty. Certainly not made for arduous work. What a pity.

Reed found himself watching the movements of her lips while she took in those breaths. She parted them slightly then closed them, parted then closed. It was like some miraculous dance designed to make him as frustrated as possible. Those lips would taste spectacular, he could just tell.

"Your riches shall be with you soon, but you must work hard for them."

He hardly heard a word. In his mind, he was pushing aside the flimsy table and drawing her hard against him. Kissing her. Touching her.

"The answers you seek are there, but you must try something different."

He stared at her mouth. Touching. Stripping. Tasting.

"Your usual plans will not work. If you are to succeed, you must accept help."

Kissing her deep. Taking her hard. Making her cry out.

"Are you willing to accept help, Noah?"

"Oh yes." The deep, sensuous tone of his voice surprised even him. He snapped his gaze to hers. "I mean, yes. Of course."

She looked at him intently and he had to wonder if she had not miraculously gained the power to see his future. Before he could say anything, the tent flap opened, and he jumped to his feet. Simen snatched Orelia and dragged her out of the tent. Reed follower her out, ready to lay out the man a second time if needs be. The mother was there too and already screaming at her daughter. Orelia tore herself away from Simen and the two women began talking over one another. Reed hardly knew what he should do so he stood between her and the drunk.

"You are too much trouble, Orelia." Her mother thrust a finger at her.

"You're just going to let him treat me like that?"

"If you would just behave..."

"I do behave, Mama. I have been working hard since we arrived. All you do is sleep and drink and—"

Simen stepped forward, forcing Reed close to Orelia.

"You treat your mother with respect," Simen demanded.

"Why?" Orelia whirled on him. "She does not treat me with any."

Her mother lifted her hands and shook her head. "Well, it does not matter anymore. I have found a new home for you."

Orelia dropped back a little. "What do you mean?"

"Cappie wishes to have you. He said he would give me coin for you. I've told him you're a hard worker, so you had better prove me right. You are too much trouble for me." Her mother gave a weary shake of her head.

The pain written across Orelia's face stung. Who was the person? And what sort of a mother would sell her daughter? It was clear Orelia had been dealing with much more than he had realized.

"You have sold me?"

"Just do as your mother tells you," Simen told her. "She does not want you causing trouble anymore."

Reed came to Orelia's side and put an arm around her. The mother scowled but made no comment.

"Who is this man?" Reed demanded. "What will he do with her?"

Simen glowered at him. "What is it to do with you, *gadje*?"

"What will he do?" Reed pressed.

"He will marry her of course. Make her his wife and put her to good use."

Orelia shook her head. "He is a bad, bad man. You know that, Mama. Why would you agree to such a thing?"

"Because you have caused me trouble since the day your father died. You are a grown woman now. You should be married."

"But to Cappie?" Orelia exclaimed.

Her mother lifted her chin. "He paid a fine amount. You shall be wed tomorrow."

Orelia gaped at her mother. Reed glanced between the people, almost unsure how to fathom such behavior. He was used to women bringing along a nice dowry to the marriage agreement but to be sold by her own mother?

"How much has he offered?"

The woman moved closer to him and peered at him. "You are very interested in my daughter's life. Be warned, once she is a wife, you will not be welcome near her."

"I'll give you one hundred pounds for her," he declared.

Orelia gasped.

Chapter Three

Her mother's eyes widened. Then she laughed. Orelia continued to gape at them all. Who did they think they were, trying to barter and sell her as if she were no more than a loaf of bread? She should not have been surprised at her mother stooping so low as to sell her to Cappie. Yet, shards of pain ripped at her heart. The man was a brute and would treat her poorly, she knew that much. How could her mother—as uncaring and as useless as she had been—be willing to subject her to such a life for what would likely be very little money?

And now this man was offering more money than she would see in her lifetime for her? Who was he? An accountant could never have that much money. He had to be lying.

"A hundred pounds," he said solemnly.

"He'll take you for a fool," Simen warned.

Her mother hushed him with a wave of her hand. "Do you have the money now?"

Noah pressed a hand into his inner pocket and drew out some notes. He thrust out one and her mother snatched it.

"This is ten."

"I am hardly likely to carry around one hundred with me to a place like this, am I? You shall have the rest tomorrow."

Orelia watched the exchange numbly. The blood in her ears roared so hard that she almost didn't hear the rest. Here she stood, as though she did not even exist, while they negotiated her future. Her mother had long ago given up caring for her, particularly when the need for alcohol took over, but she never expect to be bartered away in such a manner.

And who was this wealthy man really? Why would he wish to buy her? Icy fear swirled about her and made her shudder. Perhaps he was not an accountant. Perhaps he was criminal with some nasty fate in mind for her. She should run perhaps. Flee and hide. Let no one take her. Yet she could not help remain. She wanted to hear the outcome of this and find out who exactly he was.

She also needed to know if her vision had been true. For the first time in her life, she had held a hand and known something about a person. Goodness knows why he of all people had triggered some hidden ability, but it had to mean something. After years of seeing her mother's abilities, she knew that much.

Her mother eyed the note then peered up at Noah.

"As you will. I'll expect the rest tomorrow or there'll be trouble mind." She wagged a finger at him. "We can cause lots of trouble, you know."

"You have my word."

Simen snatched the note from her mother. "I'll be looking after that."

Her mother screeched and Simen stalked off, leaving her trailing behind, trying to grab the note from him. Orelia could only shake her head sadly. She would never know if her mother had ever loved her. Perhaps before her father had died, she had, but she could never recall such a moment.

When the drunken pair were out of sight, she propped her hands on her hips and faced down Noah. He might have bought her, but she would not go easily. She might not go at all. Though curiosity drove her, she would not be a prisoner. The Romani were free people, roaming where they wished, and nothing would change what she was in her heart.

Certainly not a stranger buying her.

"Who are you? I know you are not an accountant. No accountant is that rich."

Noah stilled a pace away from her. He seemed to be weighing her up, making some sort of a decision. Finally, he removed his cap and slowly eased off his eye patch. She sucked in a breath. His eye was healthy. Just a few red marks lingered where the patch had pressed into his skin. But he focused on her with bold blue eyes.

Then he went for his moustache. she clamped a hand over her mouth when he ripped it away.

With his face bare and visible in the light from the windows of the wagon, he was mightily handsome. She'd thought him so before the removal of that ridiculous moustache but now...well, he stole her breath.

He gave her a slightly ashamed smile and a dimple made itself known in his cheek. Why had she not noticed that before? A dimple of all things. God certainly liked to play tricks when he created man. Devilishly handsome, long lashes that a woman would be jealous of, slightly wavy dark hair that begged for fingers to trail through them and to top it all off a dimple that would be adorable or darling on a child yet was utterly devastating on him.

Her gaze inevitably fell to his firm lips that were now bare of that awful hairpiece. Now that she could see them better, there was a horrible urge to find out what they would feel like against hers. This man, whoever he was, appealed to her far too much.

Orelia took a step back, half fearful she might actually act on her desire.

"Who are you?" she demanded again.

"Well, I suppose I should not have expected you to recognize me."

She shook her head and searched for more words. None came. Her voice had fled, her common sense vanished.

"I am the Duke of Keswick."

A laugh burst from her. "Of course you are. Silly me! How could I not have known? Why I imagine the duchess is currently dressed in maid's clothes and enjoying a nice game of cards and an ale with my people."

"It is true." He pressed a hand into his pocket and drew out a golden pocket watch that glinted in the torchlight. "See here." He flipped it over and she saw it was engraved with a crest and his name.

"You're a thief!" She backed away again. Perhaps he was a dangerous man after all. Her initial instincts of liking him had been utterly wrong and he meant her harm.

"Not at all. I am the duke. I live not two miles down the road in Keswick Abbey."

Orelia shook her head and edged away until her back struck the side of another wagon. He came closer until he bore over her.

"I'm not lying, Orelia. At least not anymore. I am not Noah nor am I an accountant. I'm the seventh richest man in England and tomorrow I shall pay a mighty sum for your freedom."

"For my freedom or my body?"

A wicked grin crossed his face. "That is up to you."

She narrowed her eyes at him. "So you would pay for me, then let me free?"

"I have no need to hold women prisoner."

Noah—no the duke, no... "What is your name?" He came closer and the scent of soap curled around her. She tilted her head to eye him. "Or should I call you 'Your Grace.'"

"I think we have no need for formalities." Closer still. "My name is Reed Albinus St. Vincent."

His warm breath touched her face. Her own breaths grew shallow. Firm lips filled her vision and she clamped her hands at her side lest they fist into his jacket and pull him close.

She lifted a brow. "Reed Albinus St. Vincent. And that is not formal?"

He chuckled. "Less formal than Your Grace, anyway."

"Why lie? Why the charade?"

"I am here on an investigation." His gaze grew serious and he eased away, leaving her feeling cold. "You must not utter a word of this."

She nodded, hardly sure where this conversation would be going anyway.

"Swear it, Orelia. Swear you will not utter a word or I shall leave you to that brute."

"I swear it."

"I work for His Majesty's Secret Service. Well, I did. But I do again, if briefly. My ability to move in most social circles with ease made me indispensable to them during the war. Now, they wish to use my services again."

"Move in social circles?"

He waved the now rather floppy moustache at her.

"I am, Orelia, rather good at disguises and an incredibly good liar."

"So why should I believe you're the duke?"

"Come home with me and you'll believe it."

She pondered him for a moment, folding her arms across her chest. "Will you really give Mama one hundred pounds for me?"

"Well, it's ninety now."

A brow arched, she waited.

He relented. "Yes, I will."

"You think that I will let you just buy me?"

Noah—no, Reed—chuckled. "I think nothing of the sort. I would, however, like to buy your services."

"My services?" She shook her head. Had she given him the wrong impression? "I am not that sort of woman, whatever you think of the Romani people, I can assure you of that."

"No, no, no I did not mean that. Christ, I don't need to pay for that."

Orelia tried not to consider how many women this 'duke' might have bedded. He was handsome and if he was as good a liar as he said he was, he would have little trouble swaying women into bed. Goodness, even with that silly moustache, she'd been attracted to him and found him quite charming.

"I hope you do not intend to purchase my gift of sight, because I am afraid to say it is next to useless."

A grin slipped across his face. "Yes, I sort of guessed that."

"You made quite a fool of me, did you not?" She jerked her chin up. "I imagine it was terribly amusing when I claimed to know your occupation."

"I had little intention of fooling you. If it makes any difference, I quite enjoyed my first fortune telling experience."

"So if you do not want me for my lack of fortune-telling skills, nor my body, what do you want me for? Because I tell you, I have little intention of being a servant."

Both brows rose. "I have enough of those too." He came toward her again, making her feel as hot and slightly itchy, as though she needed to strip off her clothes. "No, Orelia. I want you to help me with my mission."

A laugh escaped her. "You make it sound so serious, as if you are a spy or something."

"That's exactly what I am. Or was." He scowled. "Or am, at least for a little while longer." He pressed the moustache into his pocket. "During the war, I worked in France as a spy, tracking down French spies and gathering information on Napoleon."

It all seemed so fantastical to her. As a gypsy, she had roamed all over the country, meeting many interesting and not so interesting people, but never a spy.

"The war is over," she pointed out and immediately felt silly for saying as much.

"Yes, but Napoleon is in exile. We are still in a precarious position."

"You believe he will try to raise an army again?"

"I think he is too old and tired to do such a thing but there are those who still see him as a risk." He paused. "Can we talk about this someplace else?" He took her arm before she could suggest anything. "Come, you want to know if I am who I say I am. I'll show you and we can discuss this on the way.

"I—" She glanced back at her mother's wagon. She wouldn't be welcome there. Perhaps she was a fool but whoever this man was, she doubted he would harm her, not when he had just paid ten pounds to save her from that brutish beast of a man. "Very well then."

Reed put on the eyepatch and cap but left off the moustache. She imagined it was dark enough that no one would recognize him—that was, if he really was the duke.

Though she had little idea what he looked like, he was known as the main landowner in the area. The fact was, they were likely on his land. but while her people would not know what the duke looked like, the locals visiting the camp would.

He led the way, slipping between the wagons and avoiding most of the visitors until they came to the edge of a field. He climbed over a sty and held out his hand to her. Hitching her skirts, she stepped over, ignoring his offered hand. She jumped down with ease and gave him a smug smile. He might be used to prim little ladies, but she was certainly no wallflower or prissy little miss.

"So what is this mission of yours then?"

He cleared his throat. "I cannot stress to you how much you must keep silent on this matter."

They began their way around the field, following the line of the fence. A deep groove was etched into the ground where countless other feet had followed the path. Crops were beginning to spring up in the field. She glanced up at the starlit sky and was thankful for the clear night. Without the light of the half-moon and stars, she would likely be needing his hand to navigate the uneven terrain.

"I will not say a word," she vowed. She meant it. While men like Simen had little honor, most of her people were good, hard-working people, dedicated to preserving their way of life. For their sake, she would never break a promise.

"There was an attempt on Napoleon's life last month."

"Oh."

"Yes. Arsenic was slipped into his wine. A specific wine that only he consumes, *Vin de Constance*. We believe the poison was placed into the bottle before it was shipped to the island."

"So how did you find out there was poison in it?"

"One of his servants decided to steal the wine. Lucky for Napoleon but not so lucky for the lad. He died."

"But surely if Napoleon is dead, that will solve many problems? Whoever tried to kill him did the country a favor!"

Reed shook his head. "Our relationship with France hangs on a knife's edge. One slip and we shall fall into a state of war again. If it is thought that we killed Napoleon whilst he was under our care, we shall be shipping our boys out to die once more. That's the last thing we need."

Orelia nodded in understanding. She did not follow the war very closely but she had seen the injured soldiers returning and even a few of their own men had joined the fight. The war with France had been too long and too bloody.

"So what is your role in this?"

"The supplies to Saint Helena—the island to which Napoleon has been banished—are taken over by ship from Portsmouth. Several deckhands have since gone missing, so we've been unable to question them. I became involved in this when your people arrived in Hampshire."

"Why?"

"Because the deckhands who have gone missing were gypsies."

Orelia paused, her hand to the fence lining the field. "You think my people were involved?"

"Yes."

"That's ridiculous. Why should the Romani wish Napoleon dead? We have little enough involvement in this country as it is. We should hardly wish to make ourselves further hated."

"That may be so, but it seems likely that they were the culprits. Everyone else has been accounted for but the gypsies and they were the only men unknown to the captain."

"If they were unknown, why did he take them on? This is so very typical. If something goes wrong, why not blame the Romani? The wine could have gone through many hands. It could have been anyone!"

He took in an audible breath and ignored her comment. As they came over the brow of the field, a grand house came into view. He gestured to the large square building.

"My home."

Chapter Four

From the top of the field, they looked down upon Keswick Abbey. Reed glanced at Orelia to try to gauge her reaction. Disbelief perhaps? Awe?

"You live there?"

"Yes."

Entirely square in shape, the abbey was not the largest house in England, but it was one of the finest. With tall arched windows that nearly reached the ceilings on the bottom floor and set in a garden his father had prided as being the best in Britain, when Reed looked at it through Orelia's eyes, he found himself taking a certain amount of pride in the old place.

"And it's only you who lives there?"

He offered a hand to help her over the next sty, but she ignored him again.

"And my brother. My mother on occasion too but she likes to travel a lot. And of course all the servants."

Orelia kept her skirts lifted and jumped down into the mud. She seemed to care little if her hems were now mud-splattered, which they likely were, though he could not tell in the dark. What a fascinating woman she was. All questions and curiosity. Most women would be bowing and scraping or praying for an offer of marriage by now, then using the stys as a fine excuse to jump into his arms, much like Lady Edith.

"Why do you not move to a smaller house?"

He laughed. "Why would I wish to do such a thing?"

"It must seem so empty. I imagine it gets lonely."

"No, of course not." He paused to consider this. "Well, I suppose..."

"And it's so costly to run."

Of course, running a place like Keswick Abbey cost a fortune. Were it not for his father's savvy investments, little of the family wealth would be left after so many years of upkeep. Thanks to his financial advisors, he kept a healthy flow of income coming in but while he was hardly stupid, he could not claim to know all the ins and outs of investing well. After all, he had spent his best years knee-deep in French society. Noah could be thanked for most of the money flowing in.

As for being lonely...well, he supposed there had been times...and those times had certainly fed his hunger for excitement. His brother tended to keep his head in the books and what with Noah being deaf, it meant things could be a little on the quiet side.

There was only so many ways one could entertain oneself all alone in such a house. Travelling to the House of Lords from Hampshire took a good day so he did it only when vital and the rest of society there bored him. Even the men he'd went to Eton with were dull and old to his mind. They all seemed to have suddenly become grey and tiresome during his time away.

Unlike the vibrant Orelia. With her colorful scarves and interestingly bold manner of speaking, no one could ever accuse her of being grey and tiresome.

They began their way down the slope toward the house. Most of the lower rooms were lit with a fine glow that spilled out onto the lawns. The stars and moon reflected off the lake to one side of the house. For the most part, he forgot how impressive the house could be. What would Orelia make of it in the daylight?

And what the devil was he going to do with her?

In truth, 'buying' her had been an ill-thought-out move. Not that he intended to keep her or any such thing. But, having seen how her mother and her mother's lover treated her, he could hardly let her be given away to some lout of a man. He'd done the easiest thing he could do and thrown money at the problem. His instincts had guided him, and they were rarely wrong. Instinct had saved him from many a sticky situation during his time in France.

If he could persuade her to help him, it would be easily worth the one hundred pounds he promised her mother.

"These places are costly, that is true," he conceded, "but they are about more than cost."

"Are they?"

"What do you think they are about?"

"Oppressing people. Making sure they know their place. Displaying wealth."

He could not help but grin at her impassioned tone. "Admittedly, my father made many of the renovations with the intent of making it fine indeed. But it was also because he enjoyed architecture and wanted this place to last for generations. Houses like these are our history."

Good Lord, he practically heard his father intoning the same words to him. When exactly had he become just like his father? That would not do at all.

She shook her head. "Your history, you mean. Not mine."

"The Romani are intent on preserving their culture, are they not?"

"Of course."

"My family is the same," he pointed out. "This is part of our culture and heritage. We want future generations to look back and see the history."

He smirked to himself. He could hardly believe what he was spouting. The truth was, he had never much thought about what it meant to be an heir to a title. It was just how it had always been. His entire life had been lived for one moment—the day his father died. It was a rather morbid prospect, truth be told.

Orelia did not respond until they moved past the lake and toward the grand entrance way. The two sides of the pale building jutted out slightly and two doors sat at either side of the massive gothic windows. He opted for the nearest, knowing he could sneak around and lead Orelia upstairs without questions from Mosley.

Pausing to remove his disguise, he shoved his hat under his jacket and motioned for her to remain quiet.

"What—?"

"Shhh."

Orelia followed his instruction thank the Lord and followed him through the secondary hallway. He kept having to tug her along as she gaped at the high arched ceilings. Her bare feet at least made no sound on the floors though the housekeeper would have a fit when she saw the muddy footprints.

Reed led her upstairs into one of the spare bedrooms. The garden room—named so because it had the best view of the gardens—was tastefully decorated by his mother for guests. Not that Orelia would be able to see that. He hastily lit a candle and set about lighting several more.

She stood in the center of the room, hands clasped together, turning to view every angle of the pale green and gold room. The curtains were heavy and tassel-lined, and the bed canopy had been made from the same expensive fabrics. A marble fireplace dominated the room but had not been lit. Thankfully it was a mild spring evening so there was no need of it.

"Orelia," he prompted when she turned again, her mouth open, eyes wide.

She stopped and looked down at her muddy feet and hem. "Why did you bring me here? I shouldn't be here."

"What else was I to do with you?"

She shrugged. "Leave me at the camp."

"I could hardly leave my investment behind."

Her eyes narrowed into slits. "It may be commonplace for men like you to see women as objects to be bought and sold but I assure you, my people do not."

"Yet your mother offered you up for a pittance," he pointed out.

She gave a huff and a smile teased his lips. What a picture she made in her headscarf and her simple, mud-streaked gown. If it was not for all the dirt, he might have found himself having a tough time denying the desire to push her back onto the bed and twine his fingers into her loose, dark hair.

A flash of an image came to him. Her hair around her bare shoulders. Breasts thrust up. Lips begging. No, apparently even a good deal of mud would not dissuade him from desiring her.

"You clearly do not want me here if you had to sneak me in."

"I was sneaking myself in," he explained. "My servants have little idea of what I do, and I have no intention of letting them know, either."

"You do not trust them."

"Never."

Orelia moved to the fireplace and used a finger to trace the swirling carvings in it. "It seems strange to surround yourself with people you do not trust."

"There are a few who have been with the house for many years whom I do trust. But maids and footmen come and go. They can rarely be trusted to keep a master's secrets."

"Perhaps you should pay them better. Then they shall be less likely to leave." She flashed a cheeky smile at him.

Minx. She liked to toy with him apparently. And he could not help but like it.

"I am a generous master I shall have you know." He took a few steps closer. "Generous indeed."

His gaze fell to her lips. It was a move he had not considered, yet at any other time, it would have been. He would have intended to use it to throw someone off balance, to draw back the power to him. However, with Orelia, he acted entirely on instinct. The problem was, he could hardly tell if that was a good thing or not.

She faced him head on, her chin lifted, her eyes daring him. "So, what do you want with me?"

"Your help."

"You said as much. Why should I help you?"

"Because I just paid for your services."

"No, you paid my mother."

He grinned. Beautiful—if a little filthy—intriguing and quick. She was quite the woman. "Very well, I shall pay you too."

Her chin dropped a little. He imagined she had not expected him to acquiesce so easily.

"One hundred pounds too," she said once she'd recovered.

"Absolutely."

Damn this mission was costing him. But if he got to the bottom of this and found the would-be killers, perhaps the government would want his services again. One could only hope after all.

"If you are willing to pay me, you had better let me know what you wish me to do."

"First, have a bath. You are filthy."

Color burst onto her cheeks, turning them a dusky pink that was far too enticing.

"*You* made me walk across the fields."

"I did, but I am offering you my hospitality in return." He scowled at her bare feet. "And some shoes. We must find you some shoes."

She gave him an exasperated look. "So I am to stay here? Is that what you are paying for?"

"No. Yes." He paused and pinched the top of his nose. Damn his instincts and rash actions. What the devil had he done? "You will stay here whilst you help me," he explained.

"And will people not think it strange and scandalous you have a Romani woman staying with you."

"Probably."

"But you do not care?"

"If you do not."

Orelia laughed. "I am a Romani. What reputation do I have to preserve? As far as my mother and my people are concerned, once she sold me to you, I am no longer an innocent."

Innocent. The words rattled his brain a little. It shouldn't have mixed with the visions he'd been having. Certainly should not have made them all the more appealing. But the idea this brazen woman had never felt the touch of a man fired something inside of him. It made him hungry to be the first to touch her.

He waved a hand. "I can weather scandal easily enough. Being one of the richest men in England tends to help smooth these matters along."

"You are really one of the richest men in England?"

He nodded.

Her lips tilted. "I never would have guessed."

"Yes, well as we both know, your gift for sight is not exactly perfect."

Her smile widened. It struck him like a bolt to the heart. That was what had intrigued him to begin with. After that first night in her tent, her smile had lingered with him the rest of the night. How easy and genuine it was. Unlike the calculated smiles of the ladies he usually associated with.

"I think I should be offended," he added.

"Do not be. It simply means you are not as prissy and uptight as most rich men."

He dipped his head, taking the compliment for just that.

"So while I stay here, what will you have me do?"

"Ah yes, the mission." The damned mission that he somehow managed to keep completely forgetting. "I need information on your people. Somehow, I have to find these men. Yet I have been unable to find out anything. Those who are willing to talk tell me little and the rest refuse to speak to me."

"I'm not surprised. We do not trust *gadje*—outsiders," she added.

"But they trust you. You can help me."

"Help you lay the blame at the feet of my people you mean."

He lifted a shoulder. "The evidence points at them."

She shook her head then thrust out a hand. He lifted a brow and eyed it.

"I will help you," she declared, "but only to prove that my people had no hand in these dealings." She motioned with her hand again. "We shake on this do we not?"

He hadn't the heart to tell her that he never shook hands with women as it wasn't the done thing, so he took it and smothered a laugh when she tried to take his hand in a crushing grip.

"We have a deal then."

He nodded. "We have a deal. Now let's get you that damn bath."

Chapter Five

O relia stood to one side while the slightly fatigued-look-ing maids brought up buckets of warm water to fill the metal bathtub. She twined her hands together and hardly dare breathe. It was not all that late if the golden clock on the man-telpiece was anything to go by, but the women looked thor-oughly annoyed with having to wait on her. She couldn't blame them. Part of her longed to tell them to go away and she would do it herself except she would never find her way down-stairs to fill it.

She glanced around the room again. What was it with rich people and their love of gold and swirls? The ceiling was covered in swirls, all picked out with gold paint. Gold trim-mings, candlesticks, picture frames. The room could easily have fit her Mama's wagon inside it, yet with all the heavy fab-rics and excessive ornamentation the room felt more cramped than it should have. Now she almost longed to be outside, sleeping under the stars.

"All done," one of the maids declared.

Before she could say thank you, they left. She eyed the tub with mistrust. It was not that she had never seen them before or even taken a bath, but she usually bathed in the river or oc-casionally filled the wooden tub and sat in that when she had the chance. But steam rose from this water and a sweet fragrance teased her. The maids had poured some concoction in it and she had little idea what it was.

Almost feeling as though something might jump out of the water at any moment, she took a tentative step forward and peered at the water.

"Silly girl," she scolded herself. She was a Romani. They were brave and bold people. They travelled wherever they pleased and faced many a foe. A little water should not scare her.

Lifting her foot, she dipped a toe into the water and mud immediately dissolved into the water and vanished.

"Goodness."

She put her foot all the way in and let the warmth surround it. "Oh goodness."

Removing her foot, she hurriedly stripped off her clothes and discarded them in a messy pile. Orelia stepped into the bath and sank down slowly. A groan escaped her.

She laid back and let the water lap over her body. Perhaps these rich people did know a thing or two. Their love for gold might be a little much but she could quite happily have a proper bath every day for the rest of her life. In truth, she was unsure how she would ever take a dip in a river again without remembering this experience.

Eyes closed, she recalled the day's events. So Reed—not Noah—really was a duke. And a spy, if he was to be believed. Her mother had sold her. She had a mighty fine bruise popping out on her cheek.

Oh, and she was going to be a rich woman.

Well, not as rich as the duke but it would be enough to give her freedom to do anything.

What *would* she do with it?

She opened her eyes and lifted a handful of water, letting it trickle between her fingers and splatter on her chest.

She certainly would not stay with her mother. Not that that was an option. She had made that much clear.

An annoying tingle started in her nose and she sniffed it away. She would not cry over that woman. Mama had never been a true mother to her. As much as she had ached for the love of a mother in her younger years, she had long since resigned herself to the fact she would never get it. Her mother was a selfish, cold woman and this was the last time she would let her hurt her.

So she would leave her people? Strike out in the world on her own?

Hopefully she would have time to think about it. She'd help Reed, but he was wrong. Her people were not responsible for this plot to kill Napoleon. As she had reminded him, the Romanis did not care about politics and wars. They had their own battles to fight and those were usually with the people of Britain.

The door swung open and Orelia clamped her hands over her chest. A squeak escaped her when a maid walked in carrying a bundle of clothing.

"What are you doing?" Orelia demanded.

"I'm just bringing you some clothes," the maid said, her tone disgruntled. "His Grace thought you might need some." She put the pile on the end of the bed. "And some shoes."

Fighting the desire to sink down into the bath and hide herself completely, she asked, "Where are the clothes from?"

"The dowager duchess," she said and put the shoes on the floor.

Even from her position in the bath, she could tell the shoes were worth more than her fee for helping Reed.

"I cannot wear those!"

"I said the same myself." The maid's lips twisted into a bitter smile. "However, His Grace commands it."

The woman left, shutting the door behind her and Orelia took a few moments to let her heavily beating heart slow.

"He commands it," she intoned.

Of course he did. He was rich and used to everyone doing as he commanded. Well, if he thought she would follow his every command, he was wrong. She was a Romani. Born free. She would never be told what to do by anyone.

Orelia dragged herself out of the bath and dried herself on the towel draped over the back of one of the chairs.

Wrapping the towel about herself, she picked up the shoes, one by one. The delicately pointed shoes were a pale blue silk, decorated with tiny dots and lace trimming. She eyed her own bare feet that, though now clean, were hardly delicate.

She'd had shoes once or twice, but they were expensive and as soon as she had outgrown them, she had not been able to afford new ones. The years had grown leaner with her mother's drinking so even once she'd stopped growing, she could not purchase any.

She turned them over in her hand, touching the delicate fabric. Who did these belong to? The dowager duchess, the maid had said. What would Reed's mother think of a gypsy girl wearing her finery?

Turning her attention to the gown, she fingered the silk.

The thought of the fabric near her skin enticed. It should not have done so, though. She was a Romani, unmoved by expensive belongings. As long as she was free, did it matter what she wore on her back?

She glanced back at her filthy clothes and sighed. She could hardly wear them in this beautiful house, so she resigned herself to wearing the duchess' clothes. She had little idea what the lady would be like, but she could imagine she would fall into a fainting fit at the idea of Orelia wearing her finery.

Orelia had to admit that picture of a fine lady tumbling over at the sight of her in all this silk made her smile.

Hopefully that was where that meeting would stay—in her imagination. She had little intention of putting herself in such an uncomfortable position.

She slipped on the chemise and gown and grimaced as her damp hair began to stain the beautiful fabric. Snatching up her scarf, she bundled her hair up and tied the scarf around it.

"You look a fool," she told herself, when she peeked in the full-length mirror in one corner of the room. "You do not belong here."

Why she had to remind herself of that, she did not know. It was not exactly unobvious. Even all the maids loathed her on sight. It would not do to get used to the comfort and space of a house like this, nor the luxury of warm water and fine clothing. Even if she did rather enjoy the bath.

Holding a breath in her lungs, she stared at herself while the candle light played across her face. She looked younger in the silk. Perhaps she even felt younger. She released the breath slowly. There was something about working so hard to survive that made her feel old and worn—far older than her one and twenty years. She imagined the ladies Reed spent time with were more youthful and innocent than she.

Reed.

Should she go find him? She needed to speak with him, understand exactly what they were to do. After all, she could hardly stay here forever. But one hundred pounds would give her a wonderful start on life. She could move elsewhere. Start a business, perhaps. An inn? She shook her head. No, the last thing she wished to do was provide alcohol to drunks.

Never mind, she would think on that later. Either way, she needed that money. If she returned to the camp without Reed, she had little doubt Cappie would make another claim on her and she would have no choice but to go along with it. It seemed she had been abandoned to lead her own life and with Reed's help, she would be able to achieve something more than simply surviving.

An uncomfortable knot gathered in her throat when she considered how easily her mother dismissed her. She swallowed it down. It was not the first time her mother had treated her poorly. If Orelia remained with the Romani, it would not be the last. She was better off this way.

Smoothing her palms down her gown, she straightened her shoulders and gave her reflection a nod. She might not be able to remain with her people, but she would clear them of wrongdoing. No Romani cared if an emperor lived or died. Whatever Reed believed of her people's involvement, it was wrong and she intended to prove that.

Chapter Six

The mantle clock ticked away the seconds in what could only be described as an ominous tone. Reed peered at the offending object. Why had he never noticed how damn loud it was? He glanced back at the footman by the door.

"Have some tea and sandwiches brought in," he ordered.

He thought it likely Orelia would be hungry. Even if she was not a gypsy, with a mother like hers, she could hardly be well-fed. He suspected Orelia had spent much of her life going hungry. After all, fortune-telling hardly put one on the road to riches.

Reed eyed the clock again. She'd spent quite some time in the bath. She was filthy but not *that* filthy, surely? He should insist someone go to fetch her except the maids were all walking around with mutinous pouts at the idea of serving a gypsy girl and he'd found he rather wanted to avoid any more rolled eyes or huffs of indignation.

Mrs. Corley the housekeeper nearly fainted at the idea of having her under the roof, even if he intended for it to be a short while. As for Mosley...well, he could have sworn the man had actually shown emotion for the first time in his life. It was all rather disturbing.

Disturbing. He traced the curve of the outside of the clock with a finger and tried not to imagine other gentle curves that were likely now wet or naked or being dressed in silk at present. *Disturbing* was a good way to describe Orelia.

Disturbing and intriguing. He could not help but admit to himself he was rather on edge awaiting her. How else would she surprise him next? What else would she do to make a smile creep across his face? Her direct manner and self-sufficiency was quite appealing. Certainly more interesting than the women his mother kept sneaking into the house. None of them would jump stys or make up fortunes or try to fleece him for one hundred pounds. Hell, half of them could barely look him in the eye.

But when Orelia looked at him, she did not see a title, nor a spy, nor his fortune. She just saw...him.

Intriguing.

The door behind him swung open. Noah strode in and stood in front of Reed, folding his arms.

Noah motioned to the door and Reed turned to see Orelia in the doorway. He hated to admit that his heart bounded a little.

In the golden light, she glowed. Her skin had a dewy look to it and the blue silk contrasted spectacularly with her dark skin. His gaze landed on the headscarf currently binding her hair up on top of her head. A few dried strands were curling around her face. She should have looked ridiculous with that one item that was so obviously and typically a gypsy scarf, yet she did not. It only served to bring attention to the long arch of her neck and the rise of her breasts beneath the gown.

He scowled at himself. Was there something slightly perverted about lusting after a woman in one's mother's gown? He could not decide.

Reed decided not to think too hard about it and just enjoy the effect of the silk on her body. The shapeless gown she'd been wearing previously was not far off a sack and had done little for her body—though he was not a blind man, he'd seen the womanly shape of her hidden there. Not to mention he had an excellent imagination.

But his imagination hadn't done her justice. Though she was clearly underfed, there were delicate curves there. Hips that beckoned to his hands, and breasts that—

"Reed?"

He snapped his gaze to his brother. Only then did he realize he'd been trailing his gaze up and down Orelia's figure without uttering a word. Damnation. As much as he wanted her help, he hardly needed to be lusting after her.

"Who is this?" his brother demanded, signing as he went.

Reed sighed. He'd rather hoped he could avoid explaining. His brother was vaguely aware of what Reed did—they never kept secrets from one another—but the fewer details Noah had the better.

Orelia glanced at them both, remaining in the doorway, her hands clasped in front of her.

"A friend," Reed replied, using his hands to sign out the words.

His brother could read lips perfectly most of the time but in the evening light, it was harder, so they had both learned signing when Noah had been younger. It had been a blessing, somewhat, that the illness that had stolen Noah's hearing had come after he had learned how to talk. It meant communicating with Noah was easy enough—and made his brother an excellent replacement for himself when he had been in France.

"She is staying here?" Noah asked, swinging a glance at her.

Reed nodded. "For a while." He motioned for Orelia to come in. She inched into the room slowly. "Orelia, I would like you to meet my brother, Noah."

"Noah?" She frowned. "Ah."

Reed imagined she now understood why he'd used that name.

"A pleasure to meet you." Noah dipped his head and his lips curved when Orelia dropped into a deep curtsey, remaining bent low for far too long.

She rose. "I—" Reed saw her chest rise with a long inhale. "A pleasure to meet you, Sir...um, my lord...um..." She glanced at Reed, a pleading look on her face.

"Noah will do just fine," Reed assured her, certain Noah had likely missed her bumbling words.

A shaky smile crossed her lips.

"Perhaps you can come and look at something later, Reed," his brother said. "I think we need to have a talk."

Reed nodded. The last thing he wanted to do was talk about Orelia in front of her, particularly not when there might be some unpleasant assumptions about her unexpected presence here. He would have to explain to Noah that Orelia was certainly not a mistress or anything else untoward, though how he would explain that he had bought her in a manner, he did not know.

"Hopefully I shall see you at breakfast, Orelia." His brother flashed a grin.

Reed resisted the urge to curl a fist at his brother's flirtatious smile. Noah was no stranger to the ladies. His mild manners and softly spoken way never failed to work on them, but Reed would be damned if he wanted it to work on Orelia.

Reed waited until his brother left the room and motioned to the sandwiches and tea that had been laid out on a coffee table. "Will you not come and eat? You must be hungry."

She threw a wary glance around and stepped forward slowly. He masked a chuckle. At this pace it would be morning before they'd eaten.

"It's not poisoned."

Her gaze darted to his. "No, of course it's not." She glanced at the door. "Your brother looks like you."

"He does."

"He is quite a bit younger than you, though?"

Reed nodded. "Seven years."

"I am afraid I gave him a shock. Or we both gave each other a shock." Color rose in Orelia's cheeks. "I did not realize he was..." She motioned to her ears. "So I am afraid I rabbited on and he probably did not understand a word."

"Noah can read lips very well, but you need to be facing him."

"And what is it you do with your hands?"

"It's sign language. It allows us to communicate when reading lips isn't so easy. Like when it's dark."

She nodded slowly and remained standing.

"Will you not sit?"

"I just...this is all very new." She cast a hand about the room and finally settled on the sofa.

"Well, seeing as I have bought you, you should make yourself at home. For the time being at least."

"Your servants are not pleased."

"No, but I do so enjoy riling them."

She paused, her hand almost to a sandwich. "You do?"

"Servants are a funny bunch. They like to complain about their masters and yet loathe anyone who does not belong."

"And you tolerate this complaining?"

He sat opposite her and placed a leg over his knee, spread his arms across the back of the chair. "Good staff are hard to come by," he explained. "And what a bore it would be if they were all beautifully obedient. Most of the servants here served my father. I think bloody Mosley—the butler—came with the house. I'm fairly certain he was born a butler."

Orelia giggled and finally bit into a sandwich. He watched the movement of her mouth.

What would it be like to kiss those full lips?

"Are you not eating?" she asked.

"I ate well enough earlier."

She stilled. "Oh."

"Is that a problem?"

"This is all for me?"

"Yes."

She sent a wary look his way. "I do not want your pity."

Reed shook his head. "And you will not get any. I am paying you handsomely for your services and I should like you to remain in full health."

He would not tell her that he was certain she hadn't eaten all day and there was some odd desire to look after her simmering its way through him.

"Oh, yes. Of course."

She began to tuck into the food with gusto, forgetting any manners. He could not help enjoy seeing the true pleasure on her face as she sampled the various fillings.

"So, what exactly is your plan to find this would-be killer?" she asked between bites.

"I had hoped to be able to find out enough to track down these gypsies who were on the ship."

"I suppose you thought you could come in with your eye-patch and moustache and simply ask us?"

He shrugged. "It would have been nice if it had been that simple."

"We do not trust *gadje*. And whilst you were hardly dressed as you are now, you did not look poor. That would give most Romani a reason enough to distrust you."

"And here I thought I did a fine job of dressing down."

She laughed. "Well, no one would believe a duke tried to buy me for certain."

"I cannot think why. You are a beautiful woman. It's surprising you are not already married."

"My mother could not do without me. At least until now. Besides, I have never met a man I would wish to spend more than one day with."

"I hope that you are willing to spend more than one day with me. I suspect tracking down these men will take a little more time than I originally anticipated."

She swiped a crumb from the corner of her mouth and Reed immediately regretted that he had not leaped forward and done the job himself—with his tongue. Then she leaned across and took a cup of tea, adding an inordinate amount of sugar and milk. What a fine job he could afford to keep her in sugar.

"I've never had sugar in tea," she explained.

He waited, practically holding her breath while she lifted the cup to her lips. She grimaced.

"Oh my."

A laugh escaped him. "A little sweet?"

"Oh dear, perhaps I did get carried away."

"One spoon usually does the job."

She placed down the cup as though it were poison and put her hands in her lap. She gave a little shudder. "I shall try again another day, I think."

"Good idea."

"You still have not told me your plan."

That was because he didn't have one. He certainly had not planned on 'buying' a gypsy girl nor had he intended to bring her to her house and bathe, clothe and feed her.

Not that he had bathed her. A mighty shame indeed. Sweeping a soapy flannel over that dusky skin would be a pleasure indeed. Why he could almost picture her—

"Reed?"

He gave himself a mental shake. Some spy he was, distracted by a girl who appeared to have little idea that she held any sexual appeal at all.

"You can find out if any of the men from your camp went out on the ships," he said.

"And that is all you wish for me to do? For one hundred pounds?"

"I can always pay you less," he suggested.

"That's not what I meant!"

"I may still have need of your services. As you've said, it is not easy for an outsider to infiltrate your community."

She shook her head. "Infiltrate. You make it sound so serious."

He leaned forward, his elbows on his knees. "It is serious, Orelia. If our relationship with France crumbles, we shall be at war again. Napoleon was powerful but there are plenty of other men ready to take up the fight for him. If we wish for no more of our men to die on French soil, these people must be stopped."

"*These people*," she scoffed. "You must think very little of my people if you believe they would stoop to plotting against Britain. If you think the poison was slipped on board, could it not have been someone else? The wine would have gone through many hands."

"I am only following the information I've been given."

"You are a mindless man who cannot think for himself, you mean. You do the bidding of your king and ask no questions. I might not be as well-travelled as you, Reed, but I have met men like you before. You shall likely have my people made guilty regardless of whether that is the truth or not."

He lifted a brow. So defensive. He supposed he should not blame her, after all her people were often blamed for everything from famine to disease. Gypsies were an easy scapegoat.

"I spent years on enemy territory with little contact from the British government. Should I have been caught, there would have been no aid or acknowledgement of me." He snorted. "Trust me, Orelia, I am excellent at thinking for myself."

And how had the Secret Service repaid this? By casting one last mission upon him simply because he was in a convenient position to investigate. But maybe if he brought these people—whoever they were —to justice, they'd realize they needed his services. After all, what else was a man who had spent far too many years lying and hiding meant to do?

Orelia appeared chastened. She glanced around the room and fingered her skirts. "So tomorrow we shall question some of the men?"

"Yes."

"And then?"

"We follow whatever leads we have. Someone must know something."

"This is a funny way to conduct an investigation."

"This is what it is. Picking at a string until it unravels. Eventually something will give, and we'll have our lead."

She laughed.

"What is it?"

"If someone had told me I would be drinking tea in a fine house with a duke and becoming a spy yesterday I would have called them mad."

"You did not drink the tea," he pointed out.

Her smile expanded. "Yes, you're right. Without the tea, it would have been completely believable."

They both laughed, and his gaze locked to hers. He froze. Her laugh ended abruptly. Some indescribable heavy weight came over them, as though a cloud of cannon smoke had filled the room—and his lungs. Breathing grew hard until he snapped his gaze away.

"You must need rest," he murmured.

"Yes, I suppose I must." She stood and dropped into an awkward curtsey that was far too appealing. "Thank you for the sandwiches, Reed."

Apparently she felt the need to curtsey but not use his title. He couldn't help like it. He stood and clasped his hands behind his back.

"You are very welcome. I'll send someone to you in the morning to help you dress."

"I would rather you did not."

He lifted a brow. "I would rather I did."

"Why?"

He coughed. "Because..." This was ridiculous. He had seen enough women naked to last a lifetime. He'd dressed many himself after a quick tumble. He'd even done up many a corset. "Because gowns like the one you are wearing are generally designed to be worn with stays."

She glanced down at herself, as though surprised to find she was not wearing any. "I don't have any."

"No. And Lord knows, I'm certainly not riffling through my mother's collection, but you could do with a maid, um, helping you tighten the fit a little."

Peeking down at her own chest again, a wash of understanding came over her face. "I see."

The fact was that every time she'd bent over, he'd had a hard time not trying to see farther down the neckline of her gown. Perhaps a nice high chemise would do the job. He'd suggest it to Vera, though it would kill him to say as much to the maid. But needs must. He certainly could not afford any distraction in the form of breasts whilst they were investigating.

"Well then, sleep well."

Another curtsey. He should stop her from doing them, especially with the whole breast situation but she looked too sweet doing it.

"Good night, Reed."

After she left, his name seemed to bounce around the inside of his head. In her voice of course. All husky and delicate. How a voice like that could spit accusations of being unthinking and practically hunting down her people, he did not know, but they had no less impact on him. If the Romani were innocent of any wrongdoing, it was in everyone's best interests that he found out as soon as possible because if they were, that meant someone else was trying to kill Napoleon and start another war.

Chapter Seven

Orelia could not help but smile when Reed pressed the moustache over his lip, donned the eyepatch and placed on his floppy cap.

"What exactly am I to call you?" she asked as they made their way from the house back up to the field they had walked across the previous night.

In the morning light, the house appeared even more grand. If that was possible. She had spent most of the morning pacing around the outside of it. She only managed three laps before he joined her. She still could not quite understand why one family needed so much house and why everything had to be gold or marbled or covered in sumptuous fabrics.

Though, she had to admit, she would not complain about the bedding. She couldn't recall the last time she had slept so well. It was certainly more pleasant than sleeping on a straw mattress next to her mother whose alcohol-tinged breath used to fill the small space so quickly that Orelia felt like she was suffocating.

"Noah, of course."

"Oh yes, I forgot."

"It was the first thing that came to mind," he confessed.

"I did not see him this morning."

"He was likely eating in the study. Noah enjoys nothing more than a morning of pouring over letters."

"And you do not."

He gave a mock shudder. "Not particularly."

"I imagine that does not make you a very good duke. I do not know much about what a duke does, but I always imagined it meant lots of letters."

"My brother makes an excellent replacement for me." He grinned.

She peered at him. His rather casual approach to being a nobleman seemed forced somehow. She could not quite fathom how or why, however.

Orelia glanced over his body, taking in the plain brown clothing. She was back in her own basic gown—that was at least now clean. He still looked dashing somehow. Although perhaps that had more to do with the knowledge she had seen him in exquisitely made breeches and a waistcoat.

The sight of him standing in the drawing room, his hands clasped behind his back while he waited for her to sit as if she really was a lady had made her heart flutter. No, more than flutter. Dance...reel...jig. Something like that, anyway.

"What am I to tell people of our acquaintance?" she enquired.

"You can tell them I'm your fiancé."

She blinked at him. "I cannot say such a thing!"

"Why not? I'm sure word of our deal will have spread. I highly doubt your mother nor your intended will have kept it quiet."

"But..." He was right of course. Blasted man. He had a slightly smug smile on his face too, as if he was quite enjoying pretending to be betrothed to a gypsy girl.

"I shall be ruined, you know," she muttered.

"Do you really intend to travel on with them once I have paid you?"

She shook her head. Of course, she didn't. How could she when Cappie would think her an easy mark after her 'husband' had vanished and she had no mother to protect her virtue. Cappie had been talking of making her his wife for years. It wouldn't be hard for him to force her.

She drew in a breath of clean spring air. Would her mother even miss her? Likely not.

"You can take your earnings and start afresh," Reed suggested. "No one shall know anything of us. You can even find yourself a handsome husband."

"I have little intention of doing that."

He offered a hand to help her over the sty and she took it before she even realized what she was doing. She snatched her hand back and jumped down. Her ankle twisted slightly, and she stumbled. Reed gave a chuckle and she narrowed her gaze at him when he nimbly made his way down.

"Why not?" he asked.

"First, I would have to give up my money to him. Secondly, I have yet to meet a man I would be willing to spend every day with."

"Perhaps you have not been spending time with the right men." A grin cracked his face. "I do believe we have spent quite some time with each other at this point and you are not fed up with me."

She thrust a finger at him. "We have hardly spent days together. Two fortunes and an evening is not exactly the equivalent to married life. Besides, you are paying me to tolerate your company."

He affected a wounded look and came to her side while they traversed the narrow path down the side of the field. "Come now, my company is not so terrible, is it?"

"I have met worse," she admitted.

"What a compliment."

She laughed. "For a duke, you're not easily insulted, are you?"

"Am I going about it wrong then? Should I be insulted? Tell me, Orelia, how should a duke behave?"

"Usually like he has a stick up his arse," she declared, then clapped a hand across her mouth. "I mean—"

"You mean the upper classes all behave like stuffed shirts."

"Well, I suppose—"

"You would be right about many of them but not all of us are so bad."

"No, of course not."

"Sometimes even us noble folk have bad reputations." He gave her a little nudge with his elbow. "I hope you shall not judge us as all the same."

Heat burned her cheeks. Had she not complained about the very same? Most folk saw her people as nothing more than the scourge of the earth but even before Reed had enlisted her help, he'd been charming and pleasant. Now she was doing the same to his people—marking them all the same.

The point on her arm where their bodies had briefly connected felt more singed than her cheeks. She rubbed it absently. "Forgive me."

"Nothing to forgive."

"I don't think you have a stick up your arse."

He paused and looked at her. "I like that."

"What?"

"How you say arse."

Orelia covered her face with her hands. "Oh dear."

He gently tugged her hands away and looked at her, his eyes warm and bright. "I seldom hear a woman say coarse words. It's refreshing. Besides, you say it so beautifully."

"Beautifully?"

"Arse." He tried to mimic her, his voice soft and high.

"Oh dear Lord," She giggled.

"Arse, arse, arse." He offered her his arm and she looped her arm through his before she had even considered what she was doing. "It has quite the ring to it."

"I suppose it does," she agreed with a smile. "You know, arse is not the only bad word I know."

He clapped a hand over his heart. "There's more? How shall I survive it?"

"And here I thought gentlemen wanted delicate ladies who never said more than two words, and certainly did not curse."

"Well any gentleman who does is a fool. I cannot understand why ladies are encouraged to be dull, and why gentleman are persuaded to seek dullness. Isn't it bad enough you have to spend a lifetime together?"

"You know, you might be the richest man in England, but we are not so different I think. Why consign yourself to a life of boredom for the sake of civility?"

"Seventh richest," he corrected.

She rolled her eyes. As if that made any difference. They still could not be further apart in circumstances. For the moment, however, it didn't seem to matter.

She let him help her over the second sty. Why, she didn't know. He really was dangerously charming. If she was not careful, she'd find herself softening completely to him. That would not do at all.

Smoke from the various campfires curled into the sky. The maze of colorful wooden wagons didn't offer the same comfort as usual, not when she knew she could see her mother or Cappie. How he would react to another man effectively outbidding him for her, she did not know. He liked to use his fists.

Though she had seen Reed fight. For a noble, he certainly knew how to brawl, something she would not have expected from a duke. She supposed his time as a spy must have taught him a thing or two. She so did want to know more of what he did in France. How envious she was that he'd travelled across the sea and visited other countries. Maybe one day she would do the same. Without Reed's money, she could never have even considered doing such a thing. At least something positive had come out of this experience.

"Who do you recommend talking to first?"

"Marko might know. He did some work at the docks when we first arrived here."

"Very well, let us find this Marko."

They came out into the center of the settlement, where the tents and various craft stalls were gathered. "I don't know how well he shall take to you. Perhaps you should make yourself busy elsewhere."

"Afraid I shall sully your reputation."

"Hardly, but if you want information, you must let me ask on my own."

"Very well." He nodded toward the ale kegs. "I shall keep myself occupied and wait here."

"Don't get into trouble."

He lifted his chin. "I shall have you know I am rarely trouble."

"I said 'get into'. And I do not believe that for one minute."

He cracked a smile and made his way to where the cheap, homemade ale was being served. She hoped he didn't drink much. It was always made from the oldest of hops and often gave people a sore head.

Orelia went in search of Marko, who preferred to spend his time playing cards and trying to beat any visitors. She found him not far from the river's edge, using an old crate as a table while he bested a young man at whist. She waited until he had beaten him and won his coin before sitting opposite the old man.

He narrowed grey eyes at her. "Little Orelia. Now, I know you do not gamble."

"I wanted to ask you something, Marko."

"Should you not be with your husband?" He glanced around as though searching for Reed and scrubbed a hand across his grey beard.

"You know of that already?"

Marko nodded. "Cappie is angry that you were given to someone else."

She grimaced. She thought he would be. Another reason for her not to remain with her own kind. "My husband is having an ale," she explained.

"I hope your mother has not given you away to a drunk. Everyone is still surprised she gave you to an outsider." He leaned across the crate. "Though I heard he paid handsomely for you. I would hope a man willing to pay so much would treat you well."

"He is treating me well," she assured him.

"Good." He picked up the stack of cards and shuffled them. "Good, good. You always were a good girl. Of course, what else could we expect when your father was an outsider?"

Orelia nodded but said nothing. Marko and many others were kind to her but there were many who didn't like that her skin was lighter than theirs and that her father had not been one of them. She didn't even remember him, so it always struck her as strange that people would hold it against her. After all, should she be blamed for her mother's choices? And was that choice so bad? As far as she knew, her mother had loved her father very much. She suspected losing him was what had driven her to drink.

"Will you play?"

"No, I will not leave my husband for long." Lord, how strange that lie sounded. "Marko, when we first arrived here, did any of the men go out on the ships?"

His brows furrowed. "Why should you wish to know such a thing?"

"My husband had some produce on a ship that sailed shortly after we came here. He said some went missing."

"So you have married an outsider and now you believe what they say about us?"

"No, of course not. I wish to prove him wrong. I wish to show him that we are not all bad people."

He made a dismissive sound. "He cannot believe you are bad or else he would not have married you."

"We are not married yet."

"And yet he has you doing his bidding already."

"He is a smart man and knows you will not speak to him. Please, Marko, if you know who went on that ship, I shall be able to tell him that they had nothing to do with the theft."

Marko shook his head. "You will have to be persuasive indeed to clear a Romani of theft."

"Ree—Noah will believe me."

"Unfortunately, I know nothing of any of our men on ships. You know how it is, little Orelia. The men come and go." He lifted his great shoulders in a shrug.

She released a long breath. Of course, she had not expected it to be so easy to find out who had gone on the ships, but it would have been nice. Marko was right. Many of their people vanished and returned at times, following work and wherever their feet carried them. Since arriving in Hampshire, many Romani had left the camp and would return before they moved on again.

Rubbing a hand over his chin, he eyed her. "There is an inn in the town where some of the men go—The Red Lion. I heard tell that they were asking for deckhands last week."

"But this was weeks ago."

Marko lifted his hands. "That is all I can tell you, my girl. Your husband seems a rich man. Can he not hire someone to find his produce rather than leaving his poor wife to ask the questions?"

"I am not his wife."

"Soon enough."

A couple of men were milling around, and Marko turned his attention to them, no doubt aware he could make some money from them.

"Like your chances?" he asked them.

Orelia recognized her dismissal and stood. "Don't beat them too easily, Marko," she murmured. "You don't want to get accused of cheating again."

The old man lifted his chin. "Marko never cheats." He wagged a finger at her. "Do not let that rich man be cruel to you."

"I will not," she promised.

She headed back to meet up with Reed. What should she tell him? The inn might be worth a visit, but Marko was frustratingly vague. They could ask some of the other men but if Marko knew nothing, she doubted anyone else would.

When she emerged from between the wagons, she stilled upon spotting Reed. Several women were gathered around him—Romani and outsiders alike. He held a mug of ale in one hand while he leaned against a stack of kegs. How was it that even with a ridiculous moustache and an eyepatch, women were still flocking to him? She curled her hands into fists and marched over.

"Noah."

He ignored her and continued regaling the women with whatever tale he was telling them. They hung on his every word, mouths open, eyes wide, all leaning in. She could have sworn he could have any one of them with ease, regardless of their own situations.

"Noah!" she barked.

His gaze struck hers, but she saw it take a moment for him to recognize his pretend name. She came to his side and took his arm before smiling sweetly to the ladies.

"If you will excuse me, I have need of my fiancé."

Mouths turned pouty and eyes disappointed before the women dispersed.

"Investigating, Reed?"

He chuckled. "Very much so."

"Somehow I do not believe you." She dropped his arm. "I don't know why I am surprised that you were trying to charm those women while I was doing your work for you."

His smile expanded. "Do you think I charmed them?"

"You know very well you did." Heat began to rise in her chest. How dare he stand there, flirting with all those women when he was supposed to be her fiancé? She swiveled on her heel. She couldn't stay here and confront him, not with too many prying eyes around.

"Orelia?"

She stalked off in the direction of the field, aware he was following. There would be no escaping him. Besides, she was walking in the direction of his house. Whether that had been a decision she'd made by choice, she was not sure, but she could hardly turn around now.

"Orelia." He hurried to her side. "Slow down."

"Why?"

"Because you need to tell me if you found anything out for a start. If you did not, we need to turn around and ask more questions."

She kept her gaze head on. "I suppose you would enjoy asking those women a few more questions, would you not?"

He laughed and the anger brewing inside her felt as though it would burst out of every limb. "I'm glad you find it so amusing! It must be lovely to be able to pay someone to do all your work for you while you spend your time flirting and drinking!"

"Orelia." He tapped her arm, forcing her to slow her aggravated pace before they reached the first sty.

"What?"

"There's no need to be jealous."

"Jealous? What makes you think I am jealous?" she demanded.

"I recognize jealousy when I see it."

"Oh yes, I suppose it's quite a hobby for you. What better way to pass your time than to make a woman jealous. Do you derive a lot of enjoyment from toying with women's emotions,

Reed, or has it become so commonplace for you that you only receive a mere jot of pleasure from it?"

"So you are jealous."

His smug smile made her want to swipe her hand across his face and tear it off. The worst thing of all was that, deep down, she suspected her anger was driven by jealousy.

"I am not. I simply hate to see my sex toyed with."

Reed inched closer. A tiny curl of soapy scent wafted her way before vanishing. She had to fight the urge to move closer and bury her head against his skin to find that enchanting fragrance once more.

He glanced around, likely surmised no one could see them between the backs of the wagons and the field fence and flipped up his eye patch.

"There is no need to be jealous, Orelia."

"I told you, I am not—"

The gap between them shrank again. "There is no need to be jealous," he repeated, "because whilst I was questioning those ladies, all I was thinking about was you."

Orelia opened her mouth to answer then clamped it shut.

"I was thinking about your eyes and the way they spark when you're angry. How in the early morning sun, there's little streaks of amber in them. As I was speaking to those women, I could only think how their lips were incomparable to yours. None were as full, as beautiful or as kissable as yours. When they spoke, their voices were but a mere shadow of your husky tones. And as for their figures..." He smirked. "Well, none were as blessed as you. None were anywhere near as enticing as you."

Her mouth dropped open again. She stared up into those blue eyes and tried to find the lies or the deliberate charm. But why should he need to charm her? He had paid her after all. She was bound to him by money.

"I—"

A finger came to her chin, then to the corner of her mouth. Tingles raced from that spot, through her body, making her ache in so many places. He pressed down on her bottom lip.

"You really do have the most beautiful mouth. Made for kissing," he said softly.

It was almost too much to process. No one had ever called her beautiful. Or told her she was made for kissing. Or admired her figure.

A nonsensical sound escaped her. Perhaps she had meant it as *stop* or *please go on*. Who really knew? She did not, for certain, but apparently Reed did. He took it as *please continue*.

He lowered his mouth to hers. For several heartbeats, he hovered there, his warm breath touching her lips. She smelled mint and that sweet scent of soap wrapped about her once more. His gaze dug deep into hers, making her heart constrict. Orelia had to close her eyes to him. At the same time as wanting nothing more than to stare into those depths forever, she could bare it no longer.

Behind the comforting darkness of her lids, she waited. And waited. Then it was there. She released the air from her lungs after the first light touch of lips upon lips.

Reed kept her chin lifted with a single finger upon her face. Another touch. This time to the corner of her mouth. Every part of her now tingled.

He swept his mouth across hers the next time. So frustratingly lightly that she wanted to grip him by his coat and press herself hard against him, but her legs and arms were frozen, rooted like an old oak tree. She was his to do with as he wished, so she waited again.

One more sweep. More frissons of sensation. Then firm lips covering hers. She sighed inwardly as warm satisfaction flowed through her. Her hands had become unrooted and she found the coarse wool of his coat under her palms. His mouth moved gently, without demand, but she almost wished he would demand.

He gave her one last firm, decisive kiss and eased away, just enough so that she could stare up into his eyes and wish for another.

"What did you do that for?" she asked huskily while she uncurled her fingers and released him.

He grinned. "Because you are too damn beautiful."

With that, he began to march his way toward the sty, leaving her staring at his back. What an astonishing few days this had been.

Chapter Eight

Reed stared at the dark canopy until the little swirls and tassels on the fabric grew visible. He normally slept excellently. Even when in France, when really any day could be his last, he had the ability to sleep like a baby. The fact was, that while he wined and dined with nobles, his job had meant travelling across the country at a moment's notice or having to move on swiftly. He had therefore learned to make the most of any rest he could get.

Not tonight, though. Tonight he had tossed and turned and finally fallen asleep while that lingering knowledge that she was a few bedrooms away burrowed deep into his gut. Then he had awoken for no reason, fully aware his body had not gained the rest it needed.

He scrubbed a hand across his face and yawned. He was never going to find sleep here, so he climbed out of bed and cursed the cool night air as it wrapped about his bare legs.

A burst of pain flared through his toe. "Damn it."

All the years he had been sleeping in this room, he should remember the layout. What a fool. He scowled at the offending chair and fumbled for his robe.

It was the blasted kiss, he acknowledged as he did up the robe and found and lit the candle at his bedside.

That blasted, delicious, enticing, searing kiss.

Who knew a gypsy girl could be so kissable?

He supposed he did, given that he'd been thinking of her lips from the first day. Still, he couldn't continue. As much as he wanted to repeat it and as much as he could not bring himself to regret it, it was becoming clear kissing Orelia wasn't the brightest of ideas. What else could he blame for his inability to sleep? Reed was hardly one to lie to himself and he would not start now.

The truth of it was, he was far too attracted to Orelia.

He shuffled out of the room and down the quiet corridor. When his mother wasn't home, the whole house seemed too empty. It was one of the reasons he had eagerly accepted the government's request to aid them. She loved to travel and visit with friends, often leaving him to fend for himself. It was not that he missed his mother's company—far from it. At least he didn't have to tolerate her meddling whilst she was gone. But it did leave the house somewhat cold and empty. Noah was not one for entertaining and Reed had not been returned long enough to arrange balls and week-long parties. No wonder Orelia thought it odd that they had all this space and hardly put it to use.

He paused outside her door. Behind there, she would be sleeping. Her hair would be loose most likely. He doubted she thought to braid it or put it in rolls before bed. Her long lashes would be fanned across her face. Maybe she'd be naked. Even if she was not, his imagination had decided he liked the image and clung to it.

Orelia, wrapped in a sheet, the tops of her breasts peeking out, her arms wide, her hair spread out. Yes, his imagination liked that very much.

He grimaced when he began to grow hard. So did his body, apparently.

He moved on swiftly. If she heard him and came to investigate, he could not imagine her reacting well to him standing there like some primitive beast, breathing heavily and sporting an erection.

Carefully, he made his way down to the main hall and progressed through the house. Clock ticks and the drip of water from somewhere echoed through the empty spaces. Moonlight drifted through the gaps in curtains, turning the belongings of his ancestors a ghostly blue. He moved through the house—hardly sure where he was intending to stop but following his instincts nonetheless. He was restless and aroused. A good walk through the house would not hurt at all.

When he came to the door of the library, he paused. Perhaps it had been his imagination which, as was obvious, was ridiculously active at present, but he could have sworn he'd heard a voice. Unless his servants had taken up midnight reading, it could only be one person.

Really, he should have turned around. Twin voices echoed in his head. The one governing his aroused state urged him forward. *Go, go, go*, it said in time with the beat of his heart. The other was quieter, more subdued. The other voice was the sensible one that told him to turn around, go to the kitchens, find a little something to eat and go to bed.

The other voice could hang. He pushed the door open.

She screamed.

Reed raced forward and caught Orelia mid-air. She had only been a few steps up the ladder resting against the bookcase, but it would have been enough to twist an ankle.

Muslin and soft skin surrounded him. He found his head buried against some breasts until he repositioned her.

"Are you well?" he asked, the words raspy.

His body was in shock, stiff and aching and hot. He could feel warm skin beneath his palm and could see the outline of dark nipples. Orelia had lit a few candles, unfortunately for him. Or fortunately, depending on how he looked at it. Mostly he looked at her breasts.

"Let me down," she whispered.

"Right. Yes." He nodded and eased her to the floor.

Though he could no longer feel a soft thigh or breast against him, he could see even more. Her breasts pressed against the shift she wore, round and full. Her nipples were hard. And still dark against the fabric. He'd hardly expected that to change from between then and now, but one could always hope. By some miracle, he forced his gaze onto her face.

"Forgive me, I did not mean to startle you."

She lifted a shoulder. "I should not have been in here."

"Not at all. You are a guest here." He nodded to the shelf of books to which she'd been climbing. "Were you looking for something to read? I do not suggest that section. My father was keen on philosophy and most of those are books he bought."

"You do not like philosophy?"

"I don't really have the patience for it. One can ponder life and all its meanings for an eternity and never come to a conclusion."

"Oh."

Reed longed to give himself a solid smack around the face. What the devil was he doing? Here he had an exquisitely beautiful woman in his library and they were discussing philosophy. Had this occurred in France, he'd have likely seized the opportunity to take some enjoyment in the chance meeting. However, this was not France and he was no longer some great spy. He had one last chance and he could not afford to mess it up.

"Were you looking for something in particular?"

Her gaze lowered. "No. I mean—" She huffed out a breath.

"Orelia?"

Her lashes lifted and the mournful look in her eyes struck him. "I cannot read. I was hoping for some books with engravings in them."

Reed seldom felt an arse. Generally, he could bluff and charm his way out of any situation. But how blind could he be? Of course Orelia could not read. When would she have been given the opportunity to learn? The fact was half of his tenants couldn't either. What a buffoon he was.

Unwilling to draw out her embarrassment, he took her hand and led her past the chairs in the center of the room and up a set of spiral stairs. The candlelight only touched the corners of the room, leaving much of it in darkness but there was enough light for him to read the titles on the leather-bound books. The scent of musty paper strengthened as he took her along the mahogany balcony that ran around the whole room.

"This library was designed by my grandfather," he explained. "He intended to fill it with books from all around the world, but he died before its completion. My father took up the mantle and did an excellent job."

"And will you continue the tradition?"

He paused and peered at the few empty shelves remaining. "I picked up a few on my travels but I've seldom had the chance to think about it. War tends to make one forget about things like family traditions."

She wrinkled her nose. "Yes, I suppose you are right, though the war never much touched us."

"War is a nasty way to pass time. I'm glad it did not."

They stopped in front of a section of books near the long windows that nearly touched the ceiling. The curtains were open and from where they were, they had a fine view over the fields in front of the house. Tiny glimmers of lamp light flickered on the hills, displaying the whereabouts of the gypsy camp.

She peered at him. "You speak of the war as though you enjoyed it."

"I was lucky. I had a skill and it was put to use. Most men were simply cannon fodder." He motioned to the books. "This is the architecture section. You shall find many engravings here. Castles and suchlike. There's even a few books dedicated to the history of the house. I'd wager they could keep you occupied for quite some time."

"But were you not scared?" she persisted.

He pulled out a book. "Ah, here. The history of Keswick Abbey. This will show you the progression of the house. It was once a Tudor manor house, you know?"

"Reed?"

He chuckled. "You are curious, are you not?"

"I've never met a spy before."

"How do you know?"

"Well, I do not believe I have but I've never met one who admitted to being a spy." She took the offered book from him and clutched it to her chest. "Was it not terrifying?"

"Sometimes. For the most part, I reveled in it. You cannot know the thrill of being so close to being caught and somehow slipping free once more."

"You miss it?"

"I do." He glanced around the room. "I am aware I am vastly privileged in my position but once you've tasted the thrill of sneaking around a country in which you represent the enemy, it's hard to find any excitement in managing farms and socializing with the 'right' families."

"If you find out who tried to kill Napoleon, will they ask you to spy for them again?"

He shrugged. "One can only hope."

"And then what of your duties?"

"Noah is extremely capable, no matter what others think."

"What of your need to sire an heir?"

Christ, she was beginning to sound like his mother. He lifted a brow. "Why should that interest you?"

"Is that not what all rich men want? An heir?"

"I'm hardly an old man."

"But the estate is in danger as long as you are without a son, is it not?"

"Yes," he admitted. "It will pass onto Noah if anything happens to me, but he does not have a son either. My mother would be devastated. But I have no intention of letting anything happen to me."

"Even if you return to working for the Secret Service?"

"I am not dead yet." He snatched up another couple of books and went the long way around the balcony, aware she followed. Reed made his way down the steps and set the books on the table in the middle of the room. "There, plenty to keep you occupied."

Orelia perched herself on the edge of the table. Damn the woman. The position drew attention to her shapely form against the muslin and how it hugged the curve of her rear. Heat rolled languidly through him, as though he had all night to simply stand and stare.

She picked up a book and leafed through it. "Did you nearly die when you were in France?"

Reed gave in then. How could he fight her? Her incessant questions and the way that cloth draped over her body had him beaten. He sank down into the plush chair opposite her and rested his head on his hand.

"Yes."

"How? Why?"

"The first time was when I had infiltrated the home of an illustrious French count." A smile creeped over his lips as he remembered how he had slipped in. "The count was thought to be funding the French army and would hold a lot of information about Napoleon's dealings."

"Goodness."

Even he could not quite believe he'd had the audacity to seduce the man's wife while he was away. The countess had been a fairly attractive woman and quite neglected by her husband. It had not been hard to charm his way into her bed.

"I was in his house one night when he returned. I was confronted by an angry man with a pistol. Really, I should have been dead."

"How did you survive?"

"Pure luck I'm ashamed to say. The pistol exploded, giving me the chance to escape." He would not add he'd been semi-naked at the time.

"But you had other brushes with death?"

He chuckled. "None quite like that one, thankfully. Let's just say, I learned from that incident."

Orelia shook her head. "I am not sure how you can seem so...so calm about it all. And I certainly do not understand why you would want to do it again. Many men did not return. Surely you should be thankful you did?"

"I am thankful, I promise you that. I might not have needed to spill blood in my line of work, but I saw enough of it. It was not all dining with nobles and dancing. There were times when I had to visit the battlefield. I would not wish it on anyone."

"And yet after all that, you wish to continue spying?"

"I wish to be useful to my country," he said, aware his voice was growing hard and defensive.

Was it so wrong of him to crave the excitement? So wrong to want to do something more useful than marry someone respectable and sire an heir? Noah had proved himself over and over. All Reed had to do was sign a few letters and check over investments occasionally.

"But the war is over now, Reed," she said softly.

Yes, it was. And he was having a tough time admitting it. The war was over, and he was no longer useful. Once this was done, he would have to return to digging through papers and touring the estate before wining and dining with the rest of nobility and finding himself the perfect wife to bear his sons. And Noah would lose the responsibilities he relished.

She slipped off the table and came to stand in front of him. Orelia reached out then hesitated. He made no movement. How could he? She held him captive with her curvaceous form against her shift. He waited, and she moved again, pushing her fingers into his hair and rubbing them across his scalp. He groaned.

"Why could you not sleep?" she asked softly.

"Who knows," he mumbled.

"I could not sleep either."

"Strange bed?" he asked, closing his eyes and savoring the delicious touch of her fingers.

"I think it is more likely the events of the day."

Reed did not say anything. He didn't have to. She referred to their kiss. A kiss that should not have happened, yet he could not bring himself to regret. He'd likely remember the day he'd kissed a wild, beautiful gypsy girl even on his deathbed.

"What shall we do tomorrow?" she asked.

"We'll visit that inn you mentioned. I also have a contact in Portsmouth I have been communicating with. I haven't heard from him for a while, but he might have some information."

Though it was a minor miracle he'd heard anything she'd told him after their kiss. Really, he was terribly impressed with himself for being able to hold a sane conversation with her once they'd returned to the house.

"And what then?" Her fingers continued to work their magic. Part of him longed to open his eyes and see her face, but he couldn't bring himself to. He was enjoying this far, far too much.

"One step at a time. You are far too keen to move into the next step before we have discovered anything."

"It's in my blood. The Romani are always on the move."

"Well you should sit still for a while. Enjoy what life has to offer."

"I think perhaps you should take your own advice." Her fingers left his head and he bit back a groan of disappointment. "You too could also take some time to enjoy life."

He opened his eyes and found her staring down at him. Reed couldn't help but curl his fingers around her hips and draw her close. He pressed his head against her stomach and she smoothed his hair with both hands.

"You know, Orelia, you and I are not so different."

She laughed.

Chapter Nine

"Surely your servants suspect something?" Orelia pressed.

Reed laughed and aided her onto the simple pony and trap. The seat was hard beneath her rear and much of it was worn. They'd collected it from a farm, some distance from the house, all in the name of keeping his identity a secret.

"They tend to believe I'm doing something very wicked whenever I sneak away."

She pressed her lips together. "Somehow I believe there were times when you were," she murmured. "What of your brother?"

"He knows enough. Noah is excellent at keeping secrets." He climbed up next to her and the trap wobbled.

She gripped the rail beside her. "Are you sure this is safe?"

"Absolutely."

Night began to fall on them, the skies turning dusky and grey. Apprehension thrummed through her stomach and couldn't even be defeated by the knowledge of sitting so close to Reed. Last night had been a strange moment. She'd gained some measure of him, she suspected, and liked what she'd discovered far too much.

Reed gave the reins a tug and the horse started slowly down the winding lane. The hedgerow brushed her sleeve. "These lanes are so tight!"

"They're old lanes. Seldom used really. They were not really designed for vehicles."

They went over a rut and she gripped the seat as it flung her against him. "I suppose at least if I fall, I shall have a nice hedge to cushion me."

He chuckled. "You shan't be falling anywhere. I will not allow it."

Orelia drew in a breath before releasing it slowly. How odd it was to think that she had touched her lips to this man's—a man so rich that he could probably feed her entire community for life. And to think that she'd been touching him, soothing him last night. Reed, of all people. Why should he need her comfort? Yet, she had wanted to give it to him. He was upon a crossroads in life like her. They were both adrift from their previous path with little clue as to what to do next.

Of course, Reed would have to settle down to his duties. Rich men like him had no choice. She had plenty of choice thanks to what he would pay her. More than she had previous, anyway. Now all she needed to do was decide what to do with her new-found wealth.

"We should have left earlier," she muttered with the skies seeming to close in about her.

She'd spent much time on the road with her mother, but they seldom traveled after dark, not with the risk of coming off the road or meeting highwaymen.

"All will be well. Unfortunately, I could not get away from my meeting with the estate manager."

No, and she had been tucked upstairs in the house, hiding away from the glares of the servants and ensuring she did not meet any of Reed's visitors. Not that he had asked her to, but what else could she do? Linger around and expect people to be polite to her. Whilst Reed seemed oblivious to her circumstances, even the servants were not. She was a dirty gypsy to them and no pretty gown would change that.

"Not to worry, the town is but four miles away. It shan't take us long."

She failed to respond. So much in her mind was awhirl. Orelia did not like it one bit. In truth, she had never had so much time to simply think. Her life had been one of hard work and survival. Her biggest worry had been where their next meal was coming from. Now she had to wonder if he would kiss her again or what she would do with one hundred pounds. All this thinking and not doing was rather exhausting.

They continued in silence. Why he was quiet, she didn't know. Estate worries perhaps or planning how they were going to find the men. It was strange how quickly she had grown used to hearing him talk. She found herself wanting to hear more of his life. Last night had offered a glimpse and she wanted more.

"What—"

The trap jerked to a halt and tilted abruptly. A strong arm banded around her waist when she tumbled to one side, her arm becoming lost in the hedgerow. Reed pulled her into him and ensured she was upright before clambering down.

"Damn." He took off his cap and pushed a hand through his hair. "Looks like a wheel has gone."

"I knew it was not safe," she declared and immediately clapped a hand over her mouth.

"Yes, thank you for that, Orelia." He gave her a stern look, but amusement tinged his lips.

He offered her a hand to help her down. She winced. Apparently her knee had taken the brunt of the crash. "Sorry, that was not at all helpful."

"No, it was not." He peered back up the lane. "There will be no fixing it and we are closer to town than to the abbey."

Moving to unhook the horse, he nodded in the direction of the dim glow of lamplight on the horizon. "It will only take an hour or so."

She nodded but her stomach bunched. It was bad enough being on wagon at night, but on foot...? It would be so easy to attack them and leave them for dead. And her knee still hurt.

Reed coaxed the horse along and nodded to the animal. "Do you wish to ride? I'd imagine you would have no troubles without a sidesaddle."

She did not know whether to be offended that he did not expect her to ride like a lady but as he was correct, she simply smiled. "You would be right. I've never ridden sidesaddle. But I would rather walk I think. I'd rather have sore feet than a sore bottom."

He chuckled. "Oh yes, we certainly cannot have that. Come then, we had better make haste. I would rather not be in the dark for any longer than we have to be."

She nodded quickly and followed beside him whilst he led the pony along.

"Orelia?"

"Yes."

"Do not be afraid, I will not let anything happen to you."

"Do I look afraid?"

He paused to stare at her. His lips slanted. "I think the only time I've seen you look afraid was when you stepped into my home."

Orelia lifted her chin. "I was not afraid."

"If you say so."

"I was not!" she protested.

"Orelia, you are the strongest woman I've ever met. Do not think that because you were a little afraid very briefly that it makes me think any different."

She drew in a long breath and released it. Was she strong? She wasn't so sure. Life threw many obstacles in her way and she fought to overcome them. Sometimes, though, she wondered when that obstacle would be so big that it would defeat her. It would happen soon, surely? Being a Romani would make it a certainty. Something would come in her way as she strove to create a future for herself. She only hoped her strength could carry her through once more.

They walked silently for several minutes, following the winding lane. The pain in her leg was not so severe, but it did make her wince. Being several miles still from the town, she did not much look forward to this walk. Something tickled her leg. Something damp, she realized.

"Reed, wait." He stilled when she stopped to lift her skirts. She grimaced at the sight of a small stream of blood trickling down her leg. Lifting her skirts higher, she found the source. A rather frightful gash upon her knee. Some of the skin had lifted away and provided a gruesome sight.

"Christ." Reed dropped down in front of her and brandished a handkerchief.

"It looks worse than it is." He pressed the cotton to her knee and she hissed.

"You should have said something."

"It was only a graze. I must have bashed it on the cart when it came to a stop. I did not think I'd done much damage."

He eyed her. "I know I said I admire your strength, Orelia, but there was no need for you to try to prove it to me. You should have told me."

She remained quiet, teeth gritted while he dabbed at the wound. She was not used to telling people of her woes. For most of her life it had been her and her mother, and they dealt with things alone. And when her mother had fallen prey to alcohol, she handled things truly alone.

Reed undid his necktie and proceeded to bind it around her wound.

"Ouch." The word slipped from her lips before she could prevent it. The pressure upon her knee was an odd mixture of relief and burning pain.

"Forgive me." He tightened the cloth then stood. "Can you walk?"

"I was walking was I not? What do you intend to do? Throw me over your shoulder like a grain sack?"

He chuckled. "If I had to." He held out an arm. "At least lean on me a little. Ease some of the burden on your knee."

"I am not so fragile."

"Just take my arm, Orelia."

He said it so wearily that she did as she was told. It brought her close to his side. Though they were dressed as relatively poor folk—well, she looked poor, Reed only moderately so—she could not help remind herself that she was on the arm of a duke. What would it be like to be wearing one of those expensive gowns while he was in his best clothing walking down the stairs of the abbey to a crowd of rich people?

Terrifying most likely but in her imagination, she had all the courage she needed to face those sorts of people.

"If we head toward the main road, we shall likely come upon someone. It will take us a mile out, but it will be quicker."

"Do you really think someone will stop for us?"

"Why not?"

The image of a beautiful gown vanished as she glanced down to look at her drab brown wool. "Because I am dressed like this and you are only just respectable. Even less so with me on your arm."

"You underestimate the impact of my charm."

"You overestimate it. No one shall give you long enough to utter a word upon seeing me."

"Have a little faith, Orelia."

They continued along the road for a while longer before branching off toward the main road. This was wider with stones marking the directions. Ahead the path sloped down toward the next rise where it then vanished on the horizon. Somewhere over it would be the town.

Grooves were dug deeply into the ground, making it uneven and hard for her to walk. However, that at least meant it was well-used and they were likely to come upon travelers. She still doubted anyone would stop for them, not when there was a risk of highwaymen but if Reed believed he could get them a ride, she would, as he had commanded, 'have a little faith.'

Soon her faith was repaid by the sound of horse hooves and carriage wheels behind them. Reed tugged her to one side and removed his hat before lifting a hand. She noted that he'd instantly adopted a charming facade, his mouth pulled into a pleasant smile, his posture unthreatening and welcoming.

The driver flicked a glance their way and a face pressed against the window of the closed carriage. Orelia watched it pass, muscles tense with expectancy.

The carriage continued.

"Damn."

She only gave him a look, knowing full well there was no need to remind him she'd told him so. The rattle of wheels faded into the distance.

"Come, let's keep moving. We shall end up out here in the dark at this rate."

He nodded. "Yes, I suppose we must. I don't much like you walking with your knee like that, though."

And she knew she was slowing their pace. Each time she moved her knee, the graze protested, sending burning pain through the joint.

They stilled again at the sound of another approaching carriage. She glanced at Reed, his charming expression back in place and shook her head.

"Give me your jacket."

"What?"

"Give me it!" she demanded and tugged at the lapels.

He hauled it off and she bundled it up then shoved it up her gown. A fierce scowl marred his brow when she forced it into a rounded shape. The carriage neared, and she waited until the passengers would be able to see her before flinging herself across Reed's arms. He gave an *oof* sound and fumbled to hold her as she lay across his arms, eyes closed.

From behind her closed lids, she heard the carriage roll past then slow down. The creak of a window. Then the shout of a man. "I say, is everything well?"

Reed hesitated. "Um..."

"Your wife fainted," Orelia hissed at him.

"Um. My wife appears to have fallen into a fainting fit."

"Goodness," said the man.

"Oh dear me. Eldon, do something," a woman said.

Orelia cracked open one eye, just a tad and spotted the woman's head hanging out of the carriage. They were wealthy by the looks of it. Not Reed wealthy, but well off enough to be sure. Not too fine that they would dismiss people in need, though. Orelia found when people were overly rich they did not care much for others at all. Reed seemed to be the exception.

She snapped shut her eyes when Reed lifted her fully into his hold and took the few steps toward the carriage. "Our mare hurt herself a few miles back and we've been walking since. As you can see, my wife is in a delicate condition."

She fluttered open her eyes and did a show of being confused. "Oh dear, what happened?"

Reed lowered her carefully to the ground and she hung on him whilst fanning her face.

"You fainted, my dear."

She rubbed a hand across her belly and peered at the gawping couple. "Goodness, all that walking must have taken its toll. I hope I did not give you a fright," she said to the strangers.

The man shook his head and ran his gaze over her clothing. A little disdain flickered in his eyes and he went to duck back into the carriage. "Ouch."

His wife glared at him while he rubbed his arm. "Where are you travelling to?"

"Just into town." Orelia smiled sadly. "I would not be travelling in such a condition, but my mother is desperately ill. I fear she shall not last much longer." Even a few tears managed to well in her eyes. She hoped Reed noticed. He wasn't the only one who could put on an act.

"Well, you must travel with us," the woman declared. "It is far too long a journey for you."

"Excellent," declared Reed.

"Oh no, we could not take advantage," Orelia clasped Reed's arm.

"You must, I insist," the woman said firmly.

The husband reluctantly pushed open the door and flicked down the steps. Reed handed Orelia up and she settled next to the woman.

She offered the stranger a warm smile. "Thank Goodness for the charity of strangers."

She turned her smile upon Reed and spotted the tiny smirk dancing on his lips. She also noticed admiration sparking in his eyes. He rather liked that she could play his game, she suspected.

The journey passed quickly enough, with a few questions as to how they ended up on the path so late at night. Reed allowed Orelia to take the lead and answer Mrs. Corbitt's questions. The husband simply glowered at Reed, even as Reed flashed him a smile. Orelia thought she put on quite the performance, describing how their carriage had broken and how excited they were for the baby to arrive but oh dear, her poor mother was sick and thank goodness there were kind people like the Corbitts in the world.

By the time they were deposited in Portsmouth, not far from the inn, Mrs. Corbitt had all but adopted Orelia as her daughter. A flush of guilt ran through her. She was a genuinely kind woman and much as she had not enjoyed taking advantage of those who were good people in need of some comfort through her 'readings', the pleasure of her performance waned when the woman stuck her head out of the carriage and wished her and the baby all the best.

Orelia eyed the carriage as it ran across the dirt street. A few lamps lit the way, catching on the woman's beaming face before it turned a tight corner past a cobbler's shop.

"What is it?" Reed asked.

She sighed. "Poor woman."

He shook his head and grinned at her. "Orelia, you were marvelous."

"That is all very easy for you to say. You're used to lying."

"And you are not?"

"Well, it's not the same," she insisted, gnawing on her bottom lip.

"You caused no harm." He cupped her face in his hands and lifted her chin. "You got us here safely, Orelia. You did a marvelous job."

The warm praise and the boyish grin on his face eased the guilt inside her. It was true. The Corbitts had been travelling this way anyway. They had made little difference to the husband and wife's journey. In all likelihood, having Reed made it safer. She'd wager few highwaymen would want to run across Reed on a dark night.

She glanced into his eyes and saw the pride sparkling there. It was a wonderful feeling. She could not help but return his grin. It was utterly infectious. Of course, that was just Reed. Infectious. In the most charming, enjoyable way.

"Well done, my girl," he said. "You are a wonderful liar."

How such words could summon up a bubble of warmth inside of her, she did not know. However, they were just about the first kind words anyone had ever said to her, so she absorbed them. It was likely in years to come, she would remember the day a handsome duke told her such things.

He closed the gap before she had quite registered him moving closer. He captured her with his gaze. Her heart picked up pace, pounding restlessly against her chest. She knew what was to come. Held her breath in anticipation. Already, she had begun to recognize that look in his eyes. His mouth sealed across hers swiftly. His hands lifted her face higher, giving him the perfect angle to kiss her firmly.

A tiny moan issued from her at the feel of his lips upon hers. When he moved away, it took all she had not to release another of disappointment. He smiled softly, his gaze holding hers while he kept her face cradled in his palms.

"I have to wonder, Orelia, if you are so talented at telling lies, what lies do you tell me?"

Orelia laughed. As if she could tell him a single lie. Reed had seen through her from the beginning and with each passing day, was burrowing deeper under her skin. He likely already knew her better than anyone.

It should have been a terrifying thought.

So why was it not?

Chapter Ten

Though the hour was late, the inn proved to be crowded. Reed hoped the eyepatch and his general demeanor was intimidating enough to keep any wandering hands from finding Orelia. The damn woman might be dressed like a peasant but that did not hide her beauty. He was acutely aware that bringing her into The Red Lion was like bringing bread crumbs to a starving man. They'd scoop her up and eat her in one go if he let them.

"Stay close to me," he murmured to her.

There was no chance they would stay here for the night. Once they were done, he'd find them a more suitable inn in which to stay. It would not be on par with some of the fine hotels in London or Bath but somewhere a little safer and quiet would do. If he'd have been alone, he might have stayed but even with knowing how well Orelia could handle herself, he did not want to be responsible for her coming to harm.

He smirked.

After all, she was his 'fiancée.'

What would his mother think?

He wondered if his mother might not be at least a little impressed at her quick thinking on the road tonight. No one would stop for him, but for a pregnant woman... and she played the role so very nicely. It seemed he was not the only one with the ability to think on his feet.

With Orelia's hand clasped in his, he guided her through to the bar area. Smoke lingered in the air, partly from the fire in the grate which was burning with poor wood and likely a half-blocked chimney, and partly from the cigarettes some of the patrons smoked. It hung like a woolen blanket around his head.

Underfoot the floor was sticky with spilled ale. He'd wager there were other foodstuffs likely added to the concoction along with rat droppings and whatever had been traipsed in by foot.

She leaned into him. "How will we know who to ask?"

"I'll speak with the innkeeper first," he told her over the din of male laughter and the general hubbub of conversation.

"I do not see any Romani."

"You can tell?"

"We do tend to stand out."

Reed shrugged. Were it not for Orelia coming from the gypsy camp, he would not have thought of her roots. Mostly he would have been considering her figure and beautiful lips. And if she had been dressed in a sumptuous gown, he probably would have thought her to be from Spain or some other warm place.

They broke through the crowds to the bar. A man with tattoos on his arms and grey, wispy hair that stood at all angles served two gentlemen before turning his attention to them.

"Two ales."

The man nodded, pulled out two jugs, spat in them and gave them a quick rub with his cloth. If this bothered Orelia, she made no mention of it. Reed could not help but grin. What a woman she was. If he had brought one of the society ladies like Lady Edith, they'd be out of here within moments. In fact, he didn't think he'd have managed to drag them through the door let alone have them stand and watch such a display. With the ales poured, he handed over some coin and leaned against the bar.

"I heard there were some ships asking for deckhands recently."

The man nodded. "You looking for work?"

"Could be."

"We haven't had anyone in for a while, I'm afraid to say. It might be worth going down to the docks and asking." The barkeeper shrugged.

"Which ship was recruiting before?"

The man paused and scratched his head, forcing his hair into more disarray. "The HMS Norfolk I believe. A few of the regular men were on it, though they haven't got work since."

"Are they here tonight?"

The barkeep shook his head and huffed. "Lord, do you want me to go out and find a job for you?" He glanced around. "No, I don't see them but then they aren't usually in until Friday." He motioned to the waiting patrons. "If you don't mind, some of us do have a job to do."

"Now what?" Orelia asked.

"Drink your ale." He thrust the mug into her hand. "Then we shall find somewhere to stay for the night. We'll have to come back tomorrow to find these men."

She peered over the edge of the mug and then at him. He took a generous drink of the weak ale. She gave him a jaunty grin and tipped it back. He watched as she gulped it down before slamming it onto the bar. Reed chuckled.

"Thirsty?"

She gave a tiny shudder. "Something like that." Taking his hand, she tugged him away from the bar and he put his own drink down on a nearby table. "Let us get out of here, we're garnering a few looks."

He peered around, surprised to notice she was right. That was unusual, and it worried him. Normally he could be counted on to know exactly what was happening around him. For some reason, he had not been so on guard, despite lecturing himself about looking after Orelia.

Careful to keep his eye on their surroundings this time, Reed led her out of the inn and down the main road. "There's a more reputable inn just down the road."

"You know Portsmouth?"

"Yes, I sailed out from here once or twice."

"Will we fit in at a reputable inn? I hate to say it, Reed, but you are not your usual, dashing self in that disguise."

"It is reputable but hardly the sort of place the nobility stay. But it has clean beds and good food. What more do we need?"

Her eyes crinkled at the corners as she swung a glance his way. "I never thought I'd hear a duke utter such words. Do you not need, oh I don't know, a one hundred course meal, and a bed stuffed with dove feathers and servants to attend your every whim?"

He grinned. "I hope you know me better than that by now." He wrapped an arm around her shoulders and drew her close as they passed another inn with several patrons sitting outside. "I certainly wouldn't complain about the dove feathers, but I can live on a lot less than my counterparts."

"Do you think them spoiled?"

He let his brow furrow. "I'm not sure. Not more than I am, I suppose, but my experience has been different. I think they just do not know any better."

Orelia gave a sigh. "I used to dream of living in a house like yours. Of course, I hardly knew what one would look like inside, but I imagined there to be a lot of gold."

"Gold?"

"Yes." She giggled. "Gold everywhere!"

"Even the beds?"

"Especially the beds. A golden bed with the softest mattress you could imagine. That's what I used to dream of when sleeping in the caravan."

"Help me with this and perhaps I shall find you a golden bed."

She shook her head and leaned into him. "I cannot deny the idea of living as you do holds appeal, but I know full well I could never fit into a life like yours."

"What makes you think *I* fit in with a life like mine?"

"Do you not?"

"Why do you think I took up the chance to go to France? Far more interesting than sitting around playing duke."

"So you decided to play spy instead?"

He motioned to an inn tucked into the corner of the town square. White washed, with an uneven roof, it was hardly an imposing building but that kept away too many visitors and would be ideal for them. He ignored Orelia's question and pulled open the heavy wooden door to let her in.

He didn't consider what he'd done playing as such. Heck, he'd been in danger several times during his years in France. But of course there had been an element of avoiding his duties. What man in his right mind wished to sit around and manage farm land? Well, Noah did. It had been all he'd ever wanted as a boy. Fleeing the country and helping the war gave them both an opportunity to do what they actually wanted.

Reed arranged them a shared room, signing them in as Mr. and Mrs. Moseley.

"Moseley?" Orelia asked once they entered the room.

"My butler."

"Yes, I remember."

"It gives me a little pleasure to imagine how he'd feel being involved in something so sordid."

"Sordid?" She did a loop around the small room that was tucked up in the eaves of the building. A tiny window looked out onto the town square under which a table and basin sat. The bed was a decent size and clean, as promised. With the low eaves, however, he would have to be careful not to strike his head.

"Well, you and I sharing a room..." He motioned around.

"Is that sordid?"

He narrowed his gaze at her. "I have no intention of making it so, but I know Moseley would think it is."

She dropped onto the bed and shoved the tip of her thumb into her mouth. "We will be sharing a bed?"

He paused to truly look at her. Sometimes he forgot she was quite young. She seemed so experienced and confident at times. Did the idea of sharing a bed with him scare her?

"I shall sleep on the chair." He tapped the side of the rather fragile-looking piece of furniture with his foot. It gave a creak, and something snapped. "Or the floor perhaps."

Orelia shook her head and laughed. "You can share with me, I do not mind. I just was not sure what was expected and I'm sure the ladies you spend time with would be shocked at anyone allowing such liberties but...I trust you."

Who would have thought three such simple words could have such an impact? She trusted him.

A grin escaped him. The words created a terrifyingly warm, fuzzy feeling inside him. What the devil was wrong with him? Yes, she was a fascinating creature and he enjoyed her company. But there were many women who had fascinated him in the past and there would surely be many more. So why on earth did gaining her trust mean so much to him?

"Well," he said, "you will be astonished to hear you are much mistaken. There are many members of the *ton* who are far more scandalous than you could imagine."

"One of my friends used to read the scandal sheets out loud to us all."

"The scandal sheets hardly skim the surface of it." He shucked off his jacket and began to flick open the buttons of his waistcoat. "What happened to your friend?"

"She married. They went to Ireland, I believe."

"And what of your other friends, will you not miss them when you do...whatever it is you plan to do?"

"The Romani community is a close one, but we have many rules. What happens in our community remains in it. That means that if a husband is a bad husband, there is little anyone can do about it."

Reed snorted. "That sounds like the *ton*."

"I am not sure I can count many of them as true friends. They are more like..." She pursed her lips. "More like family. Sometimes you do not always like your family, even if you love them."

"So will you miss your family?"

She shook her head. "I always felt I was meant for something else. To be free perhaps. I'm not sure. It is probably my English blood that does it. It means I am not quite one of them." She gave a smile. "I quite like the idea of opening a tea shop."

Reed rubbed his forehead. Of all the ambitions to have, Orelia's amounted to serving others. The woman would never cease to amaze.

"Come on, we had better try to sleep," he suggested. "We have another busy day ahead and you need to rest that leg of yours."

Chapter Eleven

Orelia rolled and eyed the plump pillow on which her head was buried. It might not be as luxurious as the bed at the abbey but it was certainly more pleasant than sleeping in the wagon. She rolled to the other side again and froze mid-stretch. Reed was standing with his back to her.

His bare back.

She swallowed and eyed the flex of muscles across his shoulders, hardly daring to breathe.

He dipped his hands into the wash basin on the table and sloshed water across his chest. Trickles ran over his shoulders and she eyed them as they trailed down his back. Her mouth grew incredibly dry. Reed was a remarkable specimen of a man. Witty, clever, funny and far too handsome for his own good. How on earth had she ended up in such a position? A gypsy girl sharing a room with a duke whilst hunting for would-be killers... If she could read, she doubted she would have ever read a story like it.

He pushed his hands through his hair and snatched a nearby towel. Her breathing grew thick while he dried himself, each flex of muscle making her heart pound harder. There was no denying it. With all these kisses and the time spent with him, she was finding herself increasingly attracted to him. But what good would that do her? She was hardly the sort to take lovers. Despite having travelled the country, her existence had been quite sheltered.

Orelia tried to turn her attention to the ceiling. However, the dark wooden beams would not hold her attention for long and it traitorously tracked back to Reed. He dropped the towel on the table and reached for his shirt. The cotton skimmed his skin. A hint of slightly whiter skin teased her at the waist of his breeches as he stretched to put the garment on. How often did he spend time out of doors shirtless, she wondered. And what would his skin feel like beneath her fingertips?

He turned abruptly, and she snapped shut her eyes. Her breaths were heavy in her ears. Had he seen her looking? What would he think if he had caught her? Did he enjoy her admiration? He was a confident man, he likely would. But would it mean anything more coming from her?

Foolish girl. Of course it wouldn't. There was some rustling and a few footsteps. She risked drawing open her eyes to find him tying his cravat. He glanced at her, a half-smile on his face and a twinkle in his eyes. Oh dear, perhaps he'd known she was watching. He was a spy after all. He'd likely be aware of everything that was going on around him.

She feigned a stretch.

"Sleep well?"

"Wonderfully," she replied. "Have you been awake long?"

"A little while."

She pushed herself up to sitting, acutely aware of her bare legs beneath the sheets. The previous night when they had been sore and tired from travelling, it seemed foolish to make him sleep on the floor or the horribly rickety chair and astonishingly she had been too worn out to worry about her legs brushing his strong hairy ones or the inappropriateness of the situation. She snorted to herself. Not that it would matter to anyone. After all, she was meant to be engaged to him. Of course, sharing a bed before they were even married would be frowned upon even in the Romani community, but no one would know, and her mother cared little for her reputation now.

Running a hand through her hair, she eyed Reed. "What was keeping you awake? Are you concerned we won't find these men?"

He gave a smirk. "Hardly."

"Then what..."

He glanced over her cotton wrapped form and the slightest darkening of his eyes told her why. He had found sharing a bed with her distracting. It should not but the knowledge warmed her. She did not feel so guilty for her voyeurism now.

"I shall see what I can rustle up for the morning meal whilst you dress," he said, snatching up his jacket. He strode out of the room before she could answer. When Reed left, the air remained thick with unspoken...desire?

Orelia washed and dressed with haste, listening out for the returning footsteps of Reed. He didn't come back until she was running her fingers through her hair and had been dressed for quite some time. He entered holding a steaming pot of what smelled to be coffee and generous slabs of bread and a pot of jam.

He placed them down on the table and ran a glance over her. "All dressed I see."

"Yes." She smoothed down her gown. "I'm ready to go when you are."

"So we shall speak to your contact today?"

"That is my hope," he confirmed, finally reaching for a slice of bread. "Then tonight, we can head to the inn again and see if your friends are there."

"They are hardly my friends."

His lips tilted. "You've defended them well, considering you don't think so."

"Because you are all so quick to judge. What if it's the captain of the ship that was behind it? What if it was someone else?"

She watched as he took a bite from the bread, admiring his even teeth and watching the crumb that dangled briefly on his lip before he swiped it away.

"I have to research every avenue, Orelia. Like it or not, your fellow Romani are the most likely suspects. After all, there are many who are not exactly law-abiding are there not?"

She blinked, having hardly heard him. A rush of heat surged into her face. She'd been too busy thinking of when those lips had been upon hers.

"There are many people who are not law-abiding, not just the Romani. We all do what we must to make sure we do not starve. I wouldn't expect you to understand that."

"I have never had to worry about starving, I shall give you that much, but I like to think that my experiences during the war mark me out a little from the usual rich heir to a title.

However, I cannot let personal experience and my own judgement get in the way of the investigation. I have to find the would-be killers."

"And if you're wrong?"

"Then I shall continue the investigation until I track them down."

"It will not be the Romani men," she said determinedly.

"If you do not eat up, then we shall never know."

She glanced at the remaining food and any annoyance vanished. He had somehow eaten his fair share of the bread while she had been getting annoyed with him. And now he grinned at her with that charming smile that made any frustration disappear like a puff of smoke.

The tension that had been clouding around her eased. They were back to where they were before, and she was grateful.

Orelia had another slice of bread before they left the inn. She didn't know the town at all so let him lead her through the busy streets. Though the hour was early, and no fashionable people were awake, merchants and poor folk hurried about their business. They passed a ribbon shop and she paused to admire the beautiful colors and fabrics with a little envy. Before long, she reminded herself, she would be able to purchase all the ribbons her heart desired.

Reed led them through the streets and alleyways to a tiny chandlery. She wrinkled her nose. The odor of hot wax hung strong in the air.

"Wait here," he ordered after leading her around the back of the building.

She glanced around the empty alleyway. A thrum of apprehension ran through her, but she could not say why. There was no one around and it was not like she had not spent plenty of time alone during her life. Her mother had disappeared many a time since she was a young girl, most likely passed out from the drink.

"I can come in with you."

"I think it best you are not known to these people."

Nodding, she clasped her hands together and leaned back against the whitewashed wall. Reed had said little of who this contact was but a spy like himself likely had many men in his pocket who were not the nicest or the kindest but knew of all untoward dealings.

"I will not be long," he promised.

She waited, the cloying scent seeming to grow steadily more suffocating. The hairs on her arms pricked and her heart pounded faster when a shadow flicked by the alleyway. She was hardly a fortune teller, but her senses were trying to tell her something was amiss.

Drawing in a breath, she eased away from the wall and stepped carefully across the ground toward the opening of the winding alley. The buildings were close here, their clay roofs nearly touching. It would be easy for someone to slip in, do her harm and never be seen.

Back flat against the wall, she peered around the entrance. Nothing.

Yet she was sure there had been someone there. Could it have just been someone strolling by? She glanced up and down the street, but no one seemed suspicious. They were all going about their day with no clue as to her eyeing them up as though they were the very murderer they were looking for.

"Orelia?"

She screamed and spun. "Reed." Giving his arm a light tap, she pressed a hand to her beating heart. "You scared me."

"I told you to stay where you were."

"I think there was someone following us."

He scowled. "You saw someone?"

"Not exactly. It was more of a feeling."

"A feeling?" He lifted a dark brow. "Well, there doesn't appear to be anyone following us now."

"There was. I'm sure of it." She pressed her lips together. "Did you find anything out?"

His expression grew grim. "My contact is in the local jail. For theft."

"Theft?"

He grimaced. "At a wine merchants."

"You think this has to do with our investigation?"

"I know so. The wine that was poisoned was of a very specific variety—*Vin de Constance*. It's the only wine Napoleon can tolerate with his current state of health."

Orelia snorted. "Why not give up the wine altogether?"

"Because old Boney cares more about wine than almost anything."

"So what are we to do?"

Reed took her arm and led her out of the alley and away from the waxy smell. "It might be best if you return to the inn."

"I do not think so. You are paying me for my services, are you not? I should like to be of use."

"If Ambrose was locked up for theft of the merchants, its likely someone is watching it. We too could end up in some strife."

She tilted her head and eyed him. "You believe this is the place that sold the wine to the people who poisoned it?"

"It seems likely. It is local and one of the few places that stocks the French wine. It is not so easy to get a hold of these days." He took off his hat, pushed a hand through his hair and replaced it.

"Is it not likely that your contact simply grew greedy and decided to earn some extra coin while he was serving you?"

He shook his head. "Ambrose is not a bad man. Down on his luck, to be sure, but not bad. I met him when he was smuggling French goods into the country. He helped me get to France once."

She glanced back at the chandlery. "Yet he spends time with dangerous men?"

Reed's lips quirked. "Were you not defending the bad choices people make only moments ago?"

She opened her mouth then closed it.

They strolled along the street, her arm still tucked carefully in Reed's as though they really were husband and wife, or a courting couple having slipped their escort. They might look no richer than the average merchant, but they were respectable and thus, respected. A few gentlemen tipped their hats to them, a couple of ladies offered meek smiles. It was astonishing what being on the arm of a man could do for her.

Had she been on her own, everyone would have been making bold movements to avoid her.

"I will need to slip into the merchants to get a look at his purchase receipts," Reed murmured. "From what Ambrose's acquaintances said, the man guards his records carefully. Likely because he's dealing with expensive and likely smuggled wine."

"Slip in?"

"As in, enter unnoticed." He flashed a grin.

"You'll end up in jail like your friend. You just said it was likely under observation."

He shook his head. "Yes, to persuade you to return to the inn." He hefted out a sigh. "Orelia, I have slipped into French encampments. Do you really think me incapable of sneaking into an unguarded building?"

She shook her head at his smugness, unable to resist smiling. "I think you capable of many things, Reed. How sneaky you are remains to be seen, however."

REED SUPPOSED HE COULDN'T blame her for doubting him. This investigation so far had been him stumbling around, searching for a loose thread and not being at all like his usual smooth self. But the fact was, he was practically alone on this. It was too dangerous for the whole of the government's spy network to be on this. If word got out that there had been an attempt on Napoleon's life, they'd be on the edge of war again and they'd lost enough men as it was.

He motioned to the entrance of the building on the opposite side of the road. "Keep an eye out for me. I'm going to see if I can climb in the back."

While they had been talking, he had been scoping out the building. There was a small window at the side of the building, tucked under the eaves. The wooden window frames were flaked and chipping. It would not take much to force it open.

"Reed," she gripped his arm. "Be careful."

"I always am."

He noted the worry in her eyes. There was something mildly appealing about it. No one had ever worried for him. Certainly not his superiors and his mother mostly worried about finding him a wife, what with her being in ignorance as to his activities. His brother was too busy to be concerned.

Shaking away such ridiculous thoughts, he glanced up and down the street and paced boldly across the dirt road. The merchants was small with two curved windows. A shabby sign hung over the door.

He moved around the side of the building after a quick glance around and eyed the various wooden crates stacked at the back. A hasty look over his shoulder told him Orelia was watching out for him. He shifted a crate on top of another and clambered onto it. It gave him enough height to loop his fingers over the window ledge and push hard against the frame. The window creaked open an inch.

His arms burned as he heaved himself up and used his body weight to push the window all the way open. He winced at the loud crack of the wooden window frame. Reed fell through head first and rose rapidly to standing, ready to defend himself if needed.

Taking a breath, he peered around the dark attic room.

Perfect.

It was the merchant's office, as he suspected. Stacks of papers were piled high on a table. A quick glance at them and he saw they were arranged by month. He grinned. It was a shame Ambrose hadn't succeeded in gaining entry or else he might have been further along in his investigation but hopefully this would be the lead he needed. If the wine had been purchased here, they might well have their would-be killer's name.

He snatched up three piles—the recent months. He had to assume the wine was bought only recently. Surely whoever wanted Boney dead would not have been willing to wait around?

His heart gave a bounce when he heard voices. He neared the window and listened. It was Orelia and a man. Was she in trouble?

No, it sounded...He scowled. It sounded as though she was flirting with the gentleman. What the devil was the woman up to?

Stuffing the papers into his jacket, he leaned out of the window. She had to be in front of the merchant's because he couldn't see her, but he could hear her clearly enough. In fact, she seemed to be talking quite loudly.

"As an expert in wine," he heard her say. "Where would you say the best wine comes from?"

He could not hear the man's response, but his pulse quickened. It had to be the owner and she was trying to distract him. He went out of the window backward, climbing out until only his fingers clung onto the ledge. He dropped onto the crate as quietly as possible.

Easing his head around the edge of the building, Orelia's gaze connected with his. If she was at all panicked she made no show of it. She gave the merchant, a short man with shabby clothing, a beautiful smile and touched his arm lightly just as he was about to turn. The man's attention remained glued on Orelia allowing Reed to slip out from the side of the building unnoticed.

He took several quick strides along the street then crossed. He crossed again and greeted Orelia with a broad smile. "Ah, there you are, sister. Have you found the ribbons you wanted?"

She shook her head and took his offered arm. "Not yet. I was just speaking with this gentleman. I was explaining that you were looking to purchase a few special vintages. It seems you stock quite the variety, do you not, Mr. Winchcombe?"

The short man, whose top lip was beaded with sweat—either because he was talking with a beautiful woman or at the prospect of gaining a new customer—nodded quickly. "I can acquire almost anything you need."

"Well that does sound promising. I think I may have to stop by again whilst I am in town, Mr. Winchcombe. But for now, I must get my sister these wretched ribbons she so desperately desires." He gave the man a *you know how women are* look and tipped his hat.

"Good day, Mr. Winchcombe," Orelia said sweetly.

The man tipped his hat and color ran into his cheeks. Apparently, despite the shabby condition of himself and his business premises, he wanted Orelia more than he wanted customers. Reed could not decide whether to be ridiculously proud or strongly jealous. A mixture of both perhaps.

"He was just about to bring a crate around the back," Orelia explained.

"So you struck up conversation."

"Yes. Thank goodness he was willing to talk. I'm sure it must have been clear I knew nothing about wine."

"That was probably your charm, Orelia. He was hoping to teach you a thing or too."

"I have charm?"

He grinned and shook his head. "You have charm. Too much, I fear. There's nothing more dangerous than a woman entirely unaware of her charm."

Chapter Twelve

The piles of paper Reed had pulled out from his coat once they'd retreated to their room made Orelia's stomach heavy.

"What are those?"

"These are the purchase notes for the three months leading up to the attempt."

"And you think this will lead us to our man?"

"I hope so. They could well have purchased elsewhere in the country but so far nothing has turned up and it's a very specific French wine. Not easy to come by since the start of the war." She swallowed and placed herself on the bed, watching as he laid out the papers in a pile. "Makes more sense to have purchased in the same town as the docks."

"So why did you go for the gypsies first? Why not go straight to the merchants?"

He secured her with a look. "Because we wanted to move fast, and they were the most likely suspects. I'm sorry to say it, Orelia, but you know why."

"Because no one trusts us."

"No one trusts outsiders. Nor do your people. But the Romani have a history of causing trouble."

She huffed. Yes, there were those of them who would do what they could for coin, safe in the knowledge that in a few weeks they would have moved on and avoided trouble, but they were not all bad.

"Show me any element of society that does not have their troublemakers. We are simply easily scapegoated, and you well know it."

He sat on the floor and spread out the piles. "Well, let us dig through these and unscapegoat your people."

She swallowed and hesitated.

"We've a long night ahead, Orelia."

"I-I cannot read."

Reed grimaced. "Forgive me, I forgot." He picked up a piece of paper and motioned to her to come and sit next to him. She did as he bid, all too aware when her leg brushed his as she sat. He lifted a piece of paper and pointed to some scribbled writing underneath several lines. "This is where the wine is listed. This letter here," he pointed, "is a 'C.'"

She eyed the curled figure and nodded.

"I'm looking for wine that begins with a C. Once I find the one I want, I'll show you the full word. Can you set aside any that begin with that letter?"

Nodding, she picked up a piece of paper and stared at the jumbled mess. There were several Cs that she could make out but none at the beginning of the words. A pang of frustration tore through her. How was she ever going to make a future for herself in business if she could not read?

Reed took her hand suddenly. "Orelia?"

She glanced at him to find her vision blurry. Her chin trembled.

"Many people cannot read," he told her. "Don't be ashamed."

"I..." She sniffed. "I suppose I realized that having my freedom will not be so easy without such skills."

"I am sure you can pay someone to help you. You're a quick learner." He swiped a thumb under her eyes, leaving a trail of hot sensation behind it.

She peered through the welling tears into his dark eyes and found herself sinking deep. How she longed to lean forward and press her lips to his again, to remember what it felt like to be kissed by such a handsome, enigmatic man.

A line appeared between his brows and he dropped his hand from her face. "Come now, it will take some time to get through these. I have faith in you."

The words warmed her from the inside out. No one had ever had faith in her. Not her mother or her people. Regardless of having been raised with the Romani, her *gadje* blood tainted her.

Reed lit some candles as the light waned and they remained on the floor, surrounded by paper, saying little to each other. There was something wildly intimate about it. When he finally found the first invoice with the wine listed on it, he helped her understand the shape of the letters that she was looking for and she kept it to compare it to every note that she looked at.

The candles shortened, and the evening wore on. Orelia suppressed a yawn. Her eyes and head were sore from concentration and her back hurt from sitting on the floor. She glanced at their pile of suspects. Two so far.

"Not many left," she murmured.

"No. Hopefully this will be it." He motioned to the two notes with the wine orders. "Should be nice and easy to hunt them down and find out if they were involved."

"How will we do that?"

Reed flashed her a grin that made her stomach twist in excitement despite her exhaustion. "We shall have to be very, very sneaky."

She chuckled. "You sound as though you relish the chance to snoop."

"I do. A far more interesting way to spend my days."

"Meanwhile your estate and people are neglected."

He frowned. "My brother has it all in hand. Just because he is deaf, does not mean he is incapable."

She opened her mouth then closed it. Then put a hand to his arm. "I meant no insult, but does he not find it too much?"

"Noah is smarter than I and far more capable, but unfortunately cursed with being the second son. Being deaf has afforded him little opportunity but my absence has enabled him to step up to the mark and prove himself. No doubt there are many who will be lamenting he was not the heir after his time looking after the estates."

"Does that bother you?"

He chuckled. "Not at all. I always knew Noah needed a chance to show what he could do. Few people would give a deaf man a chance but what choice did they have when I began neglecting my duties?"

She narrowed her gaze at him. "Did you neglect them on purpose?"

"It was not exactly a plan but once I saw how well he did, and how respected he was becoming, I made a point of taking as many missions as possible."

She eyed him. "So you put yourself in danger, so your brother could succeed?"

He shrugged. "I was not in that much danger."

"Why is it I do not believe you?"

"I have no idea." He smiled benignly. "Now back to work. It is past midnight and I am looking forward to going on the hunt tomorrow."

Orelia turned her attention back to the remaining papers. What an enigma this man was. The more she learned about him, the more she liked him. Under that playful, bold exterior beat the heart of a good and caring man. She could not help but like all facets of him.

"Oh," she exclaimed. "Another." She handed him the letter she was holding.

"Well, it is only one more. Let's hope we can have this wrapped up quickly and get your friends out of the frame."

"You are admitting you do not think they are guilty."

"I admit nothing." He gave her a tilted smile. "I am, however, never one to jump to the easiest conclusion."

She laughed. "Somehow I imagine you never do anything the easiest way."

"And why would I? When the most complicated way can be the most fun." His grin expanded. "Why, had I decided to simply barrel in and ask questions, I might never have met you." The look in his eyes shot through to her core. She glanced away.

"And you would likely have been kicked out on your arse," she said dryly.

"That too." He leafed through the last few papers. "Looks like we are done."

Trying and failing to suppress a yawn, Orelia stretched. "Thank goodness."

"Come, let us get you to bed."

She was too tired to protest when he helped her to her feet. She had not realized just how exhausted she was until the moment she had to balance her weary body on two feet. Nearly collapsing onto the bed, she only stopped herself by snatching Reed's arm.

"You're worn out."

She nodded and yawned again. He turned her slowly and before she had quite realized his intentions, he began unlacing her gown. He moved swiftly, no doubt an expert in all things feminine, and had her down to her shift in a trice. She should feel exposed, but she already spent so much time in close quarters with him, it hardly seemed to matter.

The air seemed to still around her. All she was aware of was the sound of their breaths, heavy with anticipation. If it weren't for how tired she was, she would have likely turned and flung her arms around his neck and begged to be kissed. Oh, how she longed for another kiss.

But her feet would not move. Her arms would not lift. She could not summon the words to plead.

He came closer. She felt the heat of his body nearby. Reed put a hand to her shoulder and kneaded her flesh with his thumb. She groaned.

A sharp inhale came from him and she startled when he pressed a brief kiss to the crook of her shoulder. Before she had the chance to respond, he urged her toward the bed, drawing back the sheets and helping her in. She peered up at him through half-closed lids.

"Will you be coming to bed?"

He gave her what appeared to be a soft smile but that could have been because she was hardly able to keep her eyes open.

"I will in a moment. Sleep well, Orelia."

She nodded and closed her eyes. Shortly before the darkness overtook her, she could have sworn she felt his lips brush hers in the sweetest, most tender kiss. Perhaps it was a dream, but if it was, it was wonderful. How nice it would be to live in a world where dukes kissed gypsy girls.

Chapter Thirteen

It was far too easy to watch Orelia sleep. Reed especially liked seeing how her lips parted as she inhaled. If he was in the mood for the scandalous, he could not complain too much about how her chest rose with each breath either, or how she had kicked off the sheets overnight and her long, dusky legs were sprawled just so, giving him quite the image to lust over.

He shook his head and turned his attention back to the paper. He'd already been out in the early hours, digging up what he could on the three suspects. All lived locally, within a four-mile radius of the wine merchant's it seemed. From what the young lad had said, the first address was where the rich merchants and doctors tended to live. The other belonged to an earl and the last was a poorer area. He'd try the last address first—it would be easier to investigate.

She rolled, and he tucked himself behind the paper. He could hardly be counted as the most honorable of men, but he hardly wanted to be caught admiring her bare legs.

Especially when he should be concentrating on more important things than long, long, lush legs that would be perfect wrapped...

As he shifted his position, his foot tapped the table leg. Orelia bolted upright, springing out of the bed and looking wildly around. Her fists were raised. He might have laughed had she not looked so terrified.

Reed stood too, lifting his hands in a placatory manner. "It is only me, Orelia."

She peered at him through sleepy eyes. Her breaths ragged, she slowly lowered her fists. "Forgive me..."

He couldn't help himself. He took her in his arms, completely enfolding her in them. Her body trembled a little. Why she had been so startled he did know not, but he did know he wanted to comfort her...Hell, even protect her.

Rubbing his hands up and down her back, he held her while her breaths slowed, absorbing the feel of her soft body tucked so perfectly against him. She smelled faintly of herbs and a sort of warm, sleepy scent. She burrowed her head against his chest and something inside him cracked a little.

He nuzzled her cheek and she tilted her head.

With a groan, he pressed his lips to her neck. She sucked in a breath. He kissed a trail along her skin.

"So soft," he murmured against her skin. "Why do you taste so good?"

"I...I don't know," she said, her voice trembling.

She didn't know. That was the problem. She had no idea the effect she had on him. It was growing worse and he was getting distracted. If they were not meant to be working together, he would likely have taken her to bed by now, but there were more important things than his needs right now.

He eased away but kept her held by her arms. "I didn't mean to startle you."

She gave a sheepish smile. "I must look a fool."

"Not at all."

"It was never easy sleeping in the wagon. My mother's lover would stumble in drunk sometimes and a few other men..." Color seeped into her cheeks.

Reed clenched his jaw. "Did they harm you?"

She shook her head. "None were that foolish."

"I hate that anyone scared you. You should never have been in that position."

"It doesn't matter, Reed."

"It does to me," he said through clenched teeth.

"Well, you would be the first man to be concerned for me."

And why did that hurt him? She should have had a father to protect her from her terrible mother or from nearly being sold to a blackguard of a man.

She pushed her hair back from her face and eyed his dress appearance. "Is it very late?"

"Not too late but I thought you had earned your rest." He stepped back and forced a smile. "I shall rustle up some food for us while you dress."

Reed didn't wait for a response. He left before she could say anything and headed down to the bar. The maid gathered a platter of bread and honey and some coffee quickly, but he lingered downstairs for as long as he could. He needed the distance from her. She muddled his thoughts far too much.

By the time he'd finished lecturing himself, she had come to join him, and they ate and drank in relative silence. Just a few patrons gathered in the inn at this hour, some already drinking ale and likely planning to spend the rest of the day doing much the same.

"What shall we be doing today?" Orelia asked, her voice low.

"I'd like to check out one of the addresses we have."

"But how will we know if he is guilty?"

"Ah, well that is the nature of investigation. It usually means kicking over enough baskets until something pops out."

"So we're to rile all the suspects until one confesses?"

"I hope not but that is the essence of it. Unfortunately, it is never as easy as simply finding the evidence one needs."

Orelia peered at him. "I suppose you spent much time investigating things in France."

"A lot of what I did was tracking where the army was, what their next moves were and what their armaments and supplies were like. But I also uncovered several French spies."

"Did any uncover you?"

He grinned. "Never."

She laughed. "You are so very smug are you not?"

"Always."

Shaking her head, she finished her coffee and they made their way across town to the first address. Reed grimaced as he eyed the empty building.

Orelia peered through the window. "If they did live here, they do not anymore."

Glancing around at the filthy street, Reed tugged her close. A few beggars sat in the doorways. "Let us try the next address. We won't get any answers standing around here."

They headed to the next address on foot. It took them nearly an hour to make their way to the finer part of Portsmouth. Here the houses were adjoined but not cramped together like at the previous address. Each cream home stretched three stories tall with columns in front of the doors. Servants quarters were accessed via a stairwell down.

Reed paused to eye the building, aware he was hardly dressed for entry to a house like this. A far cry from his own home it might be, but he currently reflected a humble—if respectable—income. Unfortunately, Orelia did nothing to change that assumption.

He eyed her basic gown. Was it time to find her something new to wear? Whilst it had been useful for them to stay ignored, he could not help miss seeing her in finer materials.

"What shall we do?" Orelia whispered as though the few passers-by were listening in to their conversations.

To be certain, they could not stand around on the doorstep for long, but they had to find out something about the owner or else their day would be wasted.

He grinned when he spotted a young maid, basket slung over one arm, open the gate to the servants' stairs. He nodded toward the park opposite the buildings. "Wait over there, I shan't be long."

"Reed?"

"Orelia," he warned. Damned woman needed to learn to trust him.

She nodded and shuffled off. He donned his winning smile, flicked off his eyepatch and strode over to the maid. She paused on the stairs as he leaned over the rails.

"Can I help you, sir?"

"I certainly hope so. But perhaps I can help you with that basket first, miss."

She smiled, her plump cheeks revealing two rather charming dimples. "I can manage perfectly well on my own," she said, with an amused tone to her voice.

"No doubt you can, though I hate to see a lovely young lady like yourself carrying such a burden."

She glanced at the basket, laden with a handful of vegetables. The maid chuckled. "Aye, sir, it is a heavy burden to bear, but bear it I must."

He gave a long sigh. "It looks as though you could do with some help. Does your master work you hard?"

"No, sir. He is a good master. I am a lucky girl to be working for Mr. Daventry."

"Ah, that is good to hear. My sister was in service and was not treated nearly so well. The wages are good?"

She sucked in a mock gasp. "You are bold, sir."

"I ask only because my sister is here looking for work. She has come to stay with me and hopes to settle in Dover."

Understanding came over her expression. "So you are hoping perhaps that I might be giving up my excellent position here?"

"Not at all. I can see that you are an excellent maid. But I was hoping you might know if your wonderful Mr. Daventry might be looking for some extra help. After all, as excellent a maid as you are, no doubt, one can never have enough help."

The girl chuckled. "I think your sister has a fine champion in you, she's a lucky girl."

He lifted a shoulder. "She is a good woman. I always look after my womenfolk to the best of my ability. That is why I hope to find her a position with a good house. Unfortunately, not all servants are treated as well as you, miss."

"My name is Amy," she said boldly. "And you are in luck, sir. The lady's maid is due to be married soon. The lady is none too happy to lose her. If you bring your sister here tomorrow, I shall see if the lady of the house would like to see her. Does she have such experience?"

"She does indeed. I think your lady would be a fool not to offer her a job."

"Spoken like a truly loving brother."

He grinned. "Thank you for your help, Amy. Robert Sherbourne at your service." He tipped his hat. "My sister, Anita, shall be along tomorrow. At what time can we catch you at your leisure?"

"Bring her at eleven. My lady shall be risen by then but not receiving visitors yet."

"Amy, you are a truly wonderful creature. My thanks to you."

Amy smiled again and shook her head. "Do not thank me yet. My mistress may not even accept her visit."

"I thank you anyway for your aid. I hope you have a wonderful day, lovely Amy." He gave her a wink and color rose into her cheeks. She shook her head again and headed down the steps.

Reed strolled away to find Orelia waiting under a generous oak tree, her arms folded across her chest. "Was it necessary to flirt so obviously?"

"How did you know I was flirting?"

"Anyone could see you were."

His lips twisted into a grin. "Jealous, Orelia?"

"Hardly."

She was, and he liked it. He couldn't help himself. "Do not forget that only yesterday you were charming a wine merchant."

"I had no choice!"

"Neither did I." He took her arm. "But it was worth it."

"What have you learned?"

"Not much, save that Mr. Daventry is a kind and respectable man."

"So he is not our poisoner?"

"I did not say that."

Her brow furrowed. "So why do you look so happy?"

"Because, my dear Orelia, we have access to the house. Well, to be more accurate, *you* have access to the house, for on the morrow, you shall be going for an interview to be a lady's maid."

Orelia gaped at him. "A lady's maid? Me?" She shook her head vigorously. "Oh no. I cannot—"

"You will only have to act a lady's maid, nothing more. Do not forget I have seen you play many roles quite successfully recently. Wine expert, pregnant woman in distress, fortune teller..."

She narrowed her gaze at him.

"This will be easy for you, I know it."

Huffing, she shook her head. "We are not all trained spies you know."

"Orelia, you could rival the best. I have every confidence in you."

A light blush colored her cheeks and he grinned.

Chapter Fourteen

Orelia drew in a breath and pressed her hands to her stomach. The butterflies inside it would not quell. She paused midway across the park to eye the house they had visited yesterday.

Where Reed had flirted with the maid.

She did not think herself the jealous type nor was she one to lie to herself. She had been jealous of him flirting with that girl. It did not matter to her silly heart that he was doing it merely to find out more information or that she had no claims over him. Jealousy had beat with raw intensity through her.

And now she had to be nice to the poor, unsuspecting maid who had likely simply enjoyed talking with a handsome and charming man and thought nothing more of it.

"She will know I'm not your sister," she reminded Reed.

"Yes, so you discuss how you are my half-sister." He paused, took her shoulders in his hands and eyed her. "Orelia, you can do this. You have been surviving by your wits your whole life. Find out what you can about the household and if anything seems amiss, I shall conduct further investigations."

"You mean you shall sneak in again, do you not?"

"If I must."

She sighed. Slipping into the merchants had been heart-stopping enough. Now he wished to snoop in a rich man's house? He would surely get into trouble.

"I know what I'm doing." He gave her a soft smile with no censure in his eyes.

Any other man would be annoyed at her doubting his ability and it was not even that she did really, but she certainly feared for him, no matter how pointless that fear was.

"I know you do." Drawing in another deep breath, she flattened a hand to her hammering heart in a bid to slow it down. "I, on the other hand, have little idea what I am doing."

"You do indeed. You are Anita Sherbourne. Your mother is Spanish, and she married my father two years before you were born. Your last position was working for the Duchess of Keswick."

"Let us hope they do not question your mother," she grumbled.

"It doesn't matter if they do. We shall be long gone before then. In the meantime, you have a reference from her son." He handed over the letter. "I'm sure my words will go far enough to grant you an audience with the mistress."

"I hope you're right."

"I always am," he said with a smug smile that she wanted to tear from his face.

It also made him impossibly irresistible and part of her longed to fling herself in his arms and receive his kisses. Surely that would be far more pleasant than interviewing for a position she had no intention of taking nor any experience of?

"Now hurry along or you shall be late."

Straightening her shoulders, Orelia grasped the letter of recommendation and strode over to the house. She took the steps down and knocked on the door. The door opened, and the young woman Reed had been speaking with the previous day greeted her.

"Is your brother not with you?" The woman glanced her over and Orelia could almost hear her wondering about her skin color and the difference between them.

"My half-brother," she replied with a smile. "My mother married his father not long after she came here from Spain."

The woman's expression eased, even though Orelia was aware she had just laden her with unnecessary information. If it seemed at all odd, Amy said nothing.

"Do come in. Mrs. Green, the housekeeper, will want to speak with you first. Thankfully she was not at all angry at my impertinence. My mistress has been fretting about a replacement for some weeks."

Amy led her into the kitchen area and bid her to sit down at the large table in the center. The scent of freshly baked bread filled the room, emanating from the gleaming black stove. The only other kitchen Orelia had ever been in was at Keswick and though this one was much smaller, it still revealed the luxury the occupants of the house lived in with fresh herbs growing in pots, the meal menus spread about, and silverware stowed carefully in a huge cabinet.

"Don't be nervous," said Amy. "Mrs. Green is lovely once you get to know her."

Orelia offered a shaky smile. "Does it show?"

"Your brother would not have recommended you had you not had the right experience, I am sure. He seems like he would only want the best for you."

Orelia nodded. "He is a very good man."

"Then you have nothing to fear." Amy smiled warmly.

"Have you worked here long?"

"Three years."

"R-Robert said they are kind here."

"Mrs. Daventry can be somewhat demanding at times, but she is not unkind." Amy snatched up a bundle of clothes. "The master is a very sweet man. He's almost twenty years older than Mrs. Daventry and I think she bullies him a little, but she's good for him. Keeps him young."

Before Orelia could ask any more questions, a thin woman with dark hair pulled tightly back entered. With keys slung from her belt and a dark, plain uniform, it was clear this was Mrs. Green.

"This is the girl?" she asked Amy.

Orelia stood. "Y-yes. Miss Anita Sherbourne." She somehow managed not to stumble over her new name. "I am grateful you took the time to see me."

Mrs. Green's lips thinned. "It seems your brother is quite the persuasive man." Amy blushed and scurried away, linens in hand. "But you are lucky. We were about to advertise for the new position." She nodded her head toward the papers Orelia was holding. "Those are your references I assume."

"Yes. I worked at Keswick Abbey. The duke has seen fit to write my letter of recommendation."

The woman arched a brow and scanned the letter. "He speaks highly of you. Why would you leave such a place?"

"I wanted to be nearer to my brother," Orelia intoned, recalling all the lies she and Reed had come up with in case there were questions.

"Well, you certainly seem to have the experience even if you are a bit young in my opinion. I'll see if the mistress is available to give you an audience."

"Thank you." The hammering of Orelia's heart eased a little.

She waited in the kitchen until another maid came to fetch her and lead her to the mistresses' drawing room. The young woman gave her a reassuring smile and led her in. By all accounts, the staff were pleasant. Would they be so nice if they worked for a criminal? From what little she knew of Mr. Daventry, she could hardly imagine he was the type to get involved in such a sinister plot.

She supposed she would soon find out.

REED PACED ACROSS THE park. Grass crunched beneath his boots. He paused briefly under a tree, glanced at the house and paced back.

This was taking too long. What could they possibly need to know about her? He should never have sent her in there alone.

He swiveled, looked at the house and covered the length of the park once more. She was inexperienced, damn it. What was he thinking? If something happened to her...

Stilling, he narrowed his gaze. About time!

He strode over to the figure dashing away from the building. Orelia beamed at him as she raced over. Inwardly, he grimaced. He recognized that look. It was the same as when some whelp of a man took on his first mission. The thrill of it was currently tearing through her, making her skin hot and her pulse beat wildly. She wouldn't stop smiling for the rest of the day, he'd wager.

What had he done?

"Reed," she said, her voice breathy. "Reed!"

He put a hand to her arm. "Take a moment," he said, peering around. "Let us move away from here first."

"I was so scared," she puffed while he dragged her along. "I thought I was going to get caught."

He ignored her until they were far from the house. Motioning to a small bench along the side of a quiet road, he made her sit.

"Breathe," he commanded.

She took a long inhale. "He's innocent," she spilled out. "Goodness, Reed, I thought for certain they would see through me. Your letter must have worked. The mistress wanted to see me and even the stern housekeeper seemed impressed."

"What did you find out?" he asked slowly.

"You should have seen me. I was shaking like a leaf. Thankfully they thought it was because of the interview."

"Orelia," he warned.

"Yes, well, I spoke to the mistress and when she dismissed me, I became *lost*." Her grin widened. "I made it all the way down to the cellar without being seen. You'll never believe what I found."

His stomach sank a little. She had been there to find out about their suspect, nothing more. Certainly not sneak around their house. That was his job.

"What did you find?"

"The wine!"

With her eyes all lit up, her smile wide and trusting, he could not help think how beautiful she was. She had tied her hair up carefully today to ensure she gave the right impression. It was intended to make her look more serious. Yet all he could think was how it meant he could admire her without hinderance, how it made her look so young and innocent.

How he had entirely corrupted that by involving her in underhanded dealings...

Reed forced himself to focus in on her words. "You found the wine?"

"Yes. All of it, I believe." She held up three fingers. "Not a drop had been touched."

He shook his head. "You took a huge risk."

"The housekeeper found me just as I had stepped out. I told her I was lost. Goodness, Reed, I thought I was going to be in so much trouble, but she seemed to believe me."

"You were lucky." He couldn't resist. He cupped her cheek. "What were you thinking?"

She shrugged. "It seemed the easiest solution. If I had a look around while I was there, you would not have to. It was just luck that I came across the cellar, though."

"You did that, so I would not have to go in?"

She nodded. "And now we know it is certainly not Mr. Daventry."

Reed stared at her. "Orelia, you are surely the foolhardiest of women I have ever met."

A crease appeared between her brows. Her shoulders dropped a little. "You're displeased."

Reed shook his head. "Never. How could I ever be displeased with you?" He stroked her cheek. "You have removed one suspect in the space of a day. You've done wonderfully."

That beautiful smile appeared again. It punched him in the heart. Damnation, why did she have to be so irresistible?

Leaning in, he swept his lips across hers. "You were wonderful," he assured her before doing it again.

She flung her arms around his neck and pulled him close. The kiss became frantic. He tried to hold himself back, really he did, knowing that this excitement she felt was the thrill of having done something risky, and likely nothing to do with needing to kiss him.

Or was it?

Whatever it was, he could not help himself be swept up in it too. His Orelia had done so well. Who would have thought a sweet gypsy girl could outperform some of the best spies he knew?

"You did so well," he muttered again, drinking in the sweet taste of her and the way her hands held him tight to her.

Reed kept her face in his hands, fearful of letting her go. What else would she do if he did? Solve the case entirely on her own? Confront the would-be killer? Take the poisoner in irons and hand him over to Boney? Somehow, he suspected this woman was capable of anything.

By some miracle, he forced himself away from her delicious mouth. He held her and searched her face. Breaths heavy, smile wide, it was clear the thrill continued to race through her.

"You were scared?"

She nodded.

"But you enjoyed it, did you not?"

She nodded again.

He chuckled. "Well, my dear Orelia, you will have another chance to play spy. Whilst you have been gallivanting around and solving the case, I have found an excellent opportunity to see if suspect number two is involved."

"What is that?"

"A ball." He grinned. "I am taking you to a ball."

Chapter Fifteen

"Reed." Orelia stilled on the bottom step leading into the house. "I cannot do this."

Reed grinned. "Yes you can."

She narrowed her gaze at him. "You're a bully."

"Absolutely."

He offered her an arm and she took it. His grin widened. He'd always known Orelia was beautiful and had to admit, he had come to appreciate her simple beauty. It meant no waiting around for her to dress in layers and force herself into stays and stockings. Her hair took moments to brush and tie in a ribbon.

However, tonight, he'd been very willing to wait after seeing how stunning she looked with her hair coiled high on her head. Tiny cream blossoms of some kind adorned her hair. The long column of her cream dress accentuated her elegant figure while the low neckline drew his attention to her dusky skin. She was an intriguing mix of pure innocence with those wide, dark eyes, and sensuality with her full lips and the rise of her bust. The maids had done a wonderful job with her.

"You will be magnificent," he murmured as he led her up the steps into Knowle House.

"Everyone will know," she whispered. "Once they see me, they will know I am not one of them."

He paused and moved her aside so that other attendees could pass them by. "Just remember, let me do the talking and you will be fine."

He saw her swallow and she nodded. Offering her his arm once more, he led her into the building. Her sharp inhale reminded him she wasn't used to such decadent surroundings. Knowle House was lit to perfection with glistening chandeliers. Long mirrors reflected the light and the golden frames around each huge portrait in the hallway glowed. It was not as grand as his own home could be when decked up for a ball, but it was the first Orelia had ever attended so he should not be surprised at her awe.

"You are a *marquesa* remember? You see this all the time," he whispered.

Orelia clamped her mouth shut and nodded slightly. Her grip on him tightened and he felt a tiny tremble in her body. Here was a woman who could sneak with the best of them but put her in a room with his peers and she was terrified. Were they really that petrifying a bunch?

He led her through into the ballroom. One heavy chandelier dominated the oval shaped room. Long windows looked out onto the center courtyard and lamps had been strung along the box trees to light the grand space. The scent of powder and cigar smoke lingered in the air. The trembling in Orelia didn't cease.

Reed murmured their names to the Master of Ceremonies, who announced them as the duke and *marquesa*. A
few heads spun there way.

While he nodded his greeting to several friends and acquaintances, he managed to avoid any formal introductions.
He needed to get Orelia to relax first or else she might give the
game away.

Leading her over to the edge of the dance floor, he found
them both drinks and handed one over. "Breathe," he reminded her.

The minuet had been danced and the dancers were now
onto the next dance—Lord Dalkeith's Reel he believed. He
had conjured up an ankle injury for himself so that they did
not need to dance. However, he could not help notice how
mesmerized by it all Orelia was. Though, he should not be surprised. All ladies loved to dance, did they not? Why would
Orelia be any different.

"The dances look more fun than they are," he lied.

Unfortunately, the expressions on the dancer's faces belied
his words. They were all pink-cheeked and excited, particularly the young women around Orelia's age.

"One gets very hot and bothered after a dance or two."

She nodded absently, her gaze fixed on the young ladies
while they moved.

"I never really much enjoyed them," he continued.

"I cannot believe that."

He lifted a shoulder. "For the past few years, dancing has
merely been a tool. I use it to gain information and study the
guests. I can't remember the last time I genuinely enjoyed it."

"What a shame."

The mournful look on her face tugged at his heart. He peered around the ballroom and found whom he believed to be their suspect. They had never met in person, despite similar social circles. Reed had been too busy spying while it seemed Lord Trowbridge travelled a great deal.

With excellent posture, gleaming black hair and slim figure, Lord Trowbridge had already found himself surrounded by ladies. He lost his wife to consumption just over a year ago it seemed. Many women would be hoping this night was their chance to catch his eye and become wife number two.

What would they all think if they knew this handsome chap was a potential killer?

He offered Orelia his arm and took the empty glass from her to place on a passing footman's tray. "Come, we must speak with Lord Trowbridge."

"What are you going to ask him?"

Reed shrugged. "I shall find out soon enough."

She stared at him. "How is it you are so content having no plan at all? I have never known a man to improvise so much."

He grinned. "That is because you have never known me." He lowered his voice. "I would have thought having no plans appealed to your free spirit, Orelia. Do not tell me you've lost your taste for a life of freedom."

"Never, but I still like to know what I'm doing!" she declared.

"Well, we are going to push our way through that huge gathering of ladies and introduce you to Lord Trowbridge.

Perhaps he will be so blinded by your beauty that he shall give the game away instantly."

A blush appeared on her cheeks and Reed grinned again. Christ, he loved her blush. He needed to charm her more often.

"Why do you blush?" He knew the answer, but he wanted to hear it from her lips.

"I am not beautiful."

"You are. And you should be told as much with such frequency that you find yourself bored with the words."

A half-smile flickered on her lips and she shook her head. But as much as she might brush his compliment aside, he noted the affect it had on her. Her breathing had slowed, she'd lifted her shoulders.

They made their way around the ballroom while the next dance was called. The shuffle meant several ladies had to disperse and find their partners, much to their obvious disappointment.

"Lord Trowbridge."

The man glanced over Reed before his gaze landed on Orelia. Just as Reed had hoped, a spark of admiration lit in his eyes. Reed somehow managed to keep his smug smile to himself but he could hardly blame their host for falling for her. In a bevy of pale misses, Orelia stood out like a shining gem with her intriguing dusk skin, shining dark hair and wide eyes and lips.

"Forgive me..." the lord said.

"Reed St. Vincent, Duke of Keswick."

"Your Grace, yes, of course. I heard you announced but I could not see over the crowds. Do forgive my ignorance."

"Not at all. May I introduce the *Marquesa of Ardales.*

Trowbridge dipped his head and Orelia curtsied. The moment the viscount lifted his head, he latched his gaze onto hers. "*Marquesa*? What brings you to England, my lady?"

Orelia smiled but only Reed saw the panic in her gaze.

"I'm afraid the *marquesa* does not speak a word of English. Her husband died in the war and she has come to England to learn a little English and likely find another husband. My mother has put me in charge of such a task."

"What a delightful task that must be," Trowbridge murmured.

Reed wondered if the man had forgotten she couldn't understand English already.

Orelia fluttered her fan in front of her face and offered a bashful smile. Reed smothered a chuckle. Gone was the shy, shaking, clearly terrified woman. In her place was a master of disguise. He really could not have picked a better woman to help him. He'd known she was quick on her feet from the beginning after she told his fortune—or pretended to at least—but he could not have imagined she would slip in so easily with members of the *ton*.

He tried to draw Trowbridge into discussion of his travels but Orelia did a far too fine a job of distracting him. She shook her head as she pretended not to understand him, then cocked it delicately. She giggled occasionally and managed a faint nod as though she might have comprehended just a few of his words. Everything about her had Trowbridge rapt. Of course, if Reed had not known of the act, he might well have found himself spellbound too.

Hell, he was already. By the *real* Orelia.

They began to draw a crowd of men. A few tried to entice her into a dance, but she shook her head and Reed explained she was not yet ready to dance after the death of her husband. Somehow this did not put them off. He could see the hunger in their eyes. They wanted to be the one to coax this unique beauty out of her mourning. They wanted to cure her broken heart.

At some point, the game grew weary to Reed. The men gathered a little too close, trying to outdo each other with tales of their various exploits and wealth. Even Trowbridge appeared annoyed. A possessive look came over his face as he watched Orelia fend off her suitors and Reed ground his teeth. It was just a game, yes, but that didn't mean he enjoyed someone looking at her as though he might be able to possess her.

She flicked a glance at him and jerked her head toward Trowbridge. Reed cursed himself. Here he was, getting furious over a little flirting and missing out on his opportunity to speak with the man. Whilst all the other young bucks kept Orelia occupied, Reed had his chance.

Reed cleared his throat. "I must thank you for allowing us to attend at the last moment."

"Not at all. After all my travelling, I am keen to make new acquaintances. I believe we have attended the odd event or two together in the past but never really met. I heard you travelled too, is that how you met the *marquesa*?"

"Actually, no. My mother met her whilst in France. She was married at the time and they corresponded. My mother does like to take these young women under her wing, I find."

"And you are in charge of finding her a new husband?"

Reed didn't answer.

"I am right, I see. Why do you not snap her up yourself? Has she been left penniless?"

"Not at all." Reed didn't know why he'd said that. It would only encourage Trowbridge. But for some reason, he did not want Orelia to be subjected to any derision tonight. Let her enjoy the attention of them thinking she was something she was not. After all, he knew the truth. He knew she was so much more than money and a title. Hell, he'd take that simple gypsy girl over a marchioness any day.

He took a drink from a passing footman and shrugged. "I am not ready to wed, even to a woman like the *marquesa*. Besides, I enjoy conversation. I would not enjoy a quiet wife."

Trowbridge chuckled. "You'd be one of the few. I think most men would find her to be the perfect wife. Beautiful, elegant, rich and silent. What better combination can there be?"

Reed glanced at Orelia. Some men might like their women silent, but he liked his brave and bold, and talkative with no thought of rank. He liked them like Orelia.

"Well, what can I say. She's not for me, Lord Trowbridge."

"I hope you might keep her in society for some time."

"We are to return home tomorrow. My mother is keen to introduce her to some of the local families."

"Ah, that is a shame."

"I'm sure we shall be attending more events soon. The *marquesa* is hardly one to sit around and be bored."

"Excellent. I shall be sure to extend any invitations I have to you. Can I catch you at Keswick Abbey?"

"Yes, most of the time. I do not travel as much as I used to."

Trowbridge grimaced. "Nor I. My doctor is responsible for that, unfortunately. Too much sun, he says. So, alas, we are to remain in cold, old England."

It was amusing how cold, old England did not seem so dreary now that Orelia was in it.

Reed glanced at him. "When did you return from your travels?"

"Some two weeks ago."

So after the attempt on Napoleon's life, but that did not necessarily mean anything.

"I had heard you were quite the avid wine collector," Reed mused. "Did you pick some up on your travels?"

Interest sparked in Trowbridge's eyes. "A wine man, are you?"

"Not especially but the *marquesa* does enjoy it. It seems you might have that in common."

Trowbridge grinned. "It seems we might. You think she would enjoy seeing my collection?"

"I think she would. If you cannot share a language, a love of wine must surely be the next best thing."

His grin expanded. "I'm mightily glad you attended tonight, Your Grace. You must return or come out to my country estate for some shooting, so I can thank you."

Reed smiled, mostly to cover the foolish burning jealousy that was rising inside him. Trowbridge was falling for his plan perfectly. He could not have asked for it to go better. Yet he still loathed the man's interest in Orelia.

"I shall show her after supper, that is, if I have your permission."

Reed nodded. "Absolutely, though I must insist on accompanying you."

"Naturally."

Reed had the feeling he had just made Trowbridge's evening. A shame he had no idea the reasons behind the plotting. At some point, he needed to catch Orelia's eye and explain the plan. His hope was that if they could view his wine, they'd see if there were still bottles of *Vin de Constance* left.

He did not manage to catch her until they went into supper. That hint of nervousness was about her again, showing itself in the fluttering pulse at her neck.

"Just go slowly, do not touch the wine, let me and the gentleman next to you help, and copy the other ladies," he said softly.

"I really do not think I can do this." Her voice trembled.

"You did not think you could walk into a ballroom and charm every man in England, but you did that."

"Not every man," she exclaimed.

"A few women too, I think. Quite a few were interested in being friends with the exotic *marquesa*."

"You don't know how hard it was to remain quiet."

"Keep it up," he murmured. "It's working. Lord Trowbridge wants to show you his wine collection after supper."

She swung a look at him. "You will not leave me alone, will you?"

"I would not leave you alone with him, even if I believe you can fend for yourself."

She chuckled and tucked her mouth behind her fan. "I had better return to being silent," she said when they entered the dining room.

Gold patterned wallpaper mingled with bright red swathes of curtains. The long room was punctuated with sash windows at one end and another impressive chandelier. Not for the first time, and likely not for the last, he considered how perfectly Orelia fit in here. What a chameleon she was.

She stole a look at him as they sat. His chest compressed a little. This woman was going to be the death of him somehow, he was certain of that now.

Chapter Sixteen

Orelia could not help breathe a sigh of relief once supper was finished. She had never eaten in a formal setting before and most of the advice Reed had given her prior to the ball had seemed to vanish from her mind as she sat. Thankfully remaining quiet and patient had helped, and she'd been able to mimic the other ladies at the table whilst the gentleman at her side helped serve her.

Ensuring it was known she could not speak English had been a perfect ploy. Reed really was the most cunning man at times. It meant no one expected much of her. What would they think if she blurted out something common and coarse suddenly? The idea made her giggle.

"You are enjoying yourself, I hope?" Lord Trowbridge asked.

She gave a sort of half-shrug of confusion and smiled. Smiling worked well, she had discovered. Look a little confused and smile, and it seemed all the men adored it. Perhaps that was how they liked their women—confused and smiling.

"His Grace says you are interested in wine."

She expanded her smile and nodded eagerly.

"I should like to show you my collection."

Orelia glanced around for Reed who hastened to her side. He murmured in her ear as though trying to explain what the Lord wanted. In reality, he told her how beautiful she was.

She hoped she wasn't blushing. The way he had looked at her all night seemed to have put permanent heat in her cheeks. While she certainly enjoyed wearing the finery and appreciated the work the maids had put into ensuring she looked the part, she hardly thought of herself as rivalling any of the beautiful young women in attendance.

Their host led them down to the wine cellar. He lit a candle and escorted them through the dark undercroft. A chill made her skin bump and the air smelled damp. Though the viscount seemed harmless, if a little flirtatious, she was grateful to have Reed at her side.

"An impressive collection," Reed murmured.

"Thank you. I picked up what I could on my travels. *La marquesa* here should like my Spanish collection." He motioned to a large rack filled with bottles. She could not help wonder if he ever intended to drink the wine or merely let it sit there forever.

"Do you have any French wines?" Reed asked. "They must be hard to come by after the war."

"They are but they're getting easier to purchase now." He glanced around as though someone might be listening in. "I was in contact with a few merchants who were able to sneak some in." He lifted the candle to reveal yet more rows of wine. "Here is my French collection. I hope to expand it in time now that we are trading with France again."

Orelia's heart began to pound. This was what they were looking for.

Pasting on a smile, she stepped forward and looped her arm through the viscount's. He startled slightly but settled into it rapidly, even drawing her closer. It was not horribly uncomfortable to be at his side and a slight pang of guilt hit her. If he had nothing to do with the attempt on Napoleon, she was toying with his feelings for no reason.

It would be worth it, she reminded herself. Her people would no longer be suspected, and further war would be prevented.

She motioned to the few other racks of wine ahead, indicating she wanted to look at more and Trowbridge chuckled.

"You really do like wine, do you not?"

Orelia simply smiled and urged him on. Reed lingered behind them and she prayed she could give him enough time to peer at the bottles.

After they'd strolled the length of the cellar, with Lord Trowbridge pointing out various wines and drawing them out occasionally, she stole a peek over her shoulder. Reed gave her a subtle nod and lounged against a casket in a nonchalant manner.

"Your guests will be missing you, Trowbridge," he called.

The viscount chuckled. "You are right. We had better get back. No doubt they are missing the *marquesa* too."

Orelia tried to control her blush for what had to be the hundredth time that night. She had never had so much male attention. A few kisses and a fumbled moment with one man that she regretted, yes, but there had never been all this...*flirting.*

However, though she could not deny enjoying it somewhat, she knew they only liked the mystery about her. If they knew the real her, and her true heritage, they would run for miles. She smiled to herself. Only Reed made her feel as though being a Romani was nothing to be ashamed of and that, actually, he enjoyed her company and her definite non-silence.

They headed back up to the ballroom and Orelia took Reed's arm once more. He gave her a little nudge and a smile. She wasn't sure exactly what he meant but it had to be good news.

The dancing went on for several more hours and gradually guests flitted away from exhaustion. She rather hoped to do the same, but Reed insisted they maintained their pretense for just a little while longer. She smiled and nodded and looked confusion for at least another hour more by her reckoning until he called it a night.

The viscount gave a deep dip and smiled into her eyes. The desire to look away and blush meant she had to lift her fan to cover her face. His smile only grew at this action. After a night of so much male attention, she wanted to roll her eyes. The novelty was wearing off rapidly.

How was it such apparent bashfulness and silence appealed so much to these men of society? At least with her people she was not expected to be meek and silent. Goodness knows, her mother was far from silent and there were many strong-headed Romani women.

"I hope to see you again," Lord Trowbridge muttered, his gaze seeming to cling to her.

She dipped and gave the same smile she'd been holding all evening. It was not until Reed helped her into his carriage did she feel she could let it drop.

"My cheeks hurt!"

He chuckled and tapped the roof. "You were wonderful."

She turned to him. "So? What news? Is he our man?"

He shook his head and pushed open the curtain behind him to let in a little more of a glow from the outer lamps. "Not at all. Though I began to suspect as much when he agreed to show us the wine."

"Yes, it seemed odd that a potential murderer might display his intended means of killing someone. And he was quite pleasant."

He gave her an odd look—almost pained. "Well, the wine was all there so he's not our man."

"So it must be our first man, yes?"

Pinching the bridge of his nose, he nodded. "And Lord knows where he is, but I'll put my contacts onto it on the morrow."

"At least we likely do not need to resort to anymore playacting."

She rested her head back against the plush seat. Closed-carriage riding was something she did not think she would ever get used to. All that movement and the horse hooves and yet she was unable to see a thing or feel the air on her face. She had to admit, however, after a long evening of being on her feet and smiling at everyone, it was luxurious to sit on a soft seat rather than a hard bench.

"You were wonderful," he told her again. "Too wonderful?"

Orelia straightened. "Too wonderful?"

"Yes, you had most of the male population and even some of the female half in love with you. As for Lord Trowbridge, I think he was about ready to propose."

A laugh escaped her. "I doubt that."

"He questioned your marriage prospects."

She blinked at him. "And what did you say?"

"I said that you were a rich widow, hoping to remarry."

"Well no wonder he was interested. You should have said I had not a penny to my name! It would have been the first bit of truth spoken all night."

"We needed him to remain interested in you. Though I have a feeling that at this point, he would not care one jot if you were penniless."

Orelia huffed. "I highly doubt that. But, alas, I am, and he would have been even more put off by my heritage, you and I both know that."

"Then he would be a fool."

He leaned in and the air in the coach vanished. Not even the sound of the horses moving at a pace penetrated the hard exterior. Everything seemed to fall silent. In the faint glow of the lamps, his eyes were deep and intense. She could not look away.

"I'm glad he was a fool," he muttered. "I am glad they are all fools." He stroked a finger down her cheek and dropped it onto her bottom lip. She parted her mouth and he ran his finger across her lip and up over her cupid's bow, seemingly mesmerized. "I am glad they do not see what I see. You are a Romani, Orelia, and that has made you into the strong, courageous woman I see before me. Don't regret your heritage."

"I try not to," she said, "but it's hard when people treat you so differently."

"Do I treat you differently?" His finger had come back up to the side of her face and he traced it over her cheek.

"Never."

"I want to," he whispered harshly. "I want to treat you so very differently."

"What do you—"

He shifted closer and drew her into his arms in a moment. "I want to hold you. Touch you. Kiss you."

A tiny moan escaped her.

He must have taken that as her consent. She was grateful he did. His lips hit her neck first, hot and open. Her moan was louder this time.

Reed worked his mouth up to the dip behind her ear, sealed his teeth briefly around her lobe before pressing his mouth to hers.

Orelia dug her fingers into his neck and moved with him. Their tongues clashed. This kiss was hot, demanding, desperate—as though he had been waiting all night to do it. She felt his frustration there. Perhaps it had been the same frustration as hers. Perhaps he had spent all evening looking at her and wishing he could touch her openly.

His hand came to cup her breast through her stays. She sucked in a long gasp of air. Despite the fabric between his palm and her flesh, he might as well have touched bare skin, such was the sweet, sharp relief of the pressure. He kissed her deeply, his tongue chasing hers and he smoothed his palm across her breast, teasing her nipple against the fabric of her undergarments.

"Orelia," he groaned harshly.

She released her own whimper in response. Lord, how much more she wanted. More kisses, more touches. His hands upon her bare skin. She'd known Reed was different from early on. She even understood she had never desired a man quite like she desired him. But she had never expected it quite to be like this.

The carriage jerked suddenly and came to a halt. Dazed, Orelia lifted her head but he would not release her mouth. She surrendered quickly.

"We are home," he muttered, drawing her tighter into his hold.

Home. What an odd idea that was. Keswick Abbey was far too grand to ever feel like her home. However, being in Reed's arms felt like home. She'd never understood what such a concept could be really. For the first time in her life, she comprehended it.

And actually, it held quite a bit of appeal.

A sharp rap on the door dragged them apart. Reed pushed open the door. "Do you mind, we will—"

An attractive older woman with grey-streaked dark hair and tightly pursed lips stood in the doorway. Reed cursed under his breath.

"Good evening, Mother."

His mother narrowed her eyes at Orelia. "Been keeping yourself busy I see?"

Orelia blushed from root to toe. If only the shadows of the carriage would swallow her. Or a convenient hole opened up in the ground.

"I did not expect you back so soon," Reed said lightly.

"As I can see. Now, would you like to tell me exactly why you have been taking in homeless girls and conducting scandalous behavior in Portsmouth?"

He threw a glance at Orelia and gave her hand a little squeeze.

"In time, Mother. We have had rather a busy evening and Orelia needs rest."

The look of fury on the dowager duchess's face had Orelia surprised none of them shot up in flames, such was the heat of the anger there.

Reed stepped out and helped Orelia down as though they were back at the ball and no more than an elegant lady and gentleman instead of a duke and a Romani woman. More specifically, a Romani woman wearing the duchesses dress.

Though Orelia kept her gaze lowered, she could feel his mother's hot gaze boring into the back of her. She had been right. Keswick Abbey would never feel like home. Nor could Reed's arms. She did not belong here or in the arms of a duke. What a foolish girl she was.

Chapter Seventeen

Really it was quite the miracle his mother had not exploded overnight. Or at the morning meal. As they sat in the breakfast room, the fire in his mother's eyes did a lot more to warm the room than the sun streaming through the generous windows. It seemed his brother had opted not to join them for breakfast—and Reed could not blame him one jot.

"Did you enjoy your trip, Mother?" Reed asked lightly.

Orelia, he noticed, had barely touched her food. She remained seated, her chin lowered, and picked at a bread roll. He was almost surprised she had not fled during the night but apparently his assurances all would be well before putting her to bed had worked.

How long it would take him to ensure all really was well was another thing. His mother was hardly known for her light-hearted temperament and bringing a gypsy girl into what she might as well still consider her house was hardly the best way to greet her upon her return.

"It was pleasant," his mother said tightly.

"Excellent." He kept his tone bright. "And what of Aunt Rosamunde?"

"She is well."

"Excellent," he repeated.

Though his mother had tried her best to berate him the previous night, he had allowed her little chance, declaring exhaustion and stealing away upstairs whilst reminding her she needed rest too. Telling his mother in a roundabout way that she was old and tired had not been his wisest move, but she had been so shocked, she'd been unable to reply and thus it worked quite nicely for the night. Somehow, he suspected she would not have forgotten such a comment and his ears were likely in for a blistering today.

Reed sighed. He did not much mind if his ears suffered his mother's wrath. He'd dealt with it time and again. And he knew all her objections. Orelia was a Romani. Practically worse than a commoner in his mother's eyes. She did not belong here. There would be scandal. Was he bedding her? Why could he not simply go to a brothel and be discrete? What on earth had possessed him? And, of course, why was she wearing his mother's dresses?

Oh yes, he was prepared for it all. but his biggest regret was the looks that were being slung Orelia's way. His own servants had been excellent to her after a fashion. Of course they were paid well to do so—but he liked to think he had faithful and loyal staff who would be discrete and reserve any judgement for downstairs and far away from Orelia's ears.

His mother had never really learned the art of discretion.

If Orelia could shrink any farther into her chair she would. He tried to catch her gaze to offer a reassuring look, but she refused to glance his way.

I will protect you, he longed to tell her. It seemed mightily ridiculous he was having to protect her from his own mother, but her prejudices were far deeper than his own. His mother's world view had been limited since she was a girl, being born only to serve as a lady and a wife to a rich man.

Regardless of what his mother thought of Orelia, he would not allow her to make her feel ashamed, particularly not after the previous night. This young gypsy girl had proven herself to be more quick-witted, more intelligent, more graceful than every lady in that ballroom. She had them all fooled and what a wonderful sight it had been. He could not help take some pleasure in knowing how foolish they would feel if their prejudices had been exposed upon knowing her real identity.

His mother, however, did not care much if her prejudice was visible. He'd have to remind her that this was his house, regardless of the fact he had not resided in it much these past few years and Orelia was his guest. He expected her to treat her as such.

"What are your plans for today?" he asked his mother.

"Well, I was intending to receive some guests. It seems I have missed much whilst I have been away." She slung a pointed look at Orelia who had not yet made work of her bread roll. "However, it seems I shall not be able to receive any."

"Oh do not fear, we shan't be here to get in your way. We are off to town today."

"I've heard you were staying in town for a few nights recently."

"Really?" He lifted a brow.

Who was it who was gossiping about him to his mother? She had taken her most loyal servants with her. He'd have to warn her not to continue gossiping. There was a very real rea-son most of his work had been done abroad—too many peo-ple were far too interested in his whereabouts in England. He had to wonder if he would ever be able to return to spying, even if he did complete this mission successfully.

"Pray tell, where exactly did you hear such rumors?"

His mother made a dismissive noise. "Rumors, Reed? I do not think they can be called rumors when they are in fact, truths."

"I had some business there."

"And you needed to take your...lady friend?" His mother slung a narrowed glance at Orelia.

"Orelia accompanied me, yes."

Her face reddened with obvious annoyance. "Really, Reed! I expected better of you."

"And I of you, Mother. I never expected to return to be hounded by young women thrown at me and endless invita-tions to events. I never expected to have my guest so disre-spected."

Orelia lifted her head at the sound of all the raised voices. Slowly, with great dignity, she rose. "I-if you shall excuse me..."

She scurried out before Reed could protest. He did not much like his mother running her out of the room but at least now he could fully berate her.

"Thank you, Mother. Your pomposity knows no bounds."

"Pomposity? How dare you?" His mother's dark eyes flashed. "You know that I have supported you throughout all your various adventures whilst you gallivanted about and re-fused to play the role you should. I have run your household to the best of my abilities and made excuses for you at every turn."

"You could have asked Noah."

"Noah cannot handle such responsibilities."

"He damn well can, and you know it. Just because your pride would take a beating does not mean he should be prevented from revealing to the world what he can do."

The duchess drew in a breath. He saw her clamp her hand around a spoon.

"If you are intending to kill me, Mother, I suggest you find something a little sharper."

She narrowed her gaze at him. "Why do I have such an undutiful son?"

Sometimes the desire to tell her what he did was unbearable. No son liked disappointing their mother, not even him. But he would never put her or Noah in danger or worry her any more than he had to. She might fret over his lack of a wife but he'd far rather she did that than panic over him potentially getting killed as he snuck through war zones and army camps.

"Forgive me," he said instead. "I did not aim to disappoint you." He nodded toward the spoon. "Now please put the spoon down. I have no wish to explain to the doctor how I ended up with such strange injuries."

His mother lowered the spoon, a faint smile coming to her lips. He had long acknowledged they were similar creatures—both outspoken and with a temper at times. But at least it meant his mother would not stay angry at him forever. He might not agree with some of her actions, but he didn't want things to be tense between them.

"You cannot keep her here. Why would you? Is she..." She fanned her face with a hand and leaned in. "Is she your lover? And you know I am being generous calling her that. Others would call her much worse."

"Orelia is not my lover."

Unfortunately, a dark little voice whispered.

"Well, I know you would delight in torturing me with such knowledge if she was, so you must be telling the truth."

"I am."

She leaned in. "So what is she and why is she here?"

"She is from the local gypsy camp. She is here to help me."

"Eleanor said as much."

Reed shook his head. "Eleanor needs to stop pressing the servants for information. She might be your lady's maid, but I pay her wages."

She gasped. "Eleanor has been with me for many years. You would not dare let her go."

"I would if she continues to gossip about Orelia. I want no shame brought down upon her, do you understand?"

His mother pressed her lips together.

"Mother?"

"I understand," she said tightly, "but I still do not see how you can expect me to feel comfortable with that...woman under our roof. The scandal, Reed...Sweet Lord, no one will ever marry you now."

"Yes they will," he said patiently. "I am a duke and I am rich. They shall conveniently forget anything scandalous ever happened at Keswick Abbey in weeks, if not days. Besides, I've been doing a fair job of keeping her presence here quiet."

"What of her family? Surely they want her back?"

"Unfortunately no. Her mother is a drunkard and her father, well, we're not sure about that."

She paled further, if that was possible.

"Reed, I am not sure what I ever did to deserve this."

"Deserve what?"

His mother pressed a hand to her chest. "You seem intent on sending me to an early grave."

She genuinely did look a little close to the grave, so he didn't laugh or try to antagonize her further. "I do not mean to, I promise."

"How long will she be staying?"

He shrugged. "I'm not sure yet."

"And will you tell me why exactly, we are to house her?"

Reed decided to opt for the truth. Or at least a partial truth. "Well, it seems I bought her, in a roundabout way, and now she is helping me with something."

"Bought her? How does one buy someone in a roundabout way?" She was back to picking up the spoon again.

Reed watched the silverware with a raised brow. "I ran into a situation and my morals would not let me act any other way. So I bought her from her mother."

"So it was not really a roundabout way then, was it?"

"Perhaps not."

"And she is definitely not your lover?" she pressed.

"I have not purchased myself a whore, no, Mother. As you say, there are many brothels I could visit for that, though Lord forbid it should ever come to that."

His mother pursed her lips. "I have little intention of discussing such matters with my son, but goodness knows, you could learn some discretion."

"I am perfectly discrete. None of the local families have knowledge of Orelia or the fact that I paid for her company...not like that," he reminded her. "Soon enough she will be gone, I promise, and then you can get back to thrusting clueless young ladies at me."

"Not all are so clueless," she muttered with a slight hint of a smile.

"I noticed. Though if they knew anything about me, they would not be so unsubtle."

She huffed. "That is why you favor the gypsy girl perhaps. They have little understanding of manners and subtlety."

"Orelia is nothing like that. I would hope you would take the time to discover that. Noah likes her."

"Noah likes everyone. He is far too naive."

Reed lifted a brow. "Or he is simply a better man than all of us."

His mother eyed her half-finished meal. "I find I am no longer hungry." She stood, and he followed suit. "I hope that these shenanigans, whatever they are, will not take long and you can concentrate on your duty."

"Trust me, Mother, all shall be well. Now why do you not ask Noah to help with the meetings with the farmhands today? I find myself with little time."

His mother shook her head. "Why must you force him into such situations? Do you not understand how humiliating they are for him?"

"No, Mother, I do not. He enjoys the responsibility and the farmhands like him."

She gave another huff before sweeping out of the room. He understood her reluctance to involve Noah, really he did, but why his mother could not see that he was now a grown man, he did not know. There had been times, when they were young boys before Noah had been able to lip read, that he had been humiliated in public. Their mother wanted to protect him still, but he no longer needed that. Reed had seen how well his brother had done running the estate, so why could she not see that too?

Reed eyed his not quite empty plate and concluded his appetite had gone too. He would go find Noah, instruct him as to his duties for the day then ensure Orelia was dressed for Portsmouth. They would remain in their simpler clothing to-day to draw less attention and hopefully no one would recognize her as the beautiful countess from the ball.

He found Noah in the study, pouring over some letters. He waited until his brother spotted him. "Mother is furious." He signed as he spoke.

"Why do you think I escaped here?" his brother said.

"You have to face her at some point. I've already told her you shall be taking over today."

Noah rolled his eyes. "You know she would rather do it herself. She does not think me capable."

"But she will once she sees you in action," Reed insisted.

"You have more faith than I do."

"If we could just make her see you as more than her little boy, we might succeed."

Noah sighed. "Reed, I have not been a little boy for many years. If I have not succeeded by now, I doubt I ever shall."

"I did not take you for a quitter."

"I am not." Noah signed this bit, lifting his chin and eyeing him sternly.

His brother had been through many challenges in life, first with the infection that left him deaf and then with how people treated him. He could not join the army or do anything that a second son usually did. He was far from a quitter, but Reed did fear his mother would win one day and Noah would let himself be coddled for the rest of his life by her.

"Did she meet Orelia?" Noah asked.

Reed nodded.

His brother laughed. "It went that well?"

He guessed the grimace on his face told the story well enough. "She was not happy but there is little she can do. Orelia must remain until we have discovered the culprit."

"It will be a shame when she goes." His brother tilted his head. "I think you shall miss her too."

"Of course. Why would I not? She's a lovely young woman."

Noah rubbed his chin and eyed Reed. "I think you shall miss her greatly."

"Orelia has many things she would like to do. She's a Romani, Noah. They are always on the move. I have my doubts that will ever change."

"I think you want her to stay."

Reed rubbed his forehead. Yes, he would miss her. Yes, he was trying not to think on the day when she took his money and vanished from his life. Yes, he wanted more of those stunningly sensual kisses. Yes, he longed to take her to bed and keep her there for eternity.

But had his mother's reaction not just proved how impossible any of it would be. Yes, he could keep her as a mistress somewhere, put her in a fine house perhaps and visit her to appease his needs when he so desired. However, he knew well enough that would be unsatisfactory for him and a nightmare for her. Orelia, tied to one place, awaiting his visits...no he would never even suggest inflicting such a thing on her.

Of course, he knew damn well that if he took Orelia to bed, he would not want to let her out of his sight, let alone tuck her away in the country somewhere.

"Orelia will follow her path and I will follow mine," he said, in what he felt was a particularly enlightened manner.

Noah merely laughed. "I think your paths might just intersect several times."

Reed snorted. "What do you know about women anyway, whelp?"

His brother laughed again. "More than you I think."

Muttering a curse, Reed escaped the study and stomped upstairs in search of Orelia. Damned whelp trying to school him on emotions. Apparently, all the power he'd given Noah had gone to his head. Was every member of his family intending to fight him on his plans?

He rapped on her door and waited. He knocked again.

That tell-tale sensation in his gut triggered. He knew that feeling. The one that told him to move more quickly or escape now or hide sharpish. Without waiting any longer, he pushed open the door.

Her room was empty.

Chapter Eighteen

It was not exactly running away. She had never run from anything, Orelia assured herself as she made her way up the field and followed the indented path at the side of it. She paused to pluck a daisy from the grass and twirl it in her fingers. See? Who picked flowers when they were running away?

However, she had needed to escape. It was not the first time someone looked down upon her because of her heritage and it would hardly be the last. She could not even blame Reed's mother for behaving so. What woman would not be shocked at a young woman in her home, wearing her gowns no less?

Her cheeks flamed. To think the duchess had caught her practically in Reed's arms. No wonder she thought badly of her. After all, Orelia had hardly done anything to disprove the idea that the Romani were immoral people.

The stilted conversation from the morning rattled through her mind. And, despite herself, she had paused to listen to the rest of it before his mother left the breakfast room and Orelia was forced to tuck herself into an alcove and pray with a pounding heart she was not spotted.

Samantha Holt

The duchess thought she was a whore. Reed wanted her gone. Soon, at least. They had a mission to finish and she certainly did not wish to abandon it.

An ache gathered in her throat and she threw aside the daisy and continued down the path toward the gypsy camp. Reed had promised his mother she would be gone soon enough. Why did that hurt?

Because she wanted to stay, a little voice told her.

She huffed at the ridiculous voice. Of course she would be gone soon enough. She could hardly stay at the abbey forever and why would she even want to? Once she had money, she would have more freedom than she had ever dreamed. The world would be hers. She could invest the money, as planned, or even travel more before settling somewhere. How wonderful that would be.

Would it not?

She looked at her feet and kicked a stone that sat stubbornly in her path. It tumbled a little before stopping. "I'm not running away," she told the stone.

In a few hours, she would return. They were meant to travel to Portsmouth to find the one suspect that had vanished. Perhaps Reed would be annoyed with her and go on his own. Perhaps it would be easier if she let him. Then she would have some time between seeing him again and recalling the kiss in the carriage.

That kiss...

That kiss had been unlike any they shared before. It had been filled with promise. Promise of what, she was not sure, but she had been swept along and ready to find out. How could she face him now?

"I am not a coward," she told the cloudless sky. "Am not."

"I beg to differ," came a deep voice from behind.

Her heart leapt. Though whether it was from surprise, excitement, or fright, she did not know.

She whirled. "What are you doing here?"

Reed grinned. "I should have known *I* would be the one in trouble for chasing you down."

She lifted her chin. "I was hardly running away."

"So you were...?"

"Taking a leisurely stroll."

"Toward the gypsy camp?"

"Yes."

She hated to look at him sometimes. He was too handsome, even with that silly eyepatch that was currently lodged on his head and making his dark hair stick up awkwardly. Her gaze landed on his lips of its own accord as she recalled how they'd been on hers the previous night and how she had wanted them so much more.

Darkness glittered in his gaze that made her breath catch. Was he recalling the same? Looking at her lips with the same desire?

"After last night, I would have thought nothing could scare you."

"I'm not scared of your mother. I simply thought it best I give you some time with her."

"I think my mother is unlikely to want to see me for the rest of the day."

She sighed. "I'm sorry to create problems for you."

He shook his head. "I knew full well bringing you into my home had the potential for scandal, though I think we have avoided it thus far unless my mother decides to tell her friends—which I very much doubt. I do, however, regret her treatment of you, and certainly the idea that I might have scandalized you. I suppose I never considered the impact it might have upon you, and for that, I am sorry."

A smile she could not resist slid across her lips. "I hardly think it's possible to scandalize a Romani girl. Besides, we are meant to be married, are we not? There is nothing left to scandalize. In fact, I think your mother rather handled it well. I might have expected her to drag me out by my hair."

He chuckled. "My mother has her moments but she's a good woman really. Just a little old-fashioned and determined to keep our good name as pure as possible."

"I forget how important names are to rich people."

"They are the most important thing of all," he told her, his smile wry. "We must do everything in our power to protect them. Of course, my mother forgets that my grandfather was a rake of the highest regard and somehow survived and my Uncle Felix was embroiled in political scandal some three summers ago and that had been swept aside nicely. A young, unmarried woman under my roof is the least scandalous thing to happen to us in years."

She laughed. "Well, I suppose I do not feel so bad then."

"Good." He offered her his arm. "Now, I have a trip to town to make. Will you do the honor of accompanying me?"

"I will." She took his arm. "How did you know I would be here?"

He considered this for a moment. "In spite of all this talk of being a free-spirited Romani, I thought you would return to where you know."

"You know me too well, it seems."

"Apparently so."

Orelia peered up at him. His features were silhouetted against the bright morning sun, his nose strong and his lips near irresistible. It felt as though he really did know her well, and she him. It was hard to recall a time when he was not in her life. What had it been like not to be able to talk or laugh, or even touch this man?

"I have the carriage waiting ahead," he told her.

"That explains how you caught up to me so quickly."

"You need not have run, you know."

"I was not running," she protested.

"If you say so." He aided her over the sty and the old trap, now fixed, awaited them. Reed gave her a hand up and she settled onto the hard bench.

"I hope we shall not run into any more disasters today. I've had enough excitement."

"None at all, I assure you," he said as he flicked the reins. "I had the stable master give it a good look over and as worn as it looks, it shall survive this journey quite well. I won't make that mistake a second time, even if it did give me a chance to see how devious you are."

"Devious?" she declared, affecting her most innocent look.

"Very well, quick-thinking, then."

She smiled broadly. "That's better."

They carried on at a gentle pace down the lane. The day started cool but dry and the clouds vanished altogether leaving it bright. A few bees buzzed about the hedges, searching for something sweet to settle upon. Rapeseed filled one field, covering it in a bright yellow blanket. It was funny how she had never stopped to admire the setting in which her family set up camp.

"Why did Noah not join us for breakfast?" she asked.

"He likes to avoid Mother."

"She is stern, I'm sure, but she loves you, does she not? Even I could tell that she was angry because of love."

His brow furrowed. "An odd thought, being angry because of love."

"Love is the strongest of emotions, is it not? And so anger and love go hand in hand."

He glanced her way, his smile soft. "You are so very wise, Orelia."

"I hardly think so."

"I do. Some learning cannot come from books. Heck, I've met some of the smartest men at Oxford and they were utterly clueless about the world. You have experience. It counts for a lot."

She snorted. "Not in a world where a woman is preferred to be naive and inexperienced."

"Well, not everyone thinks like that. In my field, experience is highly valued, as are quick-wits. You have both in abundance.

Would he ever stop making her blush? She could not re-call a time when she had blushed so much or heard so many complimentary words.

"Is your mother angry at Noah?" She peered at him.

"Not at all. She loves him very much. Too much perhaps."

"How so?"

"She wants to protect him," Reed explained. "He had a tough time when he was a boy, adjusting to not being able to hear. It took him a long time to be able to read lips and many people treated him as though he was a fool. I was nine when he lost his hearing and fully able to see my mother's heartache when people treated him poorly."

"So she fears people will treat him the same as they did when he was a boy?"

He nodded. "She is trying to protect him but that frus-trates us both."

"I suppose I can understand why she would wish to pro-tect him. It must be nice to have a mother who wishes to pro-tect you."

He frowned slightly. "I suppose so. Despite all her flaws, she always loved us. Lord knows, we have enough flaws our-selves."

"No one is without them."

"I am sorry if I seem ungrateful for my mother. I know your experience is far worse."

Orelia shrugged. "You cannot compare experiences. What seems devastating to one person can be wholly manageable for another."

"And it seems I have a philosopher for a companion too."

Orelia fell silent. She had little idea what he meant by that but did not wish to ask. How foolish she would look.

He must have noticed her confusion. "A philosopher is..."

"I know what it is," she snapped. "We spoke of it before, if you recall."

They fell into silence after that. She sincerely regretted snapping at him. Reed would never mean to be condescending. Look how wonderfully he treated her when he discovered she could not read. He still managed to make her feel helpful and wanted. Goodness, why was she acting this way? First running off, then speaking to him so disrespectfully.

"We'll leave the cart here," he said, motioning to a traveler's inn.

She nodded and waiting for Reed to arrange the stabling for the horses while they continued on foot. They came to the same ramshackle building as their last visit to see it looking as empty as before. Reed rapped on the door several times and they waited.

"Do you think this is our man?" she asked.

"It could well be, though how he had the coin or the resources to buy such wine, I do not know." He slammed the door knocker hard again, and the whole building seemed to rattle. "I cannot imagine what he has to gain from killing Napoleon but maybe he is but a pawn in this game. Either way, we need to find him. He is our only suspect."

They waited for a while longer and she cast her gaze up the three-story building with its flaking paint and grimy windows. There was no sign of movement anywhere. "What shall we do?"

"We could wait. See if anyone turns up," he suggested.

"We could be waiting all day, if not more."

"We could indeed." He grinned. "You might think being a secret operative for your country is all excitement but let me assure you, I have become an excellent waiter in the process."

"As well as an excellent sneaker," she said, her lips tilted into a grin.

"That too." He peered through the lower window. "I may have to put such skills to good use."

"Oi!"

Orelia whirled to the sound of the shout to see an elderly woman with her head thrust out of a top window of the building next to their suspect's.

"Get outta here!" the woman bellowed.

Reed lifted his gaze to her and squinted. "Good day, my dear woman. Forgive us if we disturbed you."

"Well you did, making all that racket."

"My apologies. I was hoping to stop by and see an old friend, but it seems he is not home."

She paused and wrinkled her nose. "Thomas?"

"Yes."

The woman made a dismissive noise. "He don't live here no more."

Reed swung a look at Orelia. "Ah, that is a shame. Pray tell, do you know where he is?"

"No, and why should I? I'm glad he's gone. He was always drinking, muttering about the war. Lord knows, everyone is grateful for his service but there's no need to go disturbing your neighbors about it. The war belongs in France not on bloody English soil."

"Of course," Reed agreed. "Tell me, where would Thomas go drinking? I should very much like to see him again. We served together you see, and I owe him a debt of gratitude."

The old woman pursed her lips. "Were you involved in that battle too? The one that left Thomas with the limp?"

Reed nodded. "That's the one."

The woman paused and leaned a little farther out of the window. "Try the Red Lion on Braggs Lane. A lot of the soldiers spend time there. The inn doesn't much care about the amount their patrons drink, more's the pity." She shook her head. "War is hell they say but living next to a drunk isn't much fun."

"Of course it isn't," Reed said sympathetically. "Thank you for your help, ma'am. We shan't disturb you any longer."

Orelia had to hide a triumphant grin. Perhaps they would find this man at the inn. If he was drunk, he might even talk about what he'd done. Already, she could see how they might garner information. She could pretend to be lost and charm him perhaps. Find out where he lived now. Or Reed could—

"She's gone," he declared. "I think I shall have a look around."

Orelia frowned. "Is there any need? We know where we can find him."

"I think so."

She narrowed her gaze at him. "I think you just like to sneak."

He chuckled. "Perhaps."

Reed glanced over the building and made his way down the basement steps. Orelia followed. Pressing his fingers against the edge of the cracked window frame, he eased it open. She winced when a crack sounded.

"Be careful," she hissed.

"Always," he said with a far too handsome grin.

He opened the small window and lifted himself up to ease in. Orelia glanced around, her heart racing hard against her ribs.

A dark-haired man slipped from between the houses and paused when he saw her. Her heart beat harder. As he approached, she tried to smile but it felt shaky. There was something sinister in his appearance. Perhaps it was the black top hat or the long length of his wiry body, dressed far too beautifully for this area. They both looked at each other, somehow aware neither of them should be there.

He took several steps toward her, forcing her to back up against the building. She could only issue a small squeak sound as she found herself looking up into dark glittering eyes.

"You need to go from here and never come back," he said in accented English.

She might be uneducated, but she had travelled enough to know he was French. The enemy still, by all accounts. Her throat grew as arid as a drought-ridden field.

"Stop looking for Thomas Moore," he hissed. He latched a hand around her throat and she squeaked again. "Do you understand?"

She nodded frantically.

The hand tore from her throat unexpectedly. Reed barreled into the man and they toppled to the floor. They tussled for several moments, both men swinging before the Frenchman scrabbled to his feet and scarpered. His once pristine clothing was covered with dust and dirt.

Reed rose, dusted himself off and hastened over to her. "Are you well?"

"Yes, fine," she said breathlessly.

"What did he want with you?"

"He warned me away. Said not to follow Thomas."

Reed frowned and lifted her chin to eye her neck. "No marks," he murmured.

"I do not think he intended to hurt me. At least, not this time."

He cursed under his breath. "I should not have left you alone."

"You could not have known that would happen." She clasped her hands together when she realized they were shaking.

Reed glanced down and took them in his hands. The warmth of his touch soothed away a little of the horror she had hardly realized she felt.

"Why would he wish us to stop searching?" he mused. "We must be close."

"He was French, I'm sure of it."

He nodded. "We must be close then. Perhaps someone on the French side wished old Boney dead. What better way to do it than pay a feckless English drunk to do it for you?"

"You think they hoped the English would get the blame?"

"Perhaps they even hoped to trigger another war. There would be those who don't want peace between our countries."

She drew in a shaky breath. "Goodness, Reed, do you not think you should ask for more help?"

A dark brow lifted. "Do you doubt my ability to handle this?"

"Never, but this seems to be becoming more involved by the day."

"I will keep you safe, Orelia, I promise. I won't leave you alone again."

She smiled at this. He would, of course, one day, but she knew what he meant and was touched by his protectiveness.

"So what do we do now?" she asked.

"The old woman said Thomas was injured in the war. We can find out about his service history from the army." He glanced around the street, checking for any more frightening Frenchmen, she assumed. "We had better return home. I shall send a missive to London right away, requesting information. With any luck, we shall have our man within the next few days."

"And what shall we do until then?"

"Why" —he grinned— "enjoy some quality time with my mother of course."

Orelia stared at him. She couldn't tell if he was jesting or not. He chuckled, and she tapped his arm. "You are a tease, Your Grace."

"I'm merely getting revenge for all the times you have teased me."

"I have never teased you," she declared.

"Oh you have, Orelia. Teased and taunted me."

He said the last part so seriously that it was all she could think on as they made their way home. What did he mean by that?

Chapter Nineteen

Orelia eyed the austere building and gnawed on her bottom lip. Reed paused by the entranceway of the hospital, glancing back at her.

"What's wrong?"

She gave herself a mental shake and stepped forward. "I have never set foot in a hospital." She shrugged. "My people do not trust outsiders to look after our health."

"With any luck, we shall not have to stay long." Reed tugged out a letter from his jacket and glanced it over. "According to the army records, Thomas was discharged several months ago but if he was still having problems with his health, this is where he would come."

The stench of sickness pervaded the air of the voluntary hospital. Orelia wrinkled her nose and tried to breathe through her mouth. Romani women would be scandalized if they visited such places—so she had little idea what they were like. From the looks of the people lining up and down the corridor, they were no better than expected.

Reed marched past the patients, somehow able to ignore the young children dressed in threadbare clothes and looking far too close to the grave or the men so frail, they hardly looked like men at all. All were in the most desperate state.

And they had to be to come here. The voluntary hospitals were their only option for care but even the Romani knew they could be just as likely to gain a new illness in visiting here. Many who entered, never came out.

"Do you think anyone will tell us anything?" Orelia murmured to Reed.

He gave her a winning smile and approached one of the nurses. Orelia resisted the desire to roll her eyes. Dressed elegantly, she had no doubt Reed was prepared to charm whoever he needed to find out what they needed to know.

She made the mistake of breathing in through her nose and nearly had a coughing fit. When she compared her life to that of these people, it almost seemed blessed. Certainly they had struggled through tough times and were often starving. The Romani still suffered the diseases these people did but at least they had their own to care for them. It seemed to her these people had nothing and no one if they were forced to turn for help here.

The nurse visibly colored when she spotted Reed. "C-can I help you, sir?"

"I hope so." There was that charming smile again. "I was looking for information on a certain patient."

The nurse gave them both a wary look. "I am not certain—"

"My cousin here very much likes to take on a charitable role." He motioned to Orelia who managed to keep her expression natural. She really wished he'd tell her what he intended to do before he did it, though.

"I see," the nurse said, confusion marring her face.

"And she was helping a man who we believe was a patient here but unfortunately she has lost contact with him," Reed continued. "It is my hope that you might be able to point us in the right direction so my cousin can continue aiding the poor man. And perhaps then I might be able to offer some...help here."

"Ah." The nurse peered around. "Please follow me." She marched across the room and led them to a smaller room filled with leather bound books. "We keep minimal records but if your, um, friend was here, we will have recorded his entry into the hospital and when he left. Do you know when he was admitted?"

"Unfortunately, no. Though it could not be any further back than three months ago," Reed informed the nurse. "His name was Thomas Moore."

She shrugged. "We have so many patients here. It is hard to remember them all. You believe he is still alive?" the woman asked.

Orelia nodded. "We know he is." She clasped her hands together and forced a gentle smile that she somehow felt might suit a rich woman looking to take up her time with charitable work. "That is, I have been told he is."

"Well these books are those who have died in the past three months." The nurses indicated to several books stacked on a desk, the top one open and ready for more entries. "And there are those who have been discharged." A smaller pile was a grim reminder of how few people left the hospital alive.

The nurse glanced over her shoulder. "I must attend to my patients. Please be quick. You should not be looking at these."

Reed nodded and flicked open the book while the nurse hastened off. Orelia leaned over his shoulder to watch but most of the words looked like nothing more than nonsense to her.

"If I skim through from three months ago, hopefully we can find record of him," he told her.

"Will you really donate?" Orelia asked.

He chuckled, running his finger down the ledger and flicking over another page. "Do you think me a liar?"

"Well, no..."

"It's clear this place needs funds." He flicked over another page. Then another. "Ah." He placed a finger on an entry. "Here he is. He left just under a month ago."

"Is there any other information?"

Reed shook his head. "The address that is given is the empty one, but it says he was admitted to bed four. Let's see if we can take a look at it."

They exited the room and found the nurse they had originally approached. "Could you show us bed four?" Reed asked. "It seems he was discharged from it three weeks ago."

"Yes, just over here. Though I am not sure what you think you will find." The nurse led them over to an empty bed. In the bed next to it was an elderly man whose eyes were sunken and his skin hung off his bones as if there was not an ounce of muscle on him. His breaths wheezed so loudly that it made Orelia flinch each time he inhaled.

Reed glanced over the bed. It was clean and made up with no sign of any of the previous occupants. Orelia sighed. How were they ever going to find this man?

"Do you not recall this patient at all?" Orelia pressed the nurse.

The nurse gave an apologetic look. "I'm sorry. We have so many people here and your friend won't have been the only occupant here."

Rubbing a hand across his face, Reed looked at Orelia. "We need to find out where Thomas went after this."

"But how?" Orelia eyed the empty bed. "Do the patients ever leave any belongings behind?"

The nurse shook her head. "If they do, it means they are dead, and we give those belongings to the churches if they're not collected by family straight away." She gave a shrug. "We do not have the room to store them for long."

"Did you say Thomas?" the man in the bed asked.

Orelia glanced at him and moved closer. "Yes, did you know him?"

The man nodded. "I've been here long enough to see many occupy this bed. Thomas was one of the few who wanted to talk."

"He's a friend of mine. I am hoping to help him." Orelia hoped lying to a probably dying man was not considered too much of a sin if it was in aid of catching a would-be murderer.

The man's thin lips stretched. "Thomas is a lucky man to have a friend like you, miss. But I do not know where he went after he left, I'm afraid." A coughing fit wracked the man.

Orelia knelt by the bed and waited for the coughing fit to subside. "What did you and Thomas talk of? Perhaps if I know where he liked to go, I shall be able to find him."

"He liked a good drink, I do know that." The man flashed a toothless grin. "What man doesn't."

"Do you know which pubs he preferred?" Reed pressed.

The man's expression turned sour and he turned his attention back to Orelia. "He never said. Though..." He screwed up his face for a moment and lifted a finger. "I do recall him talking of a club—The Clermont. He liked to gamble—too much I think."

Orelia swung a look at Reed who gave an almost imperceptible nod. This was the thread they needed. If they went to this club, perhaps they could find him there.

"Thank you, sir. You have been an immense help." She gave the old man's hand a little squeeze. "My cousin here shall ensure you are rewarded for your help."

The man gave a wave of his hand. "No point in helping me. I will end my days in this bed before long."

Orelia winced. "Well, I'm sure we can—"

"I don't need no help!" the man barked.

"Come on, you had better leave." The nurse ushered them away from the bed. "Mr. Newell is a little unpredictable."

"I'll be in touch about a donation and I would still like to ensure he is comfortable," Reed told her as they left.

"Do you think we will find Thomas at that club?" Orelia asked when they got outside.

He nodded. "Or if not, I should be able to find someone who knows him and his whereabouts."

"What are we waiting for?" She gave his arm a tug. "Let us go now."

Reed shook his head. "I know that club, Orelia. Believe me when I say you cannot step foot inside it."

Scowling at him, she put her hands to her hips. "I'm not scared."

He chuckled. "I know you're not, but it's a gentleman's club." He glanced her over. "You are most assuredly not a gentleman." He ran his gaze up and down her body that was currently encased in another borrowed gown.

"Oh."

"Yes. Oh. Not to mention it is notorious for being home to a rough crowd. Neither of us will fit in looking like we do now, even if you were not decidedly female. We'll return home and I shall head to the club tomorrow night. I imagine that's when it will be at is busiest."

"Well, just be careful, Reed."

"I'm always careful." He winked before offering her his arm.

His assurances didn't do much to quell the uncertainty in her gut, especially after that man attacking her. The thought of something happening to Reed...well, it did not bear thinking about. He mattered to her more than she liked to think about.

Chapter Twenty

"Orelia, is it not?"

Orelia took a breath and turned to face Reed's mother, who hastened along the path with a lot less grace than usual. She would not point out that the duchess knew full well what her name was but that she had never used it nor addressed her if she deemed it unnecessary. Which was about the entire time she'd been at the abbey.

She offered his mother a smile. She could hardly blame her. What a strange thing it must be to suddenly have a Romani girl in her midst—someone so far removed from her world that it was likely the duchess had never even considered people like her existed.

Part of her wanted to reassure her that she would be gone soon, that his mother's world would be perfect once more, however, she could hardly bring herself to say the words or imagine what it would be like without being near Reed.

"Can I help you, Your Grace?"

The duchess stopped. She gulped down some air and her cheeks were red. "I...I have had word that Reed was hurt in town."

"Hurt?" Orelia shuddered to a standstill. "Badly?"

"I do not know."

The distress in his mother's eyes had her softening to her. She motioned to the stone bench nearby. "You had better sit, Your Grace."

She nodded hastily and sat. Orelia perched herself next to her, careful not to get too close to the duchess's beautiful green silk gown. She took a second to remind herself that Reed was the cleverest and wiliest of men. He simply would not let himself be hurt badly. It was likely something small and nothing to fear.

She hoped.

"What has happened?"

"A young man came to the house." His mother pressed her hands to her stomach. "He said that he had news of my son that I would wish to hear if I would pay. I, of course, gave him some coin." She drew out a handkerchief and pressed it to her lips. "He said Reed was in the most dreadful of places. Someone set upon him and he is harmed." The last word came out as a sob.

"Is the man still here?"

She shook her head. "I sent him away."

"Did he say what happened to Reed afterward?"

"No, only that a tall man dragged him out of the club and...and..."

Orelia carefully eased her fingers over the duchess's arm and gave her a light pat. "All will be well."

She forced herself to ignore the horror building inside her. What if Reed was harmed? What if he was lying on a roadside somewhere, close to death? How did the man even know it was Reed? He could be in even more danger if the patrons discovered he was a duke. They could hold him for ransom or...

No. Reed would not let that happen. He was too resourceful.

"What was he doing there?" his mother asked. "Why would he be spending time at such places?" She pressed her handkerchief to her lips again and spoke from behind it. "Why does he love to torture me so? You must know. You know him better than I already, it seems. Why are you here? Why is my son hurt? What are these trips he keeps taking you on?"

Squeezing the duchess's arm, Orelia gave a little shrug. "I cannot say. It is not up to me to. But I can tell you he wishes you no ill."

The duchess stood abruptly. "He wishes me no ill, yet he disappears constantly. He spends time away from me for years on end then when I am looking forward to having him home and settled, he vanishes again."

Orelia stood too. "I shall go and find him," she said. "He will be fine, I just know it."

"Do you?"

"Yes." Orelia nodded determinedly. "I shall go to the club and speak with the people there."

The duchess shook her head. "If you go there and are hurt, Reed shall not be happy."

"If he is hurt, he will have no chance not to be happy."

The woman peered at her as though seeing her as something other than a gypsy for the first time. "You have a lot of courage," she said quietly.

"Not all the time. But I think Reed has encouraged it in me."

"Take a few of the men with you. Colin, the stable hand, is a big man. And a few of the gardeners could help. They will keep you safe."

Orelia could not help but smile. In her life there were few people who had been concerned for her safety. But first Reed and now the dowager duchess. It was an odd feeling and she liked it. Maybe a little too much.

"Very well, I shall change, though. I would not wish to wear this into a place like that."

His mother cast her gaze over what had once been her gown. "Reed really should get you some new dresses. It is most unbecoming for you to wear his mother's old gowns. I shall send for a seamstress once Reed is safely home."

"That is really not..."

"If you are going to remain under my roof for however long, then I think it best you look the part," she said sternly.

Allowing herself a smile, Orelia nodded. At least his mother was back to her usual commanding self. Hopefully Orelia would find Reed, bring him home and all would be well. She could not consider the idea that he wouldn't. What would her life be like without him?

"I will set off presently," Orelia determined.

"I shall ask Colin to round up the men and ready a carriage. You must take the quickest one."

As Orelia turned to make her way back up the garden path, she paused and narrowed her gaze at a figure strolling around the side of the house. Her heart gave a rapid jolt and her bones seemed to melt.

"It's Reed!" she declared.

His mother gave an odd shriek, a sound unlike anything she'd heard before.

They both hastened toward him. Orelia couldn't prevent a startled "oh no," when she saw his face. "What happened?" she asked, resisting the desire to take his battered face in her hands.

He grinned at her, his swollen lip stretching and making her wince. There were several grazes on his face and he appeared to have a slight limp. A generous bruise marred his forehead.

"I had a little scuffle, nothing to worry about," he assured her.

"What were you thinking, Reed?" his mother demanded. "You must stop all of this. No more vanishing to unsavory places. You are a duke. You should be behaving like one."

"I am well, thank you for your concern, Mother," he said with a wry grin.

Orelia took Reed's arm. "Your mother was worried about you. We had already received word that you were harmed, and we feared the worst."

"Someone recognized me. Let us just say some did not take well to nobility in their midst."

"And that is precisely why you should remain where you belong." His mother gave an exasperated huff. "People should stay where they belong," she directed a pointed look at Orelia.

So much for being admired for her courage. It seemed she was back to being the enemy. She had seen the concern for Reed though. As much as the duchess pressured Reed, his mother loved him dearly and she could not begrudge her that.

He opened his mouth to respond so Orelia tugged him away in the hopes of preventing an argument. "We had better get you cleaned up."

"And looking more duke-like," his mother declared.

"Honestly, can a man not get a bit of peace in his own home?" he muttered as Orelia urged him back into the house.

"Not when you worry us like that," Orelia scolded. "I knew I should have gone with you."

"I am grateful you did not. What if you had become involved?"

"I could have done something, I'm sure."

Reed chuckled. "Perhaps you could have." He winced when they followed the steps into the house. "Twisted my ankle or some such," he explained. "Nothing terrible."

"Is it true? Did they set on you because they knew who you were or was that simply for your mother's sake?"

"They knew who I was, but how, I do not know. Someone revealed me."

She frowned. "For what purpose?"

"To prevent me from finding out more I suspect."

"Did you find anything out?" she pressed.

He grinned then winced. "Yes. Before I was so rudely ejected, I found out Thomas's whereabouts. He still lives in Portsmouth."

"That's wonderful. We can go there as soon as you are healed, but first let's see if Mrs. Corley has something cool to put on your head."

He nodded, and they made their way downstairs, past the servant's hall and into the kitchen. "Your Grace!" one of the kitchen maids exclaimed.

"Not to worry, May, all is well. Please do not let me get in the way."

Orelia tugged out a chair while the girls watched them with fascination. Mrs. Corley scowled and then and flapped a cloth at the serving girls. "Leave His Grace be for a moment. He is not here to be gawped at." She folded her arms and eyed them both. "What have you been up to, Your Grace?"

"A little adventure, Mrs. Corley. Nothing more. But if you would be so kind as to find a nice cold steak or something to ease this bump" —he motioned to the bruise on his head that was indeed showing signs of swelling— "I would be most grateful."

"Of course, Your Grace. Let me see what I can find." She nodded to Orelia. "You will help him clean up, miss. There are clean cloths under the sink."

"Yes, thank you."

Mrs. Corley went to the larder in search of something cold so Orelia busied herself wetting some strips and cleaning off the various cuts and scrapes.

"What actually happened?"

"I entered the club without any problems but unfortunately it was not long before I was approached. Things grew violent quickly and when it became clear I had no riches on me, they saw fit to throw me out. Hence this," he motioned to his head. "And I was tossed about a little. I got a few punches in but there was three of them."

She shook her head to herself. "You were lucky not to be killed."

He shrugged. "I've—"

"Experienced worse I know. That does not mean you are invincible, Reed."

"Am I not?" He gave her a lopsided grin. "I had rather hoped you might think I am. It does a man's pride good to think a woman thinks him so invulnerable."

She lifted his chin and dabbed his mouth. "What if you had been killed?" she muttered, more to herself than anything.

"Would you have missed me?"

Her gaze shot to his. "What a silly question, of course I would. I-I hate to think of anything happening to you."

"And I you," he said, his smile turning soft. He lifted a finger to her face and traced the line of her cheek. "Were you really worried for me?"

"Certainly. We both were."

"Was my mother terrible to you whilst I was gone?"

She chuckled. "Not totally terrible. She even called me courageous."

"Goodness that is a compliment. Whatever did you do" —he hissed when she dabbed a particularly angry-looking scrape on his jawline— "to deserve such praise?"

"Well, I was planning on going into town and finding you."

Reed shook his head. "Whatever will I do with you?"

"Kiss me?"

The words tumbled from her mouth, unbidden and un-controllable. It didn't matter that she had just been nursing his lip and worrying about hurting him further. Now he was safe-ly home, she wanted nothing more than a kiss from him.

HER WORDS ECHOED AROUND the empty kitchen, bouncing off the shining black tiles and the hard stone floor before finally landing in his brain and rolling around in there for a while. Reed stared at Orelia. There was nothing he want-ed more than to kiss her. In truth, it had been all he'd thought about since that night at the ball. That and a few other things...

Somewhere, something nudged the words in his brain, trying to dislodge them or tell him something. Some reason why he should not kiss her perhaps, but he could not fathom that reason. Maybe it was because his ankle was screaming in pain or because his head pounded, and his lip burned.

Either way, it could not prevent him from drawing her be-tween his legs, her on her knees, and he dropping his mouth to hers. Her intake of breath made every moment of pain worth it. The sweet taste of her near numbed his discomfort. Who needed cold steaks and salve when he could have Orelia?

She gripped his tattered shirt sleeves and he tilted his head to taste her deeper. Her kisses were growing bolder of late but then was she not growing bolder in general? Trying to re-assure his mother? Threatening to come and rescue him? It seemed to him he had but only a sample of the real Orelia and every moment he spent with her, the more he learned. And the more he liked her.

The truth of it was, he had missed her. He'd been gone one night, and he'd missed her.

What the devil was wrong with him?

His mind shut down when her tongue touched his. Nothing was wrong with him. Nothing was wrong with her. This was perfect.

"Your G—"

They bolted apart. He masked a groan. Orelia grabbed a cloth and began furiously dabbing at the graze on his jaw making him hiss. He lifted his gaze to the serving girl and forced a polite smile.

"Yes?"

"Forgive me, Your Grace." The girl's gaze skipped everywhere but on him. Soon enough all the servants would know he had been kissing a gypsy girl. Still, they had probably had a fair amount of gossip about her as it was, considering she was wearing his mother's old clothes and staying in a guest bedroom.

"There is an express messenger here for you, Your Grace. From London."

"I see. Thank you. I shall be up presently."

The serving girl scurried away, and Reed eased himself up from the chair. Orelia remained on the floor, staring at the cloth in her hand.

"Well, are you to stay there all day?"

She grimaced. "Maybe. I would quite like to hide at present."

"Won't do you much good there," he said with a smile. "The servants will be returning to prepare for dinner before long."

"Then perhaps I should hide in my bedroom."

He offered her a hand and she took it, standing to face him. Her cheeks were flushed with the most adorable pink color.

"You realize my servants are discrete and shall tell no one."

"Who could they tell that I should care about? But I am not sure I like the idea of them discussing me."

"The moment you stepped foot in the house, you were discussed, Orelia. I'm sorry I cannot protect you from that but be assured, Mrs. Corley will keep them in line."

She gave a reluctant smile. "Yes, I'm sure she will."

"I had better find out what this message is. Come, help me hobble upstairs."

"I hope you heal quickly. We have more work to do."

"Oh I'm grateful you are so concerned for me," he said dryly.

"Of course I'm concerned for you." She gave his arm a light tap as they slowly took the stairs up to the main hallway. "But I do hope we can finish our investigations soon."

Reed tried not to feel like she had just stabbed him in the heart. It was not at all like him to feel melancholy, particularly about a woman. He had been fond of many women in his life, but none had been able to make him quite feel like his heart had been twisted and tugged inside his body.

Until Orelia.

"Well, in spite of what occurred, you shall be pleased to know I did actually make progress."

"Oh, that is good news." She took his arm to help stabilize him on his painful ankle and they strolled through to the entrance hall.

"I shall tell all shortly."

The messenger awaited him in the hallway, looking red and harried. He took the letter and tore it open. He'd recognized the seal immediately—one that not many would. "Damn," he murmured as he read the scrawled writing. "Wait a moment," he told the messenger. "I'll have a reply for you."

The young man nodded, and Reed moved through to the library, Orelia following close behind.

"What is it, Reed?"

He pulled out a sheet of paper and tugged the lid off the ink pot. "It was from the offices in London. There's been another attempt on Napoleon."

"Goodness."

He scrawled a quick note, assuring his superiors he was close to the culprit. However, by the looks of it, there was more than one man involved.

"What happened?" Orelia pressed.

"A ship hand snuck off and tried to shoot him. Luckily, the ship hand was shot first."

"Is the ship hand alive?"

"It does not say. I shall request more information, but chances are they do not even know yet." He folded up the paper and sealed it with a plain seal. He glanced at Orelia.

"Whatever happens, we need to find our man, and quick. If we don't, we shall be back at war once more."

Chapter Twenty-One

Reed paused and scowled. "Perhaps you should have stayed at the inn."

Orelia shook her head. "I'm not leaving you."

The area in which their culprit lived surprised even her. She could hardly claim to have been raised in the most luxurious of manners but the dank smell of the winding alleys with their house roofs nearly touching and the tiny lengths of the buildings, all lined up next to one another made her wonder why more people did not take to travelling. At least they could be afforded clean air and it seemed that even her mother's wagon had more space than these one room buildings. Several doors sat ajar, affording her a peek inside the tiny rooms with children crammed into every corner.

Or perhaps it was her experience of living with Reed that had caused her shock. She heartily hoped that was not the case. As much as she appreciated being given the opportunity, she could not let her heritage vanish.

She sighed inwardly. Even if it meant leaving Reed's life and never looking back.

"You were lucky to find any information out at the club before they attacked you."

"It was not luck," he said smugly.

She eyed the bruise on his head. "If you claim to have found out where Thomas lives by pure skill, I shall call you a liar."

"Very well, I overheard the right conversation at the right time." He chuckled. "It does not hurt to allow a man a little pride, Orelia." Reed stopped to glance at the grimy sign attached to one house, announcing they were in the right place. "I will be wasting no time," he warned her. "You may not like what you see."

She raised her chin. "I am not scared."

He smiled and gave her a swift peck that took her by surprise. Oh, how she wanted more of them.

How she wanted more of Reed.

If they were coming to the end of their quest, she could not help but think, what harm would it be if they had one moment together? Just one to get her through the rest of her days while she found herself a new identity with her money.

Would he even consider it? Or did he think her just some mild distraction. Someone worth kissing but nothing more.

"Come then, this is it."

He signaled to a building ahead. No different to the others, the tiny windows were covered in smoke and grime, making it impossible to see through them. The dark stone of the cottage added to the oppressive feel of the area. She shuddered. Give her fields and fresh air any day.

"You shall knock," he ordered. "Then I shall step in. Make sure you stay clear away until he is secured. I have no wish to harm you."

She nodded and swallowed hard. They approached the building and Reed stepped out of the view of the door. She knocked three times and clamped her hands at her side in an attempt to keep it from shaking. She waited until footsteps echoed through the building. The hinge squeaked, and the door knob rattled.

She glanced at Reed briefly before fixing a smile upon her face as the man inched the door open. Younger than expected, a gaunt face peered at her through the gap.

"Good morning," she said brightly. "Could I trouble you for some help?"

Puzzled eyes skimmed over her and he opened the door a little wider.

She moved swiftly aside, and Reed jumped into the gap, forcing the door fully open. He pushed the young man back into the room and Orelia followed, shutting the door behind them.

Darkness surrounded them. The lone candle on a wall mount flickered and stabilized. But Reed did not remain still. Thomas fought him, trying to pry off the grip Reed had on him but to no avail. He appeared to have a limp, Orelia noted and was so scrawny, there was no chance of him beating someone of Reed's stature.

Reed forced him back into the bed that sat upon a raised platform to one side of the room.

"What is this about?" Thomas asked, his hands raised in defense. "I have no money. I can't give you anything."

"I do not want money," Reed assured him, keeping his stance menacing.

If she were Thomas, she would not have even chanced a move, but the man leapt up suddenly and Reed gave him a light blow to the stomach. He sagged back down to the mattress.

"What do you want from me?" Thomas' voice trembled.

Reed dragged over a rickety chair and set it in front of the bed. He casually moved around and sat as though they were simply having tea at this man's house instead of interrogating him.

Reed eyed him. "I want information."

Thomas rubbed his stomach. "You could have just asked," he grumbled.

"I could have. But would you really have told me why you're trying to kill Napoleon?"

The man blinked rapidly. "W-what do you mean?"

Reed leaned forward. "I have enough evidence to prove that you were behind an attempted poisoning of the emperor."

He shook his head. "No...no..."

"Yes. You poisoned his wine and placed it on The Norfolk."

Something flickered in his eyes. Thomas lifted his chin. "Well, then you had better have me strung up." He glanced around the room. "It has to be better than this life."

Orelia felt a pang of pity. He was clearly injured, likely unable to work, and in utter poverty with no one to look after him. But why would he become involved in some plot to poison Napoleon? What would it achieve?

"There are others involved, are there not?" Reed pressed.

Thomas glanced away. "I wouldn't know anything about that."

Reed shifted slightly on his chair and the man raised his hands. "I don't, I swear. I know nothing. I didn't even know anything about old Boney."

Reed glanced at her. This might be the man that put the poison in but as Reed had told her earlier in the day, there was likely many more men involved than they'd first thought.

"So what do you know?"

Thomas huffed out a breath and positioned his injured leg in front of him. "I'm not proud of what I did. If I'm honest, I did not think much of the consequences and who might be getting hurt." He smacked his weak leg. "I was injured in the war. Left me useless. Now there's no work for me or any of the thousands of soldiers returning, and no one will take on someone like me."

There it was again. That shard of sympathy burrowing into her heart. She had seen the soldiers returning, travelling the country to find work and discovering nothing but poverty. Unlike her, they had no community to support them. She was surprised Reed did not seem to have any sympathy for he too had become lost after the war. So many men had been set adrift by it. Her heart hurt for them equally.

"Tell me who hired you," Reed demanded.

The soldier shrugged.

"Tell me," Reed hissed, "or you shall regret it."

Thomas gave a weak chuckle. "There is little you can do to me that will frighten me. I have seen war. What can be worse than that?"

Reed drew back a fist but paused and lowered it. "There will be more war if you do not tell me who you are working for."

The soldier shrugged again.

Orelia stepped forward and put a hand to Reed's arm. "Why do you not leave us alone for a moment?" she said quietly.

Reed scowled. "I can't leave you alone with a stranger," he murmured.

"I hardly think he's in much of a condition to do anything and I believe I can get him to talk."

He glanced back at the soldier and nodded. "Very well."

Reed stepped out of the house and shut the door. Orelia smiled at the man who had watched their exchange with a perplexed expression.

"The reason we need to know who was giving you orders is that if Napoleon dies, we go back to war." She sat in front of him and spoke softly as though to a frightened horse. "I know it can be hard to feel any sympathy, especially when it seems like the world has turned its back on you. I understand that, I promise."

"You've never seen war. You've never come back to find there's nothing left for you."

"But I understand what it's like to be on the outside. I'm Romani you see. Well, half-Romani. Caught in between you might say. Not quite pure blooded enough for either side to want me."

He peered at her. "You don't look it."

"My father was English. My skin isn't as dark as my mother's."

"I don't see why I should care what happens to Boney. He's the one responsible for this damn thing." He smacked his leg.

"You should care because if we go back to war, more men will be injured and killed. There will be thousands more men in your position."

He made a huff sound.

"My people were accused of having a role in it simply because they were on the ship. There was no proof but of course because they are Romani, it was assumed they must have done it." She leaned forward. "I wanted to prove them innocent."

"Well, you can give the crown my neck. That'll let them off the hook."

"I would very much rather give them the neck of whoever is plotting against Napoleon. And I would hope we could save you from the noose. My companion is not without compassion, I promise."

"What does it matter? I have nothing."

"So why did you do it?" she asked.

"I was promised coin."

She tilted her head. "And yet you are here?"

"Because I failed. He gave me enough to pay for this roof over my head after I was kicked out of the last place, so I can't complain."

"Who promised you coin?"

The man paused and sighed. "Look, I can't tell you much. A man took me aside at the Red Lion and said he had a job for me. Said he wanted to help soldiers. He gave me some money then and there, so I agreed to meet him."

"What did this man look like? Did he give you a name?"

He shook his head. "He was tall, wiry but not starved like I am. Dark hair."

Could it be the man who attacked her?

"Did he have a French accent?"

Thomas scowled. "No, he was British. From Yorkshire I reckon. Strong northern accent."

"Oh."

"I think he was working for someone else. He never could quite give me all the answers."

Orelia nodded. "So he was hiring you on behalf of someone?"

"Yep."

"Can I ask my friend to come back in?"

Thomas swung his gaze to the door. "He won't hit me again will he?"

She chuckled. "No, I'll make sure of it."

Thomas gave a reluctant smile. "I suppose it's hard to say no to a pretty lady."

Orelia let Reed in and gave him a quick warning to behave. "Thomas, can you tell him what you told me?"

"I don't know anything. I just met with this man who gave me money. I really can't tell you anything."

"How did you get in touch with him?" Reed asked.

"I'd leave him a note at the inn. Last time, he gave me a coin and said that was it, that it failed so I wasn't to speak to him again."

"But with Boney still alive, he might need you once more," said Reed.

"If you contact him and arrange a meeting, we could intercept," Orelia agreed.

Thomas shook his head. "I don't know if he will even meet me. I don't see why he would."

Reed glanced at Orelia and grinned. "It's worth a try though."

Chapter Twenty-Two

"Do you really think we shall get our man?"

Reed glanced at Orelia before turning his attention back to the road. The day was turning dusky, but he had been determined that they return to Keswick before nightfall so they could prepare. They were only a mile or so from his house now and she was growing weary with the gentle rock of the carriage and the melodic clop of the horses. It had been a long and rather exciting day.

Reed nodded. "I think it highly likely. If whoever it is that wants Napoleon dead has not succeeded yet, they might be willing to give Thomas another chance. Regardless, what I asked Thomas to write will gain their attention."

"Or put Thomas in danger..." she murmured.

"You liked him."

Orelia shook her head. "Not liked. Pitied."

"He was almost a murderer do not forget."

"I think it can be very easy to follow orders when you have spent most of your life doing so. No doubt he's a murderer many times over but because it was in the name of the king, it was acceptable."

He took her hand and tugged it into his lap, grasping it tight and rubbing his thumb over the back of it. She blinked at him.

"You are an incredibly astute woman, Orelia."

She frowned.

"You are clever," he explained. "You understand people. You see things that others do not." He chuckled. "And I will admit, I pitied Thomas too. I will do my best to ensure he is not harmed and when this all comes out, I will find a way to protect him from any comeuppance."

"I'm glad. I know what he did was wrong, but I can understand why he did it and he hardly seemed to have any understanding of what his part in this whole affair entailed."

"It is often the lowly footmen that bear the brunt in these political messes. Thomas is just another victim." He squeezed her hand.

Amber and pink streaks began to paint the sky. She eyed the rolling hills against the colorful backdrop and compared them to the conditions in which Thomas had been living. Whatever she did when this was all over, she could not let herself be caged in like that. If she settled somewhere, it would be like the Hampshire countryside—wild and untamed. A space where she could be free.

"You did an outstanding job of getting him to talk." He peered at her. "What exactly did you say to him?"

"I just told him that we were alike. That we were both outcasts in society. I think Thomas was hurt by that more than anything. He had gone away to fight for his country but came back to nothing and no one and no sympathy for his plight."

"Do you really think of yourself as an outcast still?"

"I'm not sure. I think I have not found my place in the world yet."

Reed nodded. "I understand that."

"You have the ability to blend in wherever you go, Reed. Even if you take your place as the duke, you shall fit in perfectly."

"Will I?" he murmured.

"I know you will." She squeezed his hand tight.

The abbey struck a perfect contrast to the soft countryside, its dark silhouette a perfect box shape against the curves of the hills. Several windows glowed from within and an oddly soft sensation struck her.

Reed drove the horse and trap around to the stable and aided her down before handing it over to the groomsmen.

Noah stepped out of the servant's entrance and leaned against the wall. "Where have you been? Mother has been fussing all day."

Reed waited until he had stepped into the beckoning light of the hallway before addressing him. "Forgive us, Noah. We had business to attend to."

"You had business to attend to here."

"And yet I imagine you handled it all perfectly."

Noah gave a shrug. "I did but that didn't stop Mother from fussing." He scowled at Reed. "Why must you always be so damned secretive?"

"A man must be allowed to have secrets," Reed declared, tugging off his coat and gloves.

"One's that involve him sneaking away with a beautiful woman and traipsing through the servant's quarters?"

Orelia felt her cheeks color, not so much as to what he was implying but because of being called beautiful.

"You shall have your brother all to yourself soon, Noah," she promised, ensuring she spoke slowly enough so that he could read her lips.

"Well that will be a pity. Does that mean you shan't be staying much longer?"

She and Reed shared a glance. "I think so."

"We'll miss you," Noah said sincerely. "It's been pleasant having a female in the house who does not wish to trap us both here forever. Not to mention you've done an excellent job of keeping any prospective wives at bay."

Her heart gave a tiny jab. Once she was gone there was nothing stopping Reed from finding a wife. No scandalous women waiting in the wings to scare away fine, young ladies.

"I am sure once you have some lovely ladies coming to visit, neither of you shall regret my absence."

"That could not be further from the truth," Reed said firmly. "Is Mother still up?"

Noah shook his head. "No, she retreated to bed about an hour ago, though she is likely still awake so go quietly."

"Thanks." Reed grinned.

"Will you be around tomorrow, or do you have yet more important things to do?" Reed's brother asked.

"I shall be here. I must take a trip into town in a few days, but I can look things over if you wish me to."

"I have everything in hand, but you ought to. Mother doesn't quite trust that I know what I am doing." Noah grimaced.

"Well I do, and I appreciate everything you do in my stead." He clapped a hand on his brother's shoulder.

Noah gave him a look. "Do not think I don't know what you are doing. You like to pretend you are selfish and idle, but I understand your motivations behind making me take on all the ducal duties."

Reed pressed his lips together. "I have no idea what you mean. I merely don't have time for these silly trivialities whilst I am socializing and...what is it mother says?—-gallivanting around the country."

Orelia watched the exchange between brothers, somewhat envious of their teasing closeness. Why, she could even find herself envious of his mother. At least she cared dearly for them both. What would it be like to be part of such a family? From the little insight she'd had, she could conclude it would be quite lovely.

Chapter Twenty-Three

Reed led Orelia quietly to her room. Thankfully his mother was either asleep or had not heard them creeping up the stairs. He opened her door and she peered up at him, her skin warm in the lamp light. She could have no idea how much he wanted to touch her. How much he'd been longing to all day.

They were onto their man. Things were unfolding quickly. Before long he'd have their culprit and Orelia would have her money. She would fly off and be free, just as she should be.

And he'd be left here. Either playing duke or praying for another job from the government.

And he'd always remember how she tasted.

He eased open her door and she stepped through it, silent.

Searching her gaze, he tried to understand what she might be thinking. Did she wonder about the future? Consider what it will be like to be apart? Did she regret that they had not had more time together? Because he certainly did.

"Good night, Reed," she said softly. She reached out to touch him but drew her hand back suddenly.

The air wrapped around him like a thick blanket. He struggled to breathe. The flickering glow of flames danced over her skin and made her eyes gleam. She wore only her cheapest gown and yet he could easily say she was as beautiful as when she had dressed up as Spanish nobility.

He wanted her so urgently, his body hurt. From his toes to his heart, he ached. He'd spent their entire acquaintance ignoring it—and sometimes not—until he could no longer.

Or could he? Should he risk their mission, their friendship for a brief moment only to pay her off and send her on her way?

He took a step back. He was stronger than this. He'd never met a woman with whom he could not control himself.

"Good night, Orelia," he said, his voice coming out as though he'd just swallowed rocks.

She went to close the door, slowly, slowly, her gaze never leaving his.

"Damn it," he hissed, shoving open the door and taking a step across the threshold.

She jumped back with a tiny cry of surprise. He kicked shut the door, his mother be damned. This was his house and he'd stomp around if he damn well liked.

Another swift step and he had her in his arms. One moment later, his mouth was upon hers. She softened instantly to him, her body molding as though made to fit against his.

"I can't resist anymore," he growled against her mouth.

"Then do not," she replied softly.

It was all he needed to hear. Their futures, this mission be damned. If he only had a small amount of time with her, he was going to use it to appreciate her fully.

"I have never met a woman like you." He kissed her neck before dragging his mouth back to her lips.

Her hands were everywhere, in his hair, touching his face, tugging his shirt, pressing up underneath to feel his back. He shuddered at the touch of her fingers upon his skin.

"I've never met a man like you," she replied, tilting her head back so he could kiss her neck again then down to her collar bone. "I never thought dukes could be like you."

"I hope that's a good thing."

"Very much so."

He bundled her to him and edged her over to the bed. Reed managed to slow down enough to lower her carefully and admire the way her hair had spilled loose from its braid and spread across the luxurious silk bedding. She might be in a simple, brown wool gown but she seemed to fit perfectly.

When he joined her on the bed, his impatience gathered pace again. He cupped a breast through the fabric of her gown and she pushed her fingers up under his shirt, tracing a path across his stomach.

She smiled up at him. "You're very beautiful."

He could have sworn he nearly blushed. He'd been called many things. Handsome, dashing, rakish. Never beautiful.

"Nowhere near as beautiful as you."

Orelia definitely did blush and he adored how regularly she did. As good at deception as she was, she could never deceive him.

"You blush a lot," he murmured.

"Only around you."

He grinned and came down to kiss her hard. Her body rose like a ship on the ocean to meet his, her breasts pressing up into his chest and her hips thrusting against his arousal.

He released a groan when she did it again. "I have been in agony for too long. You have no idea how hard it has been."

She slid a hand between their bodies. "I do now."

"Cheeky wench."

He pushed her hair from her face and vowed to kiss her into silence. He did, leaving her writhing underneath him. When he shifted to one side and hitched up her skirts, he found her wet with desire. He skimmed a finger over her sensitive nub and watched her eyelids flutter and her pupils darken.

"Orelia, have you ever...?" He paused before pressing a finger into her. He needed to know how experienced she was.

She nodded slowly. "Once."

He released a breath. As much as he would have liked to have been her first, he had no great ambitions to initiate a virgin. If she had only made love once, it would not be easy, but he could prepare her well enough and ensure she completely forgot whoever it was before.

"Are you jealous?" she asked.

"I could be. But it would hardly be fair now, would it? I am no virgin."

She smiled softly. "It was a long time ago and I hardly remember. One of my more rebellious moments. If I had been discovered I could have ruined myself in the eyes of my people. I regret that."

"And yet you are here with me?" He toyed with her folds, making her suck in a sharp breath. He couldn't help grin at her responsiveness. "You are willing to take that risk with me?"

"You are most likely my husband in their eyes by now. Besides, I will not remain with them any longer. I have no place there, I realize that now."

"You have a place here," he said, his voice raw. "In my arms." He held her close. "Christ, why do you feel so good in my arms?"

She gave a soft smile before he kissed her firm on the lips and eased a finger into her. She was damned tight. The thought of being inside her made his head swim. She gasped against his mouth and he pushed deeper. Lifting her hips, she invited him further and he added another finger.

Using a thumb to tease her, he worked in and out until she was squirming and pleading for more. Reed released her and urged her to sit up. His hands shook as he worked loose the laces of her gown. He pushed them down her shoulders, taking her shift with it and kissed the bare skin he revealed at her back. Goddamn his shaking hands. He was acting like a whelp taking a woman for the first time.

She leaned into his kisses and pulled up his shirt. Reed paused to tug it over his head before easing her dress and undergarments away.

"Dear God," he murmured, taking in the curve of her breasts and hips. He swept his knuckles over one breast and followed the curve until he brushed past one tight nipple.

Orelia closed her eyes.

Reed shifted off the bed to finish removing his clothes. When he glanced up, he found her eyes open, watching him avidly. A tiny smile curved her lips.

"What is it?"

"You really are beautiful."

He chuckled and shook his head. "Not compared to you."

Once he'd flung his clothes in a pile with little care to where they landed, he joined her back on the bed. Scooping her close, he scattered kisses across her chest and dropped down to take a nipple in his mouth. She arched her back, offering herself to him and he pressed a hand under her back to hold her close.

Again he slipped a hand between them, all the while taking every moment to taste the sweetness of her skin. He brought her close to the edge once more.

When she skimmed a hand down to touch his manhood, his vision blurred. He pulled her hand away and eased her back. Her hair now wild about her, her body naked and ready for him, he had to wonder if he was dreaming.

Reed eased apart her legs.

"Do not make me wait," she pleaded.

He shook his head. "As if I could. I feel like I've been waiting for an eternity for this."

She grasped his arms, urging him forward and she wrapped her legs about his hips. He eased into her gently at first, feeling her accept him inch by inch. Her mouth opened in a silent 'oh'. He gritted his teeth and prayed he wouldn't make a fool of himself instantly. He had to wonder, why the hell he had not taken her to bed sooner?

"Reed," she uttered as he buried himself deep and felt her heat close in around him.

He could not find the words to respond. The world went hazy. Nothing else existed apart from this woman. He focused on her, pressing a shaky kiss to her lips before retreating and pushing deep once more. They both groaned.

Smoothing her hair from her face, he kissed her deeply. Orelia's hands and nails sketched paths across his back, biting in sometimes when he thrust deep. Her cries of pleasure filled his ears. He should have known Orelia would be so damn responsive. Why, oh why, had he not done this sooner?

Hot pleasure burned through his body. Her heat began to tighten around him. He tensed his jaw and pounded into her harder. The bed rocked and creaked, and Orelia cried out his name. Her whole body stiffened and he watched as her expression crumpled. She sagged, and the pulses of her orgasm willed him on to follow her over the edge.

He thrust once, twice, and third time then followed up with several more quick thrusts. He pulled out and, with a groan, spilled on her stomach. Eyes closed, he focused on the pleasure then opened them to find her staring up at him, her lips parted and her expression a picture of pleasure.

Once he gathered his breath, he gave her a swift kiss. "Wait there."

Feeling a little too like a newborn lamb, he staggered over to the washbowl and found a cloth. He dipped it in the water and headed back to the bed.

"It will be cold," he warned.

She sucked in a breath and he cleaned her up before flinging aside the cloth and urging her under the bedding. He took her into his arms. Orelia settled in the crook of his arm, her head tucked into his shoulder. Her fingers played a path across his chest, tracing the dips in it.

"Should you not return to your bed? Your mother shall be scandalized."

Reed shook his head. "My mother is already scandalized. Besides, you forget my ability to sneak."

"Oh yes, so I did."

"But for now, I have no desire to sneak. For now, I want to hold you and taste you, and make love to you several more times."

"Really?"

"Why are you surprised by that?"

She sighed. "I suppose I thought once you'd had me..."

"I would—what?—cast you aside?"

A smile curved her lips. "Not like that. I know you are a gentleman at heart, Reed. But I did not think you would want more of me."

"How could I not?" He urged her to look up at him and kissed her. "How could I not?" he murmured once more.

How could he ever not want her? How could he ever let her go?

Chapter Twenty-Four

Though Reed could not claim to have slept much, he rose early. Having sneaked out of Orelia's room in the early hours and slipped back into his, he'd spent the rest of the morning with a grin on his face as he recalled each moment with her.

Would she still be in bed now? Perhaps recalling their time together too? As much as he needed to focus his attention on this case, he could not help but consider how much he wanted a repeat of last night.

He supposed he'd always known they would be spectacular together or else he would not have fought it so hard.

His mother's voice echoed against the soaring ceilings of the hallway and he scowled, paused to peer over the bannister and shook his head.

Striding down the stairs, he pushed a hand through his hair and demanded, "What the devil is all this noise?"

His mother turned on him, her eyes bright with fury. "First I have a gypsy girl in my house then some...some vagabond who will not leave! This is too much, Reed. It is too much."

He peered around his mother to see the vagabond in question.

The man, near filthy from head to toe, wore a battered cap and a jacket torn in several places.

"Reed?" the man asked.

He blinked at him. "Good lord, Ambrose. I take it you made it out of jail then?"

His mother uttered a faint screech.

"What is going on?" Orelia asked as she came down the stairs.

"Mother is about to faint," Reed said dryly.

The butler, a maid, and Noah had all come to see what the commotion was. Orelia came to his mother's side and took her arm. It surprised Reed that she did not shy away but apparently, she was so overcome by the sight of Ambrose that she willingly accepted Orelia's help.

"Do you know this man, Reed?" Noah asked. "Moseley said mother was screeching."

"I do indeed," Reed confirmed. "And she was indeed. It seems we might need a little time alone. Can you look after mother for a moment? Ambrose and I shall go into the library."

"Into the library?" his mother squawked. "You cannot..."

"Go and have some food, Mother," he said calmly. "You look a little pale."

He mouthed a silent thanks to Orelia as she led his mother off. The woman looked as though she aged ten years, but he knew full well it was all for effect. By tonight, she'd be blistering his ears about letting strange men into the house.

"All well?" Noah asked.

"Yes. Ambrose is an old acquaintance."

"You will have to excuse my appearance," Ambrose said, tugging off his cap and clutching it in one hand. "I've had a bit of an adventure recently."

Noah shrugged, apparently missing what Ambrose said. "Good luck assuaging Mother later."

Reed waved a hand. "I'll deal with her." He addressed Mosley who had adopted the expression of someone who smelled something terrible with firm lips and a wrinkled nose. "Some food in the library please. And tea and coffee." He turned to Ambrose. "Though I suspect you may want something stronger."

Ambrose nodded eagerly.

Reed led Ambrose through to the library and he poured them two fingers of scotch each. Handing it over, he eyed the man who had been his main contact throughout most of his years of working for the Secret Service.

"Someone finally bought your freedom then?"

"Indeed." He grinned. "A very generous man, it seems."

Reed lifted a shoulder and sat in the armchair by the fire. "Took longer than I'd hoped, though."

Ambrose followed suit. "It was not much fun being on the other side of the bars, I shall give you that, but I learned a few useful skills while I was there."

"I am glad your time was not wasted. But honestly, Ambrose, did you not have time to stop for a bath or a change of clothes?"

"Not at all I am afraid. You shall have to apologize to your mother for me."

"She'll get over it." He took a sip of the scotch. It might be early but after waking to such drama, he needed the luxurious warmth of the alcohol. "So what brings you here with such urgency?"

"It seems we have our man."

Reed paused, his glass halfway to his mouth before lowering it to the table at the side of the chair. "We do?"

"They arrested him two days ago. Got a confession."

"Damn."

Ambrose grinned. "I'm assuming you were hoping to be there yourself."

"Who was he?"

"One of the gypsy sailors. The captain of the Norfolk is back in port and fingered him as one of the men he'd taken on board. The gypsy all but handed himself in."

Frowning, Reed shook his head. "But why would a gypsy do it?"

"He wouldn't talk. But they found more of the wine used to try to poison old Boney in his belongings. With that and his confession, it's enough to close the case."

"It makes no sense..."

Ambrose shrugged. "When does killing anyone ever make sense? Come now, Reed, you've seen enough subterfuge to understand sometimes motivations aren't clear."

"Was he working alone?"

His friend nodded. "He claims the man who tried to shoot Boney was a friend, but it was only the two of them."

Rubbing a hand across his chin, Reed stared sightlessly at the row of books in front of him. It made no sense. Orelia had been right from the beginning, he was certain of it. Why would a gypsy try to kill Boney? What could they gain from it?

Or had he just been blind from the beginning? Had he allowed her to talk him away from his suspicions and lose his chance to get his man?

Because why else would someone confess at the risk of death or deportation?

The man had to be guilty.

Reed exhaled slowly. "I appreciate you coming to tell me."

"I'd heard tell you were on the path of some soldier. Didn't want you getting in any deeper elsewhere, so I thought it best I come directly to you. I certainly could not risk putting this information in a note."

"No, of course not."

Reed threw back the fingers of scotch and stared at the empty glass. It was all over then. He'd be back to twiddling his thumbs and praying for another case—which was unlikely at this point with the war over.

And Orelia...

Well, she would go do whatever it was she planned to do once she was a good deal richer. He allowed himself a smile. At least she would be looked after. That was something, was it not?

"What's with the gypsy girl?" Ambrose asked.

"She was helping me."

An eyebrow lifted.

"Not like that," Reed snapped. "She knew her community better than I."

"Ah, useful to have friends on the inside."

"Yes."

"But why is she here, in your house?" Ambrose pressed. "Surely she could have served you better remaining with her people?"

Reed shook his head. "It's too hard to explain."

But was it? Did he really need to have kept her here for so long? After all, he only needed her help briefly. Once they'd had the information of the whereabouts of the gypsies who'd been on board the ship, he could have released her from his service but instead he decided to go through this farcical nonsense of keeping her about.

He had to admit, however, there were a few moments made much easier by her canny ability to act the spy. Another smile curved his lips as he recalled her pretending to be pregnant and in need then becoming the countess for a night. He really could not have picked a better companion.

However, he needed to let her go now. He'd held onto her for too long.

"Will you be returning to London now this is done?" Reed asked.

Ambrose nodded. "No sense in me staying here, particularly when there may be one or two people not happy about my early release before standing in front of the court."

"I imagine there will be a few surprised faces when they discover you are no longer there."

"Besides, I have a hankering for a good wash and a comfortable bed. Both of which I can have at home." He chuckled.

"I'll join you," Reed suggested. "I'd like to hand over what I know and speak to this man, if possible."

"You will discover little, I fear. I'm told he refused to talk as soon as he gave his confession."

Reed scowled. "And yet we are certain he worked alone?"

Ambrose lifted a shoulder. "We've been on this case for too long. The Secret Service is happy to accept his confession."

Reed pinched the bridge of his nose. Something did not feel right about it. "When will you leave?"

"There's a stagecoach bound for London leaving at midday."

"Give me an hour and we can travel in mine."

Ambrose's grin widened. "Excellent. I wouldn't mind travelling in a little more luxury at all."

The butler eased open the door and entered with a tray of bread, sausages and bacon. Reed nodded toward the main table. "Put them there please." He stood and placed down the empty glass. "Ambrose, I shall prepare and then we shall be on our way. You eat up, you look half-starved."

His friend eyed the plate of food and nodded. "That I am. I'll stay here. Would not want to give your mother another fright."

"Good idea."

Reed strode out of the library and followed the corridor to the hallway.

Orelia slipped out of the drawing room and eased the door shut behind her. "I was about to come looking for you. Who is that man?"

"Is mother well?"

She twined her hands together in front of her. "Yes, of course. I am sure she will have a few choice words for you later, but she has calmed down."

"Her words will have to wait. I must travel to London."

"Oh." Her gaze dropped to the floor.

He looked over her features with regret. He supposed by the time he returned, she would be long gone.

Her gaze lifted. "Shall I pack?"

Shaking his head, he began his ascent up the stairs. Orelia followed close behind. "There is no need for you to come," he clarified.

"What is going on, Reed?"

He paused midway up the stairs and faced her. One step lower, she seemed small and fragile. He longed to scoop her into his arms and beg her to stay but how could he trap her here, amongst people who would never accept her?

"It's over," he said, aware his voice sounded hollow.

"Over?"

"They've caught the man responsible for trying to poison Napoleon."

Her throat worked. "That's good news, is it not?"

"Yes, I suppose it is."

She sighed. "I shall confess I was looking forward to trying to catch him ourselves but..."

"I need to go to London to speak with the suspect and debrief my superiors."

"Of course you do."

He took a breath. "Orelia, the man is a gypsy."

"Pardon?"

"The suspect is a Romani," he reiterated.

Her brow furrowed. "Whatever do you mean? We know my people were not involved. We went over that. Surely...?"

"He's confessed. He was found with the wine and the ship's captain has identified him. We've been on a damn wild goose chase."

She shook her head slowly. "No, that cannot be right."

Reed turned and continued up the stairs. She scurried after and tugged at his shirt sleeve, causing him to stop.

"You cannot really believe it was him, can you?"

He lifted a shoulder. "Why should I think any different? What man would confess to a crime that he did not commit and risk the gallows?"

"I-I'm not sure but—"

"It's over, Orelia. It's over."

Her eyes flashed. "No, it's not. We must investigate more, Reed. Whoever this man is, I don't believe he's guilty. He cannot be. Why would a Romani try to kill Napoleon? It's preposterous."

"There are many reasons people kill," he said wearily.

"So we just give up? Accept that the case is over? You are so willing to believe the worst of my people, are you not? You're no different to anyone else!"

"I think that's a little unfair. I brought you into my home—"

Her eyes narrowed. "Oh yes, I forgot. Thank you, Your Grace, for being so benevolent." She gave an exaggerated curtsey.

"Well, there's no need to be sarcastic," he grumbled.

"I suppose I was foolish to believe anyone might imagine my people innocent. I was certainly a fool to think that..." She trailed off and shook her head.

"To think what?" he demanded.

Her eyes shimmered with unshed tears when she lifted her gaze to his. She drew in an audible breath. "I see now that I have overstayed my welcome. For that, I hope you will forgive me."

"Orelia—"

"I will get out of this," she motioned to the gown, "and gather my belongings."

"You can keep the damned gown."

"And do what with it? I would look a fool travelling on foot in such a thing and all the more likely to be robbed."

"Once I've paid you, you can hire your own damned carriage if you wish."

She smiled softly. "Perhaps I shall."

He did not know why but those words felt like farewell. Like the end of it all. He dipped his head. "If you meet me in the study once you are packed, I shall ensure you are paid."

Her smile appeared forced. "Excellent."

Reed searched his mind for something to say, some way to persuade her to stay or not be angry at him or to kiss him or reach for him. But nothing came. He could hardly fathom what had happened or what he hoped would happen. It certainly hadn't been this, however.

Before he could persuade his snail's pace of a brain to work, she turned and headed to her bedroom to pack her meagre belongings. It would take her all of a few minutes, so he headed downstairs to the study. Noah glanced up from the desk.

"I would wager from that expression, your visitor did not bring good news. And I would also wager quite a sum that your dour expression has a lot to do with Orelia," his brother said.

"You would certainly win that wager, Noah," he muttered.

Noah frowned, apparently missing his comment. "Will you tell me what that was all about?"

"I will explain it all soon," Reed promised, "but first I must make arrangements. Orelia will be leaving us today and I am away to London."

"And I suppose I am not to ask why?"

"You can ask, but I cannot give you many answers." He scowled. "In truth, I am at a loss to what happened myself."

Yes, how had he gone from content and happy in Orelia's arms to feeling as though his world had crumbled apart? He straightened his shoulders and pulled open one of the desk drawers. He was a spy. He faced many tricky situations during his time. This would not be the one that would be his downfall. Orelia would not be the end of him.

Chapter Twenty-Five

I t was an odd thing to be suddenly rich. Orelia skimmed her hand along the fence that cut the field off from another. She did not look or feel any different.

Well, perhaps that was a lie. She had awoken feeling vastly changed with a smile on her face, imagining all sorts of foolish scenarios. Reed declaring his love for her perhaps. Him taking her back to bed. Her staying at the abbey forever, putting down roots and finally finding where she belonged.

But even in her imaginings, reality could not fail to slip in. She would never fit in at Keswick, and she would certainly never belong at Reed's side.

Nothing confirmed that more than his determination to believe that a Romani had tried to kill Napoleon. Every argument she'd had with him in the early days of their acquaintance still stood. Why would a Romani do such a thing, alone no less?

She climbed over the sty and jumped down the other side. Maybe he was willing to concede defeat, but she was not. Rich or not, she would not think on her future until she had proven that man was innocent—and she had found the real culprit.

The sight of all the wagons spread across the field made her smile. She hadn't seen them for weeks and had almost forgotten what a Romani camp could look like. The scent of smoke and the tune of a whistle curled through the air toward her.

Certainly, she was grateful to Reed for rescuing her from a forced marriage and so much of her knew she could not remain with her people anymore. She had seen and done too much, and her mixed heritage would forever make her an outcast, but there were many things she felt proud of about being part-Romani. For one, they never abandoned each other. And she would not abandon them now.

She ducked between the wagons and found her mother's. Drawing in a breath, she climbed the few steps and rapped on the door. There was a scuffle and the vehicle rocked before her mother flung open the door. The odor of stale alcohol clouded around her.

"What the devil are you doing here?"

Orelia eyed her mother. Was it her imagination or had she aged in the past weeks? She seemed more tired, with deeper grooves in her face.

"Shouldn't you be off with your rich husband?" the woman spat.

Orelia shook her head. She wasn't sure what she could say. It was far too hard to explain anything, and she could not very well tell her about their mission.

Her mother folded her arms. "You're not coming back here if that's what you think. There's not enough room. Did he get fed up with you?"

Any sympathy she might have had for her mother vanished. "No, Mama. I just needed to ask you a question."

"Well, what is it? I don't have much time. We're to leave in a few days. Apparently there has been some complaints and if we don't move on, the locals are likely to create a fuss."

That didn't surprise her. As fascinating as some of the population found the Romani, eventually they tired of them and wanted them moved on.

"Did you hear of the man who was arrested, Mama?"

"Oh yes, Manfri." Her mother snorted. "He should have stayed away. Now he'll be strung up."

"What did they say he did?"

She shrugged. "I heard he was thieving. Think he stole some goods from the ship a few of them went on."

"What of his family? What did they say?"

Her mother crossed her arms. "Look, girl, I need to be packing up. You never had a taste for gossip before, what is all this?"

"Do you know anything about his family?" Orelia pressed, ignoring the finger thrust in her face.

"Not a thing. They went into hiding not too long after he returned. They won't be travelling with us anymore, that I can tell you."

"So you cannot tell me where they are?"

"No, I cannot, you nosey wretch. Why don't you keep your nose to yourself and go be with your husband? You don't belong here anymore, girl, and I'm mightily glad not to have to put up with your noise anymore."

Orelia drew in a long breath and held it. It still stung a little, but this was not the first time she'd had a tirade thrown at her.

It would be the last though.

"Mama, I do love you. I probably should not but I do. I wish you all the best. I hope you stop drinking one day."

"Why you—"

Orelia ducked the backhand to her face and walked away quickly. Her hands trembled so she clamped them to her side. At least seeing her mother had confirmed one thing—she no longer belonged with the Romani.

She made her way down to the riverside and smiled at the sight of old Marko, looking as though he had never moved from his spot by the chess board.

He glanced up at her, his eyes crinkling. "Little Orelia, whatever are you doing here? Should you not be enjoying married life and creating babies?"

"You're moving on soon," she said, sitting opposite him.

"Indeed. Did you see your Mama?"

She nodded. "We said our farewells."

A grey eyebrow rose but he said nothing.

"I heard Manfri was arrested for stealing."

He blew out a breath. "Aye, and they'll be stringing him up I reckon. Or shipping him off."

"For theft?"

Marko shrugged. "He's a Romani. He could be merely guilty of begging and be strung up."

"What of his wife? And his children? He had five, did he not?"

Marko nodded. "He came back a few days ago, then they all vanished. Then came the news he'd been arrested."

"From whom?"

"Oscar Boswell. He was on the ship with him."

Orelia rubbed a hand across her face. "And why was he not arrested?"

Marko paused in laying out the chess pieces. "Why do you care, Orelia?"

"I believe he was wrongly arrested."

"Oscar said little, only that Manfri was taken in for stealing. They found some wine in his possession—very expensive wine."

"Where is Oscar?" she asked.

"Likely at one of the inns, where else?"

Orelia nodded. "Thank you, Marko."

He eyed her. "What are you planning to do?"

"I'm not sure."

"You are no longer one of us, Orelia. Why should you care for his fate? We are all resigned to it. He did wrong and now he will pay. More harshly than we would hope but we are used to such events."

She stood and paused. "Was I ever one of you?"

"To me you were. To many of us you were."

"To many, I was not, not even my mother," she said.

"I am sorry for the way many treated you. The outside world does not trust us, so we do not trust the outside world. You are between two worlds, but with that new husband of yours, you can make a world of your own."

"I intend to."

But she would do it alone.

After she discovered the truth.

ORELIA SWALLOWED THE lump in her throat and peered up at Keswick. The day had grown grey and a light drizzle had turned the sandstone color of the house to a darker brown. She swiped her damp hair from her face and moved around the back of the house. One of the gardeners spotted her and gave her a wave.

Apparently, she had not been completely forgotten these past four days.

She waved back and made her way down the servant's steps. Pushing the door open, she uttered up a quick prayer, hoping the others had not forgotten her either and would allow her access to the house.

"Orelia!" One of the maids exclaimed. "Whatever are you doing here? Goodness you are wet. Have you come to see His Grace, because he is still not returned from London?"

She could not help feel a little relieved. As much as she needed to inform him what she was doing, she did not need to do it face to face.

"I just wanted to leave him a letter. Do you think I can sneak upstairs?"

Mrs. Corley strode in and folded her arms. "Her Grace is having luncheon. Be quick mind."

"Thank you so much, Mrs. Corley. I shall be as quick as I can."

"Will we be seeing you again anytime soon?" asked the housekeeper.

"I-I couldn't say."

The woman glanced her over. "Well, I hope that we do. You were a good influence on His Grace."

Orelia failed to see how a gypsy girl could be a good influence on a duke but she merely smiled. "I shall only be a trice."

Making her way upstairs, she ignored the slight tingling behind her eyes. The decadence of the abbey had slowly faded upon living there. Instead, elements of it had become familiar. Little bits of cornicing were pleasant to run her hands over or there was that patterned wallpaper in the morning room in which she liked to see what new things she could spy amongst the swirls. Each bold portrait of various stern ancestors had begun to feel like seeing friends.

This, she supposed, was what having a home felt like.

Unfortunately, she could not waste time greeting the portraits or staring at wallpaper. She had a mission to carry out.

She hastened around the corner and emerged upstairs. Stepping through to the hallway, she straightened her shoulders and strode over to the table at one side of the room. If she left it here, Reed would see it soon enough. She wasn't sure she dared try to sneak into his room and she certainly did not want to get any of the serving maids in trouble with the valet.

Once she had done this, she would head, on foot, into town, and finish what they started. She would find Thomas again and arrange the meeting. After speaking with Oscar Boswell, it was clear Manfri was not the man behind this. He'd done what he needed to do for the coin, nothing more. But she still did not know who had put Manfri up to the false confession.

She placed the letter down, aware it shook in her hand. She grimaced at the scrawled writing. With the help of one of the elders, she had penned this note. She only prayed it said what she wanted it to as even if her reading skills were naught, Marko's were only usually enough to get by.

Turning, she stilled at the sound of a door opening. "Orelia?"

She rotated slowly to see the duchess emerge from the morning room. "F-forgive me. I only wanted to..." She motioned to the letter.

The duchess moved slowly toward her. "For Reed?"

Orelia nodded.

"He is not here at present."

Orelia twined her hands together. How odd. His mother did not look angry that she was here. "Yes, I was told."

"He's been in London the past few days. I have no idea what he is doing."

"I'm sure he shall be home soon."

A wash of sadness came across his mother's face. "I had hoped he might not disappear anymore with you around. You seemed to settle him a little."

"I did?"

She gave a light shrug. "Even as a boy, he wanted to be free. He would slip out of the house when he was meant to be studying and would disappear for hours on end only to come back muddy and wet—but always with a smile upon his face. He worried me horribly, however."

Orelia smiled at the memory. She could picture a young Reed doing just that.

"I never thought he would grow up to be the same, though. All the men in my family stopped travelling and adventuring as soon as they inherited a title or took on new responsibility."

"Reed is not much like other men."

"That he is not," the duchess agreed. "And you are not much like other women. I think that is why you were good for him."

Orelia tried to keep the surprise from her face. "Whatever do you mean?"

"For the first time in a long time, Reed no longer seemed trapped by the house. Certainly, he was still off adventuring with you, but he appeared to genuinely enjoy being under this roof. I see now that it was you who was the difference."

"I'm not sure..."

Reed's mother took a step forward. "I am. He may keep secrets from me, but I know my son. He was utterly in love with you, Orelia."

The word didn't seem real for a moment. Love? How was that possible? It seemed to drift about her before finally settling in her mind. Reed loved her?

"No, you must be wrong."

The duchess smiled. "I am never wrong, my dear."

Orelia fought for some kind of response for several moments before giving up. Did this mean the duchess did not loathe her after all? Did Reed really love her?

Orelia glanced around. "I-I must go."

"Of course."

"T-thank you." Orelia gave an awkward curtsey and scurried out of the house via the front door. Her heart beat a horrible staccato beat of uncertainty. She hardly knew what to do now. Wait for Reed to return? Force him to confess his feelings for her?

And what of hers?

She paused and laughed at herself. Of course she loved him. Who could not? What a fool she was to think otherwise.

But for now, she had to discover the truth. Then she could worry about what to do about Reed.

Chapter Twenty-Six

Reed held up a hand before his mother could say anything. His journey home from London had been long and tiring. His body ached, and his mouth was dry. All he wanted was a coffee, something good to eat and a bath. Then hopefully a long, long sleep.

The last thing he needed was his mother quizzing him about what he had been up to.

"Reed," she tried again.

Moseley aided him with his coat and he handed over his hat and gloves. "Not now, Mother. I've had a long journey."

And a pointless one at that. He handed over the information he had but it was dismissed. With the testimony of the captain, the wine in the gypsy's possession, and the confession, the courts had their man. He'd see trial and most likely be deported or hung.

Frustration made Reed clench his jaw. It still made little sense. He'd even demanded an audience with the man, but the gypsy refused to say anything.

"I'm going to my room," he said forcefully and he began up the stairs.

"Do you not want to read this letter from Orelia?"

He froze. Taking the two steps down he peered at her. "What letter?"

His mother nodded to the table. "She left it here two days ago."

"She was here?"

"That is what I just said, is it not?"

Reed picked up the letter and eyed his name, scratched awkwardly onto the parchment. He suspected she'd had help writing it.

His mother eyed him eagerly. He gave her a glare. "What is it, Mother? Can a man not read his correspondence in peace?"

She huffed. "I am not sure what I do to deserve such behavior. Here I am, fretting for your welfare then you return and tell me to leave you be. Can a mother not be interested in her son?"

He sighed. "Forgive me, Mother, I did not mean to be rude. I am tired and hungry. But why you should be interested in what Orelia has to say to me, I do not know."

"If it is interesting to you, then it is interesting to me."

He wasn't even going to ask what she meant by that. Frowning, he tugged open the string. The writing inside was as awkward as the writing on the outside and several words were misspelled but he understood the contents well enough.

"Damn," he muttered.

"What is it? Should I have sent it by urgent messenger?"

"Damn, damn, damn."

"Reed?" his mother demanded in a tone far too high to be comfortable.

"I need to go to Portsmouth."

"What is the matter? Should I have made her stay?"

Reed smirked. "I do not believe you could have made her stay."

She thrust her hands in the air. "Then what is going on?"

He leaned in, gave her a kiss on the cheek and squeezed her hand. "I will tell you everything soon, I promise. No more secrets, but for now, I must find Orelia."

Somewhat mollified by his promise, his mother nodded. He would tell her the truth, he decided. After all, if she had known what was happening and why Orelia was here, she might have been able to prevent her from dashing off and playing spy.

For the moment, however, he had to concentrate on finding her. If what she said was right—that the gypsy had been ill and had been paid to confess—then she could be throwing herself into a dangerous position, trying to track down the contact that Thomas had used.

He marched through the house to find his brother in the study. He didn't look up from his books until Reed placed a hand on the table in front of him. Noah lifted his head. "Oh, you are home." He scowled. "What is it?"

"I need your help," he said. "Get your pistols."

"Pistols?"

Reed nodded. "Orelia could be in trouble and it's all of my making."

Noah stood. "You know I shall gladly help, but what is this all about?"

"I'll explain all on the way."

"I should bloody hope so if I've got to shoot someone," Noah said dryly.

THEIR SWIFT PACE ON horseback meant Reed could do little explaining. It was not until they reached town that his brother began questioning what this was all about. Reed had been somewhat grateful for the time to gather his wits. All he could think on was Orelia.

Was she well? Had she already done something foolish?

Noah grabbed Reed's arm before they entered the inn. "I thought you were going to tell me what this was all about."

He faced his brother long enough to tell him, "I will," before ducking through the door of the inn.

Orelia did not know Portsmouth like he did so he would have to assume if she was in town, she would stay here. Maybe she was even in the room they had shared previously. His heart gave a jolt of remembrance as he recalled waking up with her, her hair tousled and her eyes heavy-lidded.

Damn the woman. And damn him. Why had he left her behind? He should have known she would go and do something reckless.

He found the innkeeper whose eyes sparked with recognition, no doubt recalling the generous tip Reed had left him last time.

"Good evening, sir. How can I be of service?" the short, wiry old man asked.

"Is my wife here?"

His brother made a strangled sound.

"No, sir. She arrived alone yesterday but I have hardly seen her. Spent a lot of time at The Red Lion, I believe." He peered up at Reed. "I was not all that keen on having a lone woman here, but she was very insistent."

"Alas, I was delayed in joining her, but I must thank you for your diligence. I'm grateful for you keeping my wife safe."

The man shrugged. "Well, as I say, I don't know where she is now. A busy lady, your wife."

"Do you have the key to her room? Perhaps I can await her there. My brother and I have had a long journey."

The man glanced over their attire and his brows dipped. Reed had hardly considered how they might look. He'd divested himself of his cravat and jacket long ago but even then, there was no mistaking the rich cut of their clothing or the expense of their hessians.

"My patrons trust me," the innkeeper said. "And I don't like trouble."

"There will be no trouble, I promise you." Reed took one step forward. Apparently, the man had decided they were no good. It amused Reed a little that his humbler disguise had given him a better advantage in a lowly inn. "But I must remind you, she is my wife. Her person and belongings are mine and I should very much like to have her back."

The small man eased back a step. "I told you I don't want trouble." He moved behind the bar and snatched up a metal key. "Here. It's the room at the top."

"Thank you." He offered a smile. "I assure you there will be no trouble."

The innkeeper eyed them both with distrust as they ascended the stairs.

Reed unlocked the door and pushed it open. The bedsheets were rumpled but there were few signs Orelia had been in the room. Clearly she had not yet used her wealth to buy anything. Aside from a hair brush and some ribbons, it seemed she had little else.

He shut the door and Noah spied the ribbons. "We missed her?"

"Yes. The innkeeper said she has been spending most of her time out."

Noah nodded. "He formed his words badly. I could hardly keep up."

"He's not all that keen on either of us being here it seems. Thinks we're trouble."

His brother smirked. "And are we?"

"Potentially."

"So we are to track her down?"

"Yes." Reed fingered a ribbon absently.

"And how shall we do that?"

Reed kept his face toward his brother. "I think I know where she'll be. Or at least will have been."

"And will you finally explain what this is about?"

Reed took in a breath and met his brother's inquisitive gaze. He did not much relish the knowledge he had lied to his family for many years, but it was better that than putting them in danger.

"There was an assassination attempt on Napoleon." Reed pushed a hand through his hair. "The suspect was a gypsy. Hence why I brought Orelia onboard."

Noah took a moment to digest the words. "Why should a gypsy wish Napoleon dead?"

"Orelia said the same. She was right, of course, but once given a lead I had no choice but to follow it."

"With Orelia's help," his brother added.

"Yes. She could help me move about the Romani community." Reed spoke deliberately slower, aware it was a lot of information for his brother to take in. "However, the longer we followed this lead, the clearer it became this was some other plot. But before we could uncover it, a gypsy man was taken in and he gave his confessions. I went to London to see this man in person."

"And you do not think it was him?"

"I know not." He tugged Orelia's letter out of his pocket and thrust it at Noah.

His brother unfolded the letter and ran his gaze over it. Reed waited until he finished and was looking at him before speaking again. "The gypsy did it for money. He was paid off by whoever we were tracking previously."

"If the Romani was sick and dying, what would it matter if he was hung or deported, as long as his family was well-looked after."

"Exactly. It seems the man struck a deal and his family would be richer than they had ever been while he was hung or shipped to Australia."

"So someone is trying to cover their tracks?"

Reed nodded. "Which means we were close."

"What would Orelia be doing?"

He pushed a hand through his hair, snatched up his hat and thrust it back on his head. "Going through with our original plan, I suspect." He grimaced. "And most likely putting herself in a very dangerous position.

Chapter Twenty-Seven

The smoky atmosphere of the inn combined with her nerves made breathing incredibly hard. Orelia pressed a hand to her stomach to try to still the turmoil inside. She glanced over at Thomas who looked as nervous as she. Sweat glistened on his brow in the candlelight.

She peered around again, assuring herself that the men were in position. She'd hired two of them and they were twice the size of her. As long as they waited for her signal, all would be well. Thomas would let her know when his contact entered, and her men would seize him.

After that, she was not quite sure what she'd do with him. March him back to Keswick Abbey perhaps, but what if Reed has not returned yet? She could hardly hand him in to the local courts. Who would believe her?

Never mind. She had time to worry about that. Her hired thugs were paid well enough to keep the contact locked away until she could at least get a message to Reed. It really was astonishing how much easier money made life.

Orelia nursed a weak ale and kept her cloak tucked over her head in an attempt to not draw attention to herself. She had only been here about an hour but already several patrons were drunk and singing. She took a sip of her drink and managed not to grimace. It would be worth it, she assured herself. The truth would be worth it.

The candle on her table grew short as the evening passed. She eyed the globs of wax as they poured down into the metal holder. The singing ceased and a few snores emanated from the patrons who had started drinking early on in the day. Several were slumped across tables and benches. She didn't envy the innkeeper when the time came to clear them out.

Her hired men gave her a look of frustration. No doubt they had been looking forward to getting their hands dirty. She looked at Thomas who shook his head.

Sighing, she stood and approached the men. "Looks like you will not be needed tonight. Can you return tomorrow?"

The largest one nodded. "If we get paid."

"Of course."

He glanced at his friend. "Then we'll be back tomorrow."

She turned to Thomas who sidled up behind her. "Let's leave it for tonight. He's clearly not coming."

Thomas nodded. "I am not sure he'll come at all. Maybe he won't."

"Maybe, but we must try. Will you come back tomorrow?"

He grimaced. "This is dangerous."

"It's surely more dangerous to have that man out there. What if he decides you know too much?"

His face paled a little. "I'll be here tomorrow," he said, his tone resigned.

They stepped out of the inn and something in the periphery of her vision made her turn. Too late though.

Everything went dark. She couldn't breathe. She scrabbled at the sack thrown over her head, but her hands were pinned in the embrace of what felt to be a brawny man. She screamed against the fabric, but it was muffled. She heard Thomas's stifled shouts. Had he befallen the same fate? What was happening?

Panic engulfed her. Her breaths grew shallow and her head swam. The more she fought, the fainter she felt. The iron grip around her body would not ease so she forced herself to relax. Taking breaths against the thick fabric of the sack was not easy but her head cleared enough for her to analyze the situation.

Someone had her and Thomas captive. The man holding her lifted her, so her feet dangled. He had to be tall. The world tilted briefly, and her side hit the ground hard, making her cry out. Shards of pain speared her side and knocked the air from her.

While she fought to drag in breaths with the fabric covering her mouth, someone grabbed her legs and bound them together. She tried to kick but succeeded in only having her legs tied more tightly. Next her hands were tied behind her. The ropes dug into her flesh and made her hands tingly. If she tried to move, the ropes burned into her skin.

There was a thud beside her and she felt a body next to her. She rolled into it and placed her hands onto who she assumed was Thomas. She called his name and he made a muffled response. They were both bound, their heads covered. For whatever reason, someone wanted them captured. Perhaps she had been too clever telling Thomas the culprit wanted him dead.

It was quite likely they would want them both dead, especially if they had known how close to the truth she was.

Her throat tightened. She wasn't ready to die. She had only just begun living. Reed had given her that. Not only financial freedom but he had opened her eyes to a world outside of the Romani life. Romanies prided themselves on being free yet how free had she really been? Warm tears trickled down her cheeks.

A door slammed shut and the floor beneath her moved. A carriage, she realized. They were in a carriage. Where were these people taking them?

REED AND HIS BROTHER arrived at the inn shortly before closing, having fought their way across town through late evening traffic. Reed barreled inside and approached the first man he could find. Then the next, then the next. None of them had seen Orelia. He glanced at his brother, who kept a pistol tucked carefully under his jacket folded across his arm. They were putting themselves in real danger, presenting themselves in their finery at this inn but it was necessary.

Had he missed her? Or had he been wrong? Perhaps she had no intention of going through with their plan.

"I've seen a woman," a large man leaning against a wooden pillar said.

Reed whirled. "Dark hair? Beautiful?"

He shrugged. "Wouldn't say that beautiful but she had dark hair. Slightly dark skin too."

Eyeing the giant of a man, Reed neared. "Was she here tonight?"

"Yes. Got herself in a pickle too."

His heart thrust against his chest. "What do you mean?"

"Think she was up to no good. She paid me and my brother there" —he thrust a thumb toward another large man pestering the innkeeper for more drink— "to kidnap someone. Only they never turned up."

Reed held back a groan. Noah would not be able to see the man's lips clearly enough to understand the conversation but he clearly sensed things were not good. He shifted closer.

"We are drawing attention, Reed," he hissed.

Reed nodded. "Where did she go?"

The man hefted up one shoulder. "She was with some man. He had a limp. There was some kind of scuffle and they were put into a carriage."

"Put?"

The man smirked. "Very well, they were tied up and thrown into a carriage."

"God Almighty. Why the hell did you not do anything to stop them?"

He shrugged. "What could I do? They were long gone before we realized what had happened and neither of us knew who she was. Damn shame. We were hoping to earn a bit more money off her."

Reed curled a fist then released it. "Where did they go?"

"Headed down Queen Street. Toward the docks I suppose."

Icy fear washed over him. He could only think of one reason to tie someone up and take them to the docks and it was certainly not to catch a ship.

He didn't bother saying anything else to the man or to Noah. Grabbing his brother's arm, he raced out of the inn and mounted his horse. His brother followed him. All he could do was pat his arm and sign 'trust me' due to the limited visibility of the street lamps.

He set off at as brisk a pace as the cobbled streets allowed, weaving between the buildings. If she had only just been taken, he might catch up with her.

What would he do if he did not?

Life without Orelia was inconceivable. He'd known that since he'd left for London.

He eased the horse to a trot once they neared the first buildings around the docks. Several ships could be seen farther out, their lamps reflecting on the dark sea. The creak and tinkle of the ropes against wood was about the only sound. Reed came to a stop and dismounted before signaling to his brother to do the same. He pressed a finger to his lips and tethered the horses on a nearby post. Whoever had taken Orelia could not know they were there.

He tugged out his pistol and Noah followed suit. They loaded them and edged around the buildings. Sure enough at the end of the main road to the docks was a carriage, its doors wide open.

They inched around it. Crates were scattered across the area between the ships and the buildings, so they used them as cover. He checked back to ensure his brother followed. A muffled scream made them still. Reed peered over the crate they had hidden behind, and his chest felt like it had been crushed in a vice.

He would recognize her anywhere, even with a bag over her head.

There were three men that he could make out. Two were trying to handle a wriggling Orelia while the other dealt with another man—also bound with a sack over his head. Reed had to assume it was Thomas. The men dragged Orelia closer to the water and Reed's worst fears were realized. What better way to rid themselves of someone causing trouble than to tie them up and let them drown? No one would find the bodies if weighted and no one would come looking for them.

Apart from him.

He tapped his brother's gun and motioned to the men. He ensured his own pistol was ready. He had no idea if the men were armed but they at least had their hands full with a wriggling Orelia.

"Stay," he mouthed to his brother who nodded. 'Shoot,' he motioned. "Soon."

He trusted his brother to decide when the best time to shoot would be.

Reed's time to act was now, however. Any longer and Orelia would be in the water. He sprinted forward and barreled past the first man toward the second, drawing their attention. A fist came toward him, but he ducked it, bringing his own up in return and striking the second man on the jaw. Agony tore through his knuckles as they struck bone.

He whirled, pistol in hand and brought the butt of it down onto the first man's head as Reed scrambled to his feet. The man collapsed. As Reed turned his attention to the other two men, a gunshot echoed through the night. He froze only for a moment when something hot seared his arm. Another gunshot followed and in the chaos it took him a moment to realize the second man was down. He glanced back long enough to see smoke coming from his brother's position.

Reed lifted his own pistol at the final man who responded by lifting his own weapon. Orelia wriggled in the man's hold. With his brother's shot already used, Reed had only one shot. With Orelia so close, he could hardly risk taking it, not with how unreliable pistols could be.

"Give her to me," he said quietly, "or my brother will shoot you."

Orelia gave a muffled squeal against the sack at the sound of his voice.

The man shook his head. "I don't think so. I don't think he has another shot."

He would, in time. But they didn't have time.

"Give her to me or you will die."

The man smirked, raised his pistol higher and pushed Orelia into the water.

"No!"

Reed leapt forward. He shot at the same time. Bangs ricocheted around him. A blur of movement revealed his brother jumping onto the man and beating him with the butt of his gun. Both of their shots had gone wide it seemed. Or he hoped. All he could think on was getting to Orelia.

"Go," his brother said.

He wasted no time kicking off his boots and diving into the water. Orelia's body bobbed for a mere moment before going under, sinking into the inky blackness of the ocean.

The shock of the freezing water stole his breath. He instinctively reached out. She had to be here, only feet from him surely? He opened his eyes but could see nothing. Only dark emptiness surrounding him. He kicked up and took a quick breath, searching the surface for her. A tiny trail of bubbles popped on the surface.

Pushing back under, he went deeper, reaching out.

There. Fabric. He snatched it and pulled. He pulled again until he felt the weight of it. He prayed it was her. Dragging her, he surfaced and hauled her into him. With shaking hands, he yanked the sack from her head and continued to kick to keep them afloat. Orelia could do nothing but gasp for air and keep her weight on him.

"Reed," she gasped, her teeth chattering.

"I've got you."

"Reed," she only managed to say again.

He helped her over to the edge of the docks, swallowing a good deal of water in the process. With the aid of his brother, he pushed her up to safety then Noah helped him haul his sodden self out of the water.

He slumped back to catch his breath before rolling onto one side. Noah sliced away the ropes from Orelia's ankles and wrists.

"Is...he...alive?" Reed asked of the third man, motioning quickly with his hands.

"Yes," Noah confirmed. "Though he will wake up with a nice headache. That one is dead." He tilted his head toward the one whom Noah had shot. "And that one is tied up."

He peered around at Thomas who was nursing his sore wrists and keeping watch over the first man. Then he turned his attention to Orelia who lay next to him. "Are...you...well?"

She gave him a weary smile. "Yes." Her eyes widened. "You were shot!"

He peered at where she was looking. Lifting away the torn fabric, he spied the scratch from a bullet. It had created a decent path through the muscle of his arm and looked a little grizzly but was clean enough. "I'll survive." He reached for Orelia and drew her into him. They lay in each other's arms for a moment—a wet, breathless embrace. "Do not do that to me again," he scolded.

"Never."

"At least not without me."

"Never," she promised again.

"Reed?"

Noah's uncertain tone made Reed lift his head. He hastened to standing at the sight of a man with a pistol aimed at Noah. Orelia released a tiny cry and tried to stand but Reed positioned himself in front of her, lifting his hands slowly.

His heart sank to his toes. Even though it was dark, he remembered this face—the Frenchman who tried to hurt Orelia at Thomas's old house.

The man swung his gaze between him and Noah. Reed's brother had his own gun aimed at the man but Reed doubted he'd managed to reload. Reed could rush at him but he risked the man shooting Noah.

He uttered a curse under his breath.

A scrabble of movement from Orelia caught Reed's eye and the Frenchman hesitated for a moment. It was enough. Reed barreled forward at the same time as Orelia did and they pushed the man to the ground. The pistol flew from his hand and Orelia raced to snatch the weapon and aim it at the man.

"*Non, non, s'il vous plaît.* I mean you no harm." The Frenchman lifted his hands from his position on the ground.

"Why did you try to hurt me then?" Orelia demanded.

"I could not have you English interfering." He lowered his hands slowly and pushed up to standing while Orelia kept her weapon pointed at him.

Reed eyed the man. "Interfering?"

"The attempt on *l'empereur...we feared it was a French-man—one of the men on St. Helena. There are those that wish to go back to war but it has taken too great a toll on our country.*"

"Still no reason to attack her," Reed said through gritted teeth.

The man swiped his hands down his trousers and straightened. "If you found out that we suspected Napoleon's most trusted man, it would put all agreements with the English in jeopardy. I am sorry for harming you, mademoiselle, but we could not have you discovering the truth."

"These are not Frenchman, *monsieur,*" Reed pointed out.

The man nodded and drew in a long breath. "*Oui.* We were wrong it seems. I received word from France that our investigations had come to nothing. Then I followed you and it became clear the English were behind it. Though, why, I have yet to fathom."

Reed motioned to Orelia to lower the pistol. "What have you told your superiors?"

"I reported back, and they wanted me to keep an eye on the situation. I saw the mademoiselle here taken but I do not know this town like you do, *monsieur*. I regret it took me longer than I would have liked to catch up with them." The French spy gave Orelia a regretful look. "The government has no wish to go back to war. If you can uncover the people behind the attempts, we will interfere no longer."

Reed nodded slowly. "You will return to France right away?"

"*Oui*. I do not do well in this cold climate."

Chuckling, Reed motioned to the injured men. "We shall have them talking before long."

The Frenchman blew out a breath. "I wish you luck, *monsieur*."

Reed drew Orelia into him. Somehow, with her at his side, he suspected he did not need it.

Epilogue

"Stop touching!" Reed's mother barked.

Orelia dropped her hand from her hair and whirled away from the mirror she'd been standing in front of. She drew in a breath and faced the dowager duchess, twirling the large ring that adorned her finger.

"And stand straight," the woman commanded, moving closer.

Orelia drew in a breath and straightened her shoulders. Resplendent in jewels, feathers, and silk, Reed's mother came to Orelia's side, walking as though she were gliding across the floor. Orelia suspected she could be wearing a servant's dress and still look like a duchess.

Unlike herself.

She looked at the floor where delicate slippers peeked out from underneath her lemon-yellow gown.

The dowager duchess put a finger under Orelia's chin and lifted it so she could not shirk her gaze. "Do not look at the ground. Carry yourself with grace. Carry yourself like the duchess you are."

Swallowing, Orelia tried to crush the swarm of nerves curdling her insides. She'd been a duchess for all of a week now and she could still not get used to it. After a rather rushed wedding, she and Reed had not had time for a honeymoon what with questioning the men from the docks and chasing down the final leads. Still, after tonight, their mission would be complete and they would be able to have some time alone. Perhaps that would give her the time she needed to get used to her new status.

She took a sideways glance at the mirror and grimaced at her reflection, eyeing the curl she'd managed to tug free. How could anyone ever get used to such a thing, especially a Romani?

Reed's mother moved around her and artfully tucked the curl back in place, restoring the careful hairstyle the lady's maid had taken so much time over. "You look...beautiful, Orelia."

Orelia opened her mouth then shut it. The slightly soft look in her new mother-in-law's eyes made her tongue feel like it was tangled. The dowager duchess had not been thrilled at the idea of their marriage, but she seemed to be softening, especially after Reed announced he would be spending more time at home, splitting the ducal duties with Noah.

"Like a true duchess," the woman added.

Orelia's gaze shot to hers. "Truly?" The word came out choked.

A smile curved her mother-in-law's lips. "You really do. Just carry yourself with that courage I know you have."

"I'm not certain I feel courageous today."

"A duchess is always assured of herself." Reed's mother tweaked the jewels around Orelia's neck. "You are a strong woman, Orelia. That's all that is needed to carry out such a role. Strength. And love for my son helps too."

Orelia managed a shaky smile. "I have plenty of that."

"Good to hear." Reed entered the hallway as he pulled on his gloves. "The carriage is waiting. Shall we?" He offered his arm to Orelia, his eyes warming when he glanced over her. "I have plenty of love for you too," he murmured in Orelia's ear.

Her insides did a gentle flip. She suspected her husband would always have this effect on her. All he needed to do was look at her and her knees grew weak, her breaths heavy. Especially now that he was well and truly hers. She peeked back at the house as they climbed into the carriage. Surely this all had to be a dream?

"Is everything in place?" she asked when the vehicle began to move.

He nodded. "Several men are in place at the house, ready to escort Lord Windham."

Orelia shook her head in wonder. Once they had the two men in custody, they had given up their employer quickly enough. Reed had done an excellent job of playing them against each other.

"It is thanks to you we have confessions." Reed took her hand and twined his fingers between hers.

"Hardly. You were far better at it than me."

"You know how to appeal to a man's softer side I think. You broke them before I did."

She gave a light laugh. "Breaking them sounds a little extreme." She glanced down to where their gloved hands were linked. "It is hard to understand why a rich man like Lord Windham would participate in an assassination attempt."

He lifted a shoulder. "Well, we shall confront him tonight and have our answers, but it does not change what he did. I nearly lost you because of him and I will not forget that easily."

"You did not lose me, however." She squeezed his hand.

"No, I managed to gain a wife somehow."

She gave his arm a light tap. "You asked me to marry you, remember?"

Reed chuckled. "That I did. I could not wait another moment. After all, I needed to get good value for my money."

Orelia rolled her eyes and smiled. No matter how glib he was being, she would never forget the moment he asked her to be with him forever, his words tremulous and his eyes filled with emotion.

The nerves began to twist her gut when they arrived at the manor house, reassuring her that this was no dream. If it was, she would not have to be attending another ball where everyone would turn and stare at her. However, this was for the good of the mission.

"What if someone recognizes me?" she hissed to Reed when he helped her out of the carriage and took her arm to escort her up the steps.

Lanterns lined the road up to the sizeable house. A golden glow emanated from the open door between two long stone columns. The house radiated decadence and wealth.

"I should hope they do," murmured Reed, introducing them both to the master of ceremonies. "You are my wife, after all."

"I meant as the Spanish noblewoman," she muttered.

He waved a dismissive hand. "You're a duchess now. Whatever reason we make up for the subterfuge will be accepted."

She lifted her eyes to the ceiling at his nonchalant attitude. Sometimes she forgot that a man of his rank and wealth could do almost anything he wanted.

The master of ceremonies announced them as the Duke and Duchess of Keswick. She tried to keep her smile from shaking.

Reed tightened his hold on her arm. "Just breathe, Orelia."

"Everyone is looking at us."

"Everyone is looking at you. As they should be. You're beautiful."

Though Orelia appreciated the comment, she knew that was not the only reason people were looking at her. Her heritage might not be fully known but she was aware there had been plenty of gossip surrounding her sudden marriage to Reed. A few disapproving looks were sent their way.

She lifted her chin and concentrated on drawing in breaths to steady her heart. "It seems even a duke cannot get away with everything."

"Perhaps not." He drew her straight onto the dance floor as a waltz started up. "But I only care about what you think," he said in her ear as he held her close and guided her through the steps that were still a little alien to her.

She glanced into her husband's eyes and all trepidation vanished. After all, a ball was no more terrifying than any of the other adventures she'd had with Reed. Not to mention she had one less uncertainty to worry about—Reed loved her, and always would. That knowledge fed her strength and she held herself tall whilst her husband led her around the room for all to see.

His arms cradled her body just so and allowed her to relish the strength of him and draw in the intoxicating scent as well as view the promise in his eyes. Perhaps balls were not so bad.

They remained off the dance floor for the rest of the evening, and while there were those who gave Reed what he called the 'cut', many were still interested in talking to them. Orelia struggled to pay attention to the talk, particularly when there was only one person they were interested in seeing and he had yet to appear.

She waved a hand in front of her face. The atmosphere in the crowded ballroom was thick with perfume and heat. "Where is the baron?"

Reed plucked the fan from her wrist and flipped it open. She grimaced. She'd forgotten she even had such a thing. Wafting it rapidly in front of her face, she gave a sigh of relief. How people danced all night long in thick gowns and with such little fresh air, she did not know.

"I do not believe he has even stepped foot in the room," Reed told her. "Since the death of his son, he does not attend these events."

"Even though he is hosting this?"

"Well, Lord Windham's eldest son is hosting this really. It's rather obligatory, I'm afraid. One is expected to entertain when one has rank."

Orelia made a face. "Does this mean we shall be hosting balls?"

"Only a handful, but yes." He chuckled at her horrified expression. "Do not fear, I shall ensure a waltz is played at every single one. I would not pass up on an opportunity to dance closely with you."

She gave a half-smile. "I suppose that would be acceptable."

"Spoken like a true duchess."

Orelia observed the dancers and those huddled around the edge of the dance floor. "So where are we to find this baron?"

"I heard tell he likes to spend time in his study." Reed kept his voice low. "One of the serving girls said he is at home so we need to find him before the ball ends."

"I still do not know why we have to do this so subtly."

Reed gave a wry smile. "The benefits of rank and wealth, Orelia. We cannot have this hauled through the courts, anyway. The attempts on Boney cannot become common news or we might have war on our hands regardless of having caught the culprit. I hope we can persuade him to come quietly."

She pursed her lips. The Romani man who had been paid to falsely confess had not been given the benefit of such delicate handling. Thankfully once they gained the confessions of the men who had tried to drown her, Manfri admitted to giving a false confession and had been released. Thomas had also been treated sympathetically but she suspected Reed had a lot to do with that.

"Come, I think we have put in enough of an appearance. Let us see if we cannot find him now." Reed took her arm and led her out of the ballroom, muttering something about her needing some air for anyone who might be paying attention.

"The study should be down here." He paused outside a door and looked at her. "He tried to kill you, Orelia." His voice cracked slightly when he said her name. "I nearly lost you."

"But you did not," she reminded him again.

Reed's chest rose as he took an audible breath and he pushed open the door. Orelia swiftly followed him in, her eyes taking a moment to adjust to the dim light. Only lamps were lit, one on a desk and the other on a side table. Hunched over the desk, was a frail, aged man.

Orelia gasped. This was not how she'd envisaged the man who had wanted to kill her and Thomas. His eyes were gaunt, his hands boney. Little hair lingered on his head and his clothes appeared to fit poorly.

His head snapped up. "I told you—" Lord Windham scowled. "What are you doing in here?"

Reed stepped toward the desk. "We know what you did, Lord Windham."

His scowl deepened. "What the devil are you blabbering on about?"

"We have confessions. We have letters. We know all we need to know." Reed leaned in. "You tried to kill Napoleon."

The man's gaze narrowed at Reed and a few moments passed. Suddenly, he slammed his fist onto the table, making Orelia jump. "The bastard deserved it! He deserves to die!"

"So you did try to kill him?" Reed pressed.

"Why our country thought it right to let him live, I do not know," the man snarled.

Reed shook his head. "It was the best way to keep peace. If he dies under our watch, the war continues."

Lord Windham's jaw tensed. "He killed my son and now he gets to spend the rest of his days alive? No, it shall not be borne. The man needs to die."

"And Orelia here. She needed to die too?"

Reed curled a fist and Orelia moved close in case she needed to step in. She had wanted Lord Windham to be punished for what he did but it was clear the man was eaten up by grief. Whatever they did to him would be inconsequential. Perhaps her heart was too soft, but she almost felt sorry for him.

Lord Windham gave her a quick glance over. "My men told me you were getting too close. I had no wish to harm anyone else, but Napoleon has to die."

Reed folded his arms and shook his head. "If he dies, more sons like yours will be killed in battle. We cannot allow you to try again."

The baron's defensive stance drooped. "My son was young. Innocent. He had no idea what war was like. I never wanted him to go but he insisted he needed to fight for his country. I can never forgive the man who started this war." He swung his gaze between them. "What will you do with me?"

"You are lucky, Lord Windham, that the Secret Service has no wish to make this event known. You will be allowed to go into exile—under watch," Reed told him. "I hope you like hot weather."

The man's gaze hardened. "So I get the same treatment as Napoleon, all because I tried to kill one man. He killed hundreds of thousands and gets to live the rest of his days in comfort."

Reed slammed both his hands onto the desk and bore down on the man. "You tried to kill my wife," he said through clenched teeth. "Be grateful that I am not a vengeful man."

Lord Windham eyed Reed then glanced at her. He sighed. "I am sorry that you were hurt."

Orelia made no comment. It was hard to imagine this tired old man ordering someone to kill her, but she could still remember plunging into the freezing water, the darkness swallowing her.

"There are men stationed in and around the building," Reed informed him. "They will escort you to the docks tomorrow morning. I suggest you ensure you are ready."

The baron gave a resigned sigh. "I have nothing left here anyway."

"You have your other son," Orelia pointed out. "You have so much more than many others. It hurts to lose people, but you could have done so much good."

She could see her words did not infiltrate. Grief had shaped the baron into an empty shell of a man. That pang of pity struck her.

"I think we have our answers," he murmured to Orelia. She nodded and Reed took her arm. "If you will excuse us, Lord Windham, my wife and I have a ball to attend."

As they stepped out of the room, Reed nodded to a man dressed as a servant waiting at the end of the hall. The man stepped past them into the study, shutting the door behind him.

"I feel sorry for him," Orelia confessed to Reed as they walked back to the ballroom.

"He tried to hurt you. I'm afraid I cannot feel the same." He paused and twisted to face her. He skimmed a palm over her cheek, cradling her face and tracing the shape of her mouth with a thumb. "However, if none of this had happened, I would never have found you."

"And your life would be much simpler." She grinned.

"That it would," he agreed, chuckling at her gasp of indignation. "But who wants simple?"

"Do you regret that there will be no more missions?"

He shook his head. "The Secret Service may have small tasks for us, but I have no desire to leave England again—not when my beautiful wife resides here." He leaned in and brushed a tender kiss across her mouth before easing back to look into her eyes. "What of you? You made an excellent spy, Orelia. Will you not miss it?"

Her body tingled from his kiss and her heart swelled with love for this wonderful man. She shook her head. "I have all the excitement I need right here."

His smile reached his eyes and he kissed her swiftly and firmly then drew back. "Come then, shall we dance once more and truly scandalize everyone here?"

She nodded and took his offered hand. A strange wash of sensation came over her as an image fluttered through her mind—one of a long marriage and many children.

"Lead the way, Your Grace."

After all, she did not need a vision to tell her what she already knew—her future was Reed, and what a wonderful future it would be.

"I love you," he murmured, stealing one more kiss before they entered the ballroom.

THE END

About the Author

Samantha Holt lives in a small village in England with her twin girls and a dachshund called Duke. When not writing, she loves attending music festivals, sweating to death on the treadmill, and exploring the many beautiful stately homes and castles in her area.

www.samanthaholtromance.com

Made in the USA
Lexington, KY
09 July 2018